1990

NEIGHBORS

NOVELS
BY THOMAS BERGER

Little Big Man
Killing Time
Regiment of Women
Sneaky People
Who Is Teddy Villanova?
Arthur Rex
Neighbors
The Feud
Being Invisible
The Houseguest
The Reinhart Series:
   Crazy in Berlin
   Reinhart in Love
   Vital Parts
   Reinhart's Women

NEIGHBORS

A NOVEL BY

THOMAS
BERGER

DELTA/SEYMOUR LAWRENCE

A DELTA/SEYMOUR LAWRENCE BOOK
Published by
Dell Publishing
a division of
Bantam Doubleday Dell Publishing Group, Inc.
666 Fifth Avenue
New York, New York 10103

ISBN: 0-385-28682-1

Reprinted by arrangement with Delacorte Press/Seymour Lawrence

Printed in the United States of America
Published Simultaneously in Canada

One previous Delta edition
New Delta edition—October 1989

10 9 8 7 6 5 4 3 2 1

OPM

TO HERMAN SINGER

NEIGHBORS

CHAPTER 1/

IT would have been nice," said Earl Keese to himself as much as to the wife who sat across the coffee table from him, "to have asked them over for a drink."

"We can certainly do that tomorrow," said Enid. "Nothing is really lost."

"But of course tomorrow won't be the *day they moved in,* will it?" Keese reflectively sipped his transparent wine. "I find that if something is done when it should be done, it is not forgotten. Still, I suppose it's no tragedy. We could probably get away with giving them no formal welcome whatever. It's scarcely a true obligation."

"You mean, like giving food to a starving person?"

"Exactly," said Keese. He rose and headed for the kitchen. While passing through the dining room, which was papered in a pale-gold figure, he bent slightly so that he could see, under the long valance and over the window-mounted greenhouse, into the yard next door. Despite what he believed he saw he did not break his stride. In the kitchen he looked again: it was a large white dog, in fact a wolfhound, not a naked human being on all fours.

Were Keese to accept the literal witness of his eyes, his life would have been of quite another character, perhaps catastrophic, for outlandish illusions were, if not habitual with him, then at least none too rare for that sort of thing. Perhaps a half-dozen times a year he thought he saw such phenomena as George Washington urinating against the wheel of a parked car (actually an old lady bent over a cane), a nun run amok in the middle of an intersection (policeman directing traffic), a rat of record proportions (an abandoned football), or a brazen pervert blowing him a kiss from the rear window of a bus (side of sleeping workingman's face, propped on hand).

This strange malady or gift had come upon Keese with adolescence. Never had he been duped by it. Indeed, the only inconvenience it had brought him had been by reason of the unusual skepticism it had engendered. On occasion reality *did* take a bizarre turn: there *were* persons who kept pet pythons, which escaped and were subsequently discovered sleeping peacefully at a drive-in movie three miles from home. If Keese saw such a phenomenon he assumed it was the usual illusion. He had doubted his eyes when seeing a nude fat man ascend the front steps of a public building. But this man had been real, and a rearview photo of him appeared in next morning's newspaper. (He had eluded the police, and his motive remained obscure.)

Keese admitted to himself that, very rarely, some outlandish vision of his might be to some degree or even wholly authentic; but since he had no standard of measurement he must, in self-preservation, consistently reject the evidence of his eyes. In this basic way he was at odds with the rest of humanity as to one of its incontestable truths: seeing is believing.

He now opened the refrigerator and found the bottle of wine, which lay horizontal. As he had feared, it was leaking at the cork, and a little pool had formed on the lid of the crisper below. While wrinkling his nose at this he heard a tapping at the glass of the back door. Pleased to be so distracted, he straightened himself and went in response. While on this route he expected to view the caller through the large clear pane of the door-glass, from which furthermore the curtains had been temporarily removed for laundering. But he saw no one until he reached and opened the door, and then he espied the wolfhound, some eight feet off and loping. He supposed that the animal could have done the tapping: no other candidate was, at any rate, in evidence.

He took the bottle of wine to the living room.

"They must have a dog," he said to Enid.

"That could be bad news," his wife replied, placing her stemmed glass judiciously on the coffee table. For a number of years now Keese had observed his wife only by means of what she did: that is to say, he saw the actor only through the action. She was invisible to him when motionless.

"Well, let's hope not," said he, making a wry toss of the chin and elbowing an imaginary companion.

Enid stood up. "I imagine that some dinner wouldn't be amiss."

"At this juncture," said Keese, completing the old family-phrase, the origins of which had been mislaid: some movie or play of twenty years before.

Normally a tall woman, Enid looked markedly larger than usual, but dwindled to her usual size as she left the room. Keese realized that the sofa, where he sat now, was subtly lower than the chair he generally used at this time of day. Not only did he see reality from a somewhat less favorable situation, but the thickness of his middle body knew an unpleasant pressure from his belt buckle. Being alone in the room, he had no reason to suppress a tendency towards extravagance, and making a hideous expression, he positively hurled himself erect.

He was heading for his habitual chair, in which, by contrast to its thick upholstery, he felt thinner, when the doorbell, a dull gong, sounded. Keese was now sufficiently old (viz., forty-nine) to hear as ominous all summonses for which he had not been furnished with advance warning, and he was especially dubious about any that came in those few hours which constituted dinnertime for persons of his sort.

He went apprehensively to the door, opened it partially, and exposed to the caller a diagonal view of the entrance hall of his home as well as about four-fifths of himself, keeping a forearm and a calf concealed and readied for leverage if needed.

For a very brief instant, looking headwards as he was, he could not identify the person by sex, for he saw a turban and under it a face which though not that of an East Indian was colored almost olive. It wore no make-up, and while the skin was flawless the features were not so delicate as to require a feminine designation.

But then Keese saw the two remarkable cones that projected themselves from her thorax. Though beneath the glistening, hard-finished blouse of oysterish synthetic they connoted more of rocketry than mammalia, once he had identified her sex he was no longer in doubt as to his own style.

"Hello," said he, showing a pleasant face, "and what may I do for you?"

"Anything you like," said the person on his doorstep. In age she had apparently just crossed Keese's arbitrary line between girl and young woman. He had not been prepared for her literalization of his greeting, which was a piece of standard usage and not a cliché to be derided. Nevertheless, with his bias towards a creature of her sex and years, he decided that he was himself at fault and he listened smilingly to the punch line which completed her opening speech: "The problem is what you want in return."

Having made her jest, she glowered momentarily and then produced the sort of laugh which seen on silent film would suggest by its physical violence that the original had been deafening, but in point of fact very little sound was heard. Her teeth were huge.

Keese fell back a centimeter in mock horror, with an appropriate flash of palms. "Miss, I assure you my intentions are honorable." He liked nothing better than such banter.

But the young woman seemed suddenly to show anxiety. Staring fearfully at him, she said: "I'm Ramona." Her next statement was almost a question. "I moved in *next door?*"

Abruptly disenchanted, Keese knew an urge to reply: "How should I know? Why aren't you certain?" But of course he did not; he was never sardonic with ladies newly met. "Welcome to the neighborhood," he said instead. "We were just talking about inviting you over for a drink—and decided against it only because we thought you'd probably be exhausted today. But come in, come in."

He did a little uncertain dance at this point, from threshold to top step and back. The problem was to hold the screen door open for her entrance and yet allow her sufficient space in which to move. Keese was no sylph. There was a further complication in that Ramona seemed oblivious to his effort: the simple thing would have been for her to catch the screen door against her outer wrist once he had thrown it open; thus he could have retreated into the hallway as she entered.

But she took no hand in her own entrance, and stretching to widen the route of ingress, he was forced to lower his elevation by one step. She raked him with her breasts as they passed: despite appearances, those cones were yielding and real, and it was quite the most exhilarating encounter with an unknown woman that Keese had had in time out of memory.

In the living room she waited as if for an invitation to sit down, but having received it she whirled without warning, went swiftly to the piano, seized the photograph there, and said: "Whoozis? Your girl?"

Keese had been drifting in spirit, but he stiffened now. The word was ambiguous, surely, and it could have been appropriate here had the subject of the portrait been younger. "If you mean 'daughter,' " said he, "then, yes, that's mine."

Ramona put both hands on her hips. She wore steel-gray slacks beneath the metallic-looking blouse. Her turban was of streaked lilac.

"No, I meant was she your chick." Again the quick glower, followed by the almost silent howl of laughter. Had it not been for the touch of her resilient breasts Keese might have found her irony repulsive. The portrait was an accurate depiction of his twenty-one-year-old daughter, who was thought even by strangers to be remarkably pretty. It was indeed unprecedented that anyone, male or female, had looked at her picture without making this observation aloud. But Ramona, perhaps empowered by envy, was sufficiently bold to remain silent. Keese's daughter had golden hair and fair skin and eyes of blue. No greater contrast could be provided than Ramona, though for that matter his "girl" bore little resemblance to his wife and none to him.

"Who plays?" Ramona asked now, having strode away from the piano, but obviously putting it in reference. She had a low-slung, long-lobed behind, though some of that effect was due to the high-waisted trousers. She wore spike-heeled sandals which exposed red-painted toes.

"*I* do," he lied, suddenly desperate to appear talented. Easy enough to pretend some infirmity of hand if she asked for a performance. But, as he had hoped, she did not make such a request.

"Who's 'we'?" she asked. "You and your girl?"

"My wife and I. And by the way, my name is Earl Keese." He took himself near her, should she wish to shake hands, but she made no use of the opportunity. Instead she stared so keenly below his waist that he feared his fly was open, and he turned away and looked discreetly down. The zipper was snugly closed.

Relieved, but also annoyed with himself, he took the initiative. "So you've moved in, have you? Nice house. The Walkers took awfully good care of the place, I believe."

Ramona asked harshly, with the implication of a demand: "Is your wife here now?"

"In the kitchen. I'll go get her. She certainly wants to meet you." He had already put one foot in the direction which would be appropriate to his proposal when he saw that Ramona was shaking her head.

"No," said she, "I don't want to meet her." She seized his wineglass, which he had refilled before answering the door, and drank from it.

Keese felt humiliated, and he was also indignant that she had not, since ringing the bell, given him a second's peace in which to meet the requirements of hospitality. She was rude to him in his own home, the sort of thing that was unprecedented except with one's relatives. It would now have been pointless to get her a glass of her own, which would only coarsely demonstrate that she had swiped his wine. Therefore he took for himself the empty goblet that had previously served Enid. But while he was reaching for the bottle Ramona drained in one prolonged swallow the contents of her glass, and as he was about to serve himself nonetheless, she forcefully extended her hollow vessel.

He filled it.

"I hope we can be friends," said Ramona when she had received her wine.

"I'm sure we can," said Keese. "We were certainly always on friendly terms with the Walkers, though we didn't really know them intimately. They were a good deal older."

"I didn't mean that polite social kind of shit," Ramona said.

This extraordinary speech resulted not in encouraging Keese

but rather in frightening him. But as luck would have it his means of resisting fright was to simulate boldness—alone at night on a darkened city street he would invariably, teeth tightly occluded, steer himself *towards* any threatening shadow that offered itself, on the principle that all malefactors abhor the initiative of others.

"O.K.," he said heartily, "you're on. We're friends. We'll start there and work backwards. I don't even know your last name and whether you have a husband. I've seen your dog but nothing else. You were all moved in by the time I came home."

"Dog?" asked Ramona. Having got her refill she had put the glass down and not touched it since. There had been only an inch of wine left in the bottle for Keese: he decided to forgo it.

"Wolfhound?" he asked. "I assumed it was yours. I thought I knew all the dogs in the neighborhood."

"Why don't you sit down?" She grimaced. "You make me nervous, standing awkwardly there like that, holding that bottle."

Keese was too startled to resist. His favorite chair was nearby. He went to it and complied with her order.

As if she had not displayed sufficient effrontery even yet, she said: "Now, doesn't that feel better?" He winced visibly. Not being as insensitive as she seemed, Ramona added: "That's what I mean about being friends: you talk turkey with your friend. If he doesn't like it he can always throw you out."

Keese had a faint suspicion that he might get onto her style eventually. Meanwhile he *was* mollified by this exposition of her rationale. He waved his hands. "Thanks, I'm quite comfortable now." He could not resist settling in, lifting one haunch and then the other, though he was aware that it marked him as being hopelessly middle-aged.

As if reading his thoughts Ramona said sweetly: "You're not so old, but you are too fat."

Had she finally gone too far? Apparently not, if Keese could ponder on the question. At any rate, he felt no impulse whatever to protest. Accepting the insult took much less of a toll than would have the display of an ire which furthermore he did not feel. After all, what she had said was no more nor less than the truth, and he was proud of his courage to face facts.

Nevertheless, he pulled his abdomen in while addressing the table at his elbow: "I have a feeling that you seldom resist an urge to say whatever's on your mind."

"Maybe I'm just testing you," said Ramona. "Anyway, I'm nobody of importance. I can say what I want because it doesn't matter. Who cares anyway?" She stood up. "Is your wife making dinner?"

Keese had no time to deplore her self-deprecation, had he been so inclined. "Afraid so," he answered, rising with a foolish feeling of guilt. "Look, do you have anything to eat over there? The stores hereabout shut their doors at five sharp, and the one restaurant in town is closed for renovation at the moment. It just occurs to me that you may not have eaten dinner. Would you like to eat with us? And is there more of your family?"

Ramona took his hand in hers. "Earl—is that your name, Earl? You just trot out first and ask your wife if it's O.K." Her fingers were almost as long as his but not of course so broad; and though her toes were painted her fingernails were not.

He had his pride to defend. "I buy the food," said he. "I think I might have some say as to who eats it."

She raised her free arm and pointed. "Now go! Don't argue like a bad boy, Earl, or you'll be sorry."

It was preposterous to be manhandled like this in one's own living room, and by a girl! But with mixed glee and shame he realized that he was aroused—at least physically.

He was pleased that the kitchen lay at the farthest extremity of the house. While he was still in the dining room he heard the outside door open and close, but when he stepped into the kitchen Enid was at the refrigerator, across the room from the door, and furthermore holding a burden in both hands: some plastic box she had just taken from the freezer.

"Huh," she said, "does the sight of frozen succotash elate you so?"

"Do we have enough for a guest or two?" asked Keese, allowing for the possibility that Ramona had a mate—of whom, strangely, he was not jealous.

Enid drew back in what seemed excessive dismay. "As it turns out, we have virtually no food at all." She marched to the stove, carrying the plastic container before her as if it were a crown on a velvet pillow.

"You can't mean it!"

Enid stared boldly at him. "I was wrong."

Keese felt the onset of an awesome despair. But this soon proved to be needless, for the answer could not have been more simple. He punished one of his hands with the other and said: "We'll go out for dinner. Yes!"

"No," said Enid, turning in curiosity. She had not even yet put down the container of succotash. "The Coachman's closed for renovation."

"Sometimes," said Keese, ebullient now, "our life is too circumscribed. We are not alone in the vastness of the tundra. We are but four miles from a prize-winning eatery, nationally renowned: La Nourriture, hey?"

Enid performed a reverse whistle. "Can you be serious?" Now she lowered the plastic box at last. "Are you in some kind of trouble?"

"What a bizarre question," said Keese. "Would I want to celebrate trouble with a meal costing say twenty dollars a plate?"

"At the minimum," said Enid. "But you might sooner do that than feed upon a success: I've known you for a long time, my friend."

Ordinarily he did not mind her applying to him the results of, apparently, an analysis of someone else; indeed, he was often flattered to hear of some trait or taste of which he had ever been innocent (e.g., "you know that hot temper of yours"; "like you, my father doted on stuffed breast of veal"). But her current misjudgment of him seemed to carry a negative implication, and he was made impatient by it.

"Be that as it may," said he, "if you want to come along to La Nourriture you will go now and get dressed."

Enid sighed and looked dismally at the container of succotash. "I suppose you won't believe this, but I really don't want to go out."

Keese felt an alarming focus of heat at the base of his neck, though he wore a knitted shirt with an open collar. He recognized the surge of blood as an anticipation of dining alone with Ramona.

"You mean you want to stay home, but you have no objections to my going?"

"That's exactly my point," said Enid. She was quite a handsome woman, better-looking, actually, than when she had been younger, so that it was routine for people to believe she had once been a beauty who was now faded. Naturally, no one made this observation directly to Keese, but he sensed it, and thought it was unfortunate that she did not get her due. She had marvelous breasts, and he was still charmed by her freckles in a certain light. She was—but he caught himself here: he was being grateful to the point of hysteria.

"I haven't even told you whom I was thinking of entertaining," he said now.

"Why not let it be a surprise?" suggested his wife, and he agreed, without having any real sense of what she meant, and he went, almost at the jog, back to the living room and rounded the turn from the hallway and said—

Nothing whatever. The room was empty. Ramona had departed—if indeed she had ever been there. Had his old trick-of-the-eye now moved towards the command of all his faculties?

He went quickly to the dining room and looked out the window that gave onto the narrowest portion of his own yard and, beyond, the widest segment of the lawn of the house next door. He saw nothing animate for a moment, and then the ubiquitous wolfhound came into view again. The dog seemed to be grazing, like a herbivore. Ramona was nowhere in evidence. Crazy little bitch! She had ruined his Friday evening, perhaps even the whole weekend.

He wandered disconsolately back to the living room. She had drunk the remainder of the white wine. He possessed nothing more in the way of an alcoholic beverage, and there was only frozen succotash for dinner. His watch assured him that the village market had closed an hour ago and that the liquor store would lock up in half a minute.

Once again he was asking *Why,* when without warning a male stranger briskly entered the room. A tall, muscular man with a head of blond curls, he had apparently, without invitation, let himself into Keese's house!

CHAPTER 2/

FOR an instant Keese considered fetching the poker from the fireplace and beating this intruder to death, but then he stopped trying to impress himself with bluster and realized that he should be seriously indignant about the invasion—unless of course the fellow was some repairman, an electrician or the like, summoned by Enid to perform a technical function. But the mystery was soon dissipated.

"Hi, Earl," cried the blond giant, and he threw out a hand large as a shovel. Keese was prepared to be maimed by the handshake, but he found that in point of fact the man's grip was reassuringly spongy. "I'm Harry. I imagine Ramona's mentioned me."

"No doubt," Keese said warily. "You're her—?"

"Sure I am," said Harry, in the airy fashion of someone who has boldly not listened to that to which he is pretending to respond. He looked to be at least six four and had enormous shoulders and an otherwise flat body: not burly, but, uh—Keese searched for the word, which was not one that he liked, because neither the look nor the sound of it seemed to support the meaning, which was essentially an expanded sort of wiriness—*rangy:* there it was. Keese himself, though not always as stout as now, had always been compact of body, and naturally, for reasons of survival, he preferred his own sort of build, while at the same time despising it.

He had by no means forgiven Harry for barging in uninvited, but nothing was to be gained by being surly in the face of a *fait accompli.*

"Well, Harry, welcome to the end of the road." Not only was this designation another old family saying, but it was less dispiriting than *dead end.*

Harry shrugged and said pleasantly: "What's on the menu? I'm famished." He actually brought his two large palms together and abraded them.

With horror Keese remembered his invitation! "Oh, my God," he said, "yes. Well, I am really humiliated, Harry. I spoke too quickly. Afraid only some frozen succotash's in the larder, you see. And the stores are closed." His failure to consider the French restaurant was not due to active suppression: he had honestly forgotten the project so ecstatically conceived.

All good feeling (whether bogus or not) receded from Harry's smile. For a moment he could have been on the point of hurling himself at Keese's throat—or at any rate, so Keese felt. Harry's right eye twitched, an ugly sneer was insinuating itself into his lower nose. But then all at once he rose above his apparent disappointment.

"Well, me bucko," he roared jovially, "then I'll just go and get some takeout."

Keese smiled. "I can see you just moved out from the city," said he. "We've got no edible takeout in these parts, only the standard burgers and dogs, pizza."

Harry leaned down and winked, and then he said in an unpleasantly confidential way as if he were making an indecent proposal: "You just leave it to Harry."

Keese puffed out his lips. "I've lived here for twenty years, but I—"

"Always more to learn about anything!" cried Harry, and he seized Keese by the crook of the elbow and propelled him across the carpet for a few feet, then slapped him on the rump, in the mode of athletes at moments of high spirit. Keese had never participated in sports since this gesture had come into fashion, and he had never liked seeing it delivered on television, but receiving it was a horror to him.

Had he known it was coming he might actually have thrown a punch at Harry to forestall him, but again he was confronted by the accomplished fact.

Harry had unhooked his elbow now and swung around to face him. Keese was aware that Harry would be called handsome by some, perhaps by most, but he himself was never favorably impressed by a prominent aquiline nose (it seemed an impropriety), nor in fact did he much like blond hair on a man, where the objection was usually that, far from being fair, it had turned muddy, perhaps even with a greenish tinge. But Harry's was almost bright; he must touch it up; that seemed even worse.

"Look here," said Harry, speaking down his chest as if rolling stones from the summit of a hill, "you just let me find the edibles." Again he threw out his right hand, which looked larger than ever. Keese could find little reason to shake on this, but anything that would encourage Harry to be on his way was surely to the good. Even though Harry's return might be regarded as inevitable Keese would have some respite, and perhaps he could fashion a style in which better to meet his new neighbor's assault.

He put his own hand towards Harry's, but Harry frowned and drew away, twitching his fingers at Keese. "I meant money, old chum," he said reproachfully. "If I do the running, you can bloody well pay the tab." He laughed horsily.

Keese went for the wallet he carried old-fashionedly in the one rear pocket (on every pair of trousers) which could be buttoned. While obviously designed as a deterrent to pocket-picking, in practice (he had read) it was none. The wallet, having been half sat upon for many years, was slightly curved so as to conform to Keese's upper ham. He now plucked out a sheaf of three bills at random: they proved to be two twenties and a ten. In truth he had not bought takeout at home since before Elaine had gone away to college, and in those days ten dollars' worth of deep-fried chicken or superburgers inundated in fragrant garbage would have been enough to feed a regiment.

But keeping up with the times he chose a twenty and then, so as to err generously, added the ten.

Harry scowled at the bills when he had received them, and he derided Keese: "Chintzy!"

Keese disliked being thought mean, but he dreaded the spending of cash. It had become almost a superstition with him to retain folding money, whereas he could be profligate with credit cards. But it was ridiculous that whatever Harry had in mind should cost more than thirty dollars.

Keese winced, and still held on to his remaining twenty. "You're not going to drive to the city?"

Harry squinted and said in a tone of tease: "Just don't you worry about old Harry. Hand over that loot."

Keese seemed to have no other option. He stoically forked over the twenty. Harry showed his teeth at it and then looked up quizzically at Keese. "Whatzis, a two-dollar bill?"

It was, of course. Keese hadn't seen one for years. He worried that someone had palmed it off on him as a twenty, relying on his probable failure to notice. No doubt he looked a pushover to some people, among them Harry and Ramona.

He now set his jaw in belligerence and said: "Yeah. If thirty-two bucks isn't enough, then forget it. We'll eat the succotash."

Harry seemed impressed. He threw up his hands as if in

defense, backed up, and said: "O.K., O.K., I didn't personally make the inflation."

Keese was mollified. "You know, you don't want to be cheap, but you know . . ." He realized he was apologizing again. He and Harry grinned in each other's faces for a moment.

Then Harry returned to the attack. "Let's have your car keys, Earl. I'm out of wheels. My fuel pump gave up just as I swung into the drive next door. But lucky it happened there, huh?"

"Then the only thing that makes sense," Keese said firmly, "is that *I* go for the food. After all, I'm supposed to be being neighborly to you: you're the guest. Why should you do anything? Just sit down here, and Enid will come in and keep you company. Unfortunately there's nothing to drink, and there won't be an answer to that problem tonight. The liquor store's closed by now and so's the next nearest, over in Allenby. What's your source for the food? Maybe I can talk them into selling me a bottle of wine under the table?"

"I can't permit that, Earl," said Harry, with a strange look in his eye. "If I let you pay for the grub, brother, then I'm going to fetch it." Again he seemed to be on the verge of committing a violent act, and he was certainly large enough to make it ugly. Only at such times was Keese afraid of him. But Harry weakened the force of his physical threat by his next speech, which relied on spite for its effect. "I just won't tell you where my source is!"

Keese decided he was but a big harmless fellow. He raised his hands as though he were being held up and told Harry: "We'll go together. I'll get my keys." He started towards the staircase in the hallway, but a muffled sound came from behind him, a kind of strangulated raspberry, not quite a full-fledged lip-fart, but it was bizarre enough to cause Keese to turn.

Harry however was not caught with contorted mouth (had he actually, outrageously, broken real wind?). Whatever, he soon distracted Keese with a display of wounded feelings. "Think I'd steal your car, is that it? Well, sir, if—" He seemed to have lost his breath again, and he sought it with a gasp that probably explained the earlier sound. "I'm sorry I brought up the matter. Forget it, fellow!" He sank his incisors into his lip, though that might have been an illusion, for no blood welled up. His jaw-joints were surging.

Keese was back in the soup with regard to Harry. He believed him unbalanced, a dangerous state in one so large, who merely by falling could destroy much.

"No offense intended," he hastened to say. "Certainly I wasn't implying you would steal my car."

"I say you were," Harry insisted stridently.

Keese realized at this point that he should terminate their association, but he was not sufficiently deft, he feared, to do so without incurring Harry's resentment. And to have an outright enemy as one's nearest neighbor, when one lived at the termination of a dead-end road, with only a wooded hollow beyond, a weed-field across the street, was unthinkable. For example, Harry could effectively impede Keese's egress by car at any time he so decided—and pretend, if the police were called, to have done so accidentally: it was not a thing that could easily be proved. Keese was in fact defenseless against any form of revenge that a demented adversary might choose.

"I wasn't accusing you of anything," he assured his neighbor, and added a supposedly amiable chide: "And speaking of offense, I'll take my own if you insist on feeling wounded. I'll get the car keys." He would, then, let Harry drive his automobile away, but he balked at the thought of leaving him alone in the living room, a place that somehow seemed more seriously vulnerable, owing to its very immobility. "Come along and meet Enid." He feinted towards the kitchen, but he failed to stir Harry.

"I'll just hang on here," said the big fellow. He sauntered

to a wing chair that was probably sturdy enough to withstand his attack, but Keese winced as he watched Harry fall into it and heard the asthmatic gasp of stuffing and muffled shriek of articulated wood.

Keese then decided to fetch Enid and have her stand guard in the living room while he went upstairs. He saw no irony in this: not only was Enid more durable than the furniture, but for some reason, perhaps his impression of Ramona, Keese doubted that Harry was dangerous to women.

He started for the kitchen, but stopped again at the sound of Harry's protest. "Where do you think you're going?"

Keese could not bring himself to confess: *to fetch my wife so that she can keep an eye on you.* It did not occur to him to explain in the flattering way, i.e., to assure Harry that Enid would be charmed to meet him. Instead he lied in panic.

"To get my car keys."

"You don't carry them on you?"

Was Harry making this an accusation? Keese said: "Not at all times."

Harry flashed his full grin, which on a face that large was ingratiating. "No quick getaways for you, then? You stand your ground and face the music."

Keese was somewhat embarrassed by the honorific platitudes. "That's putting the best face on it. Maybe I'm just lazy." He regretted having said that, for Harry's grin turned sardonic as he watched.

"You still don't trust me, do you?" the large man asked. He hurled himself up from the wing chair. "I have a feeling that if you go around the corner you might climb out a window or something. All I'm asking is that loan of your car to go get food for us all, for God's sake. I'm not going to use it to rob a bank. I'm hardly going to sell it! And for that matter, where could I at this time of day?"

Keese was embarrassed to hear the situation put in these

terms, and he tried to alleviate the feeling by taking the initiative from Harry. He asked suspiciously: "What I still don't understand is precisely where you intend to get the food? Really. I'm an old hand in these parts, and I don't know of—"

He was interrupted. In a wounded tone Harry said: "Just because I'm the new man on the block here doesn't mean that I don't know this area or that I have no resources locally."

Keese shrugged. "O.K., I'm sorry if I hurt your feelings." On Harry's example he grew bolder. "But you have a way of avoiding detail."

"Because of fear, do you think?" asked Harry. "Are you saying that I don't dare reveal my plans because I'm yellow?"

Keese was amazed. "What's fear got to do with *naming a restaurant,* for God's sake?" The tension had built up in him. He tried to laugh it loose. "Do you realize that we're two grown men, two neighbors who hardly know each other, and we are arguing about nothing? How did this begin, anyway?"

Harry sat down in the wing chair again, this time with less impact. "If you want to know," he said sighing, "it's a new place, just opened, just beyond town, where the warehouse was, on the other side of the railroad station. Italian."

"I commute," Keese said, "and go by there twice a day, to and from the station, and I haven't seen any change in that warehouse."

"Are you calling me a liar?" Harry asked quietly, his eyes almost closed.

"Certainly not," said Keese. He cravenly added: "I'm just confessing to a failure of observation."

"They don't have their sign up yet," Harry said. "You'll see it soon. Cute name: 'Caesar's Garlic Wars.' "

It was unlikely that he had made that up on the spot, and therefore Keese found it credible. In relief he put himself into a good mood. "Swell. Get some ravioli, huh? I just love those darn things! And stuffed clams—and scampi . . ."

Harry lifted his wrist almost to his nose. "Whatever I get, I will first have to *get going*, Earl."

"Sure." Keese went into the hall and up the stairs. His car keys were on the dresser. He had scooped them up and was prepared to hasten back downstairs, for believing in the reality of the Italian restaurant had little effect on his assessment of Harry's reliability when alone in a room. But someone wrapped in an oversized bath towel lay on the bed in the gathering twilight of the April evening. He pretended it was Enid, though he knew it was not, and he began to tiptoe out, as if not wishing to disturb her. Whereas his real reason was to play for time: the recumbent figure, apparently naked under the towel, was easily recognized as Ramona.

He had reached the threshold when, so to speak, the dagger struck him between the shoulder blades: so did he think of her voice, which literally, however, was neither pointed nor keen-edged but rather blurred and almost expressionless.

What he thought he heard her say was: "Are you going out?"

When he had deciphered these words the worst of his apprehensions were relieved. If she were half-asleep, perhaps he could get away with some soporific mumble in reply, slip downstairs, send her husband off for food, then return and persuade her to dress before Enid discovered her and before Harry returned.

He murmured a soft, blunt sound that was intended to be reassuring and waited for the result. She made no response and was therefore judged to be asleep. He turned and softly mounted the threshold.

"I took a bath," Ramona said clearly. "I hope you don't mind. There's a dead rat in the tub over there. I couldn't face cleaning that up."

"No," Keese said neutrally, "I don't mind." Which was

more or less true, but (1) why couldn't she have asked? (2) why the repose? He asked neither of these aloud, however, and once again sought to steal away.

She persisted. "You'd tell me if you did?"

"Of course."

"I took a pill. I'm hyper enough as it is, but moving—"

"You're taking a little nap?"

"You do mind, don't you?" Ramona asked accusingly, and suddenly she sat up, the towel falling away from her naked breasts. But her back was to the window, from which furthermore came a failing light that had grown dimmer even as they spoke. Also, amazement affected Keese's vision. For all these reasons he saw no intimate particular of her flesh before she retrieved the edge of the large towel and covered herself again. What was shocking was really the sheer *idea* of her lying naked on the bed he had shared with Enid for more than a fifth of a century. He had never had another woman in that place—and in fact few in any other. Keese was a romantic; he had never been a lewd man.

He forced himself to smile. "Harry is just going for Italian food. I imagine you'll be hungry at the end of a long moving day. You'll want to join us downstairs."

"I'm not all that hungry," said Ramona, "if the truth be known. Physical exercise tires me out, but never gives me an appetite."

Keese could sense her reluctance to get up. She might well persist in some damnable way, and how could he dislodge her if she did?

He tried now at least to counterfeit some determination. "I'm sure," he said, "that your absence would be deplored by everybody. So come on down and meet my wife. By the time you're dressed Harry will be back with the food."

"Why," asked Ramona, "are you so ill at ease at this moment? Are you afraid they'll think we are fucking up here?"

Keese maintained his composure. "I just thought you'd be ready to come downstairs and join the party."

She fell back into the supine position and maintained total silence.

"I didn't mean to offend you," he said helplessly. "Stay here as long as you like." He decided to find Enid, after he gave the car keys to Harry, and put as good a face on it as possible, perhaps insisting that Ramona had fallen ill: one could not in decency oppose the will of a sick person. He bowed out of the bedroom and went down the stairs.

He was not truly surprised when, from the hall, he saw Harry probing into one of the cubbyholes, or even an upper drawer, of the secretary desk in the corner of the living room. He had feared something of that sort. At the outset he had identified a criminal aura around the man. But Keese *was* furious. Had he held a loaded shotgun (he believed) he would have discharged it into Harry's wide back, blown a huge gory hole there; being subsequently convicted of manslaughter and sent to prison for ten-to-twenty he would have had to come to terms with the loss of respectability—and also the sexual deviation that was rife behind bars.

Having gone through this sequence and ended in absurdity, he could make a joke of it. "Harry," he cried in ironic joviality, "are you robbing me?"

"Looking for a paper and pencil," Harry said impatiently, without turning around. He slammed the little drawer in its slot, and opened the small door in the middle of the superstructure. Enid, who managed the family funds, kept her financial records there: bank statements, recent canceled checks, deposit slips, and the like.

Harry found the stub of a checkbook and riffled through it negligently, but focused in keenly on the last page. "Three hundred and twenty-seven dollars?" he asked incredulously. "Is that all you had at the end of February?"

Keese had now been pushed too far. He marched across the room, snatched the check stubs from Harry, and returned them to the cabinet and closed its door. Harry loomed above him, but offered no resistance. Neither was he apologetic. Indeed he leaned around Keese and would have probed further into the desk.

"Get away from there," Keese commanded him. "Stay away from my private files."

Harry shrugged and moved across the room. "I still don't have a paper and pencil," he said stoically.

"Why do you need writing materials?" Keese asked. "I thought you were going for Italian food?"

"To write down the order, for God's sake," said Harry in wincing exasperation. "You named five or six things before. This is likely to be complicated."

Keese said: "Why not make it absolutely simple: spaghetti and meatballs, green salad. Enough for all, period. Jug of red wine, if possible. Or a whatchumacallit of Chianti, you know. . . ." He finally remembered, with no help from Harry. "A fiasco." He expected the obvious pun to be made of this, but Harry apparently never did the expected.

"No minestrone?"

"None for me," Keese said solemnly. "Get what you want for yourself and—" He found that he could not mention Ramona's name with a straight face; he felt a growing grimace as he approached the moment for it, and he turned away.

"O.K.," Harry said, "the only thing that is not simple is how I'm going to get to the restaurant."

"I agreed that you could use my car," said Keese.

"Then how can I get it started?" Harry said this between his teeth.

"Oh, sorry! Here are the keys."

Harry lost no time in departing. He slammed the front door and, too short a time afterwards, could be heard to make the engine roar horribly as he put Keese's car in motion. At the turn from the driveway into the road he evoked from the tires a scream which had no precedent.

Keese's nerves by now were so taut that he had the illusion that his belly was a stringed instrument, like a zither, and could have been strummed. He was about to search for Enid when she appeared by her own devices.

"There really is nothing in the house but that succotash," said she. "That's not a hoax." Enid quite sensibly washed the gray from her hair, but quite as reasonably did not seek to reproduce the flaming red hair of her youth. She was now of a subdued auburn hue of head. Perhaps because of Ramona's presence in the house Keese found himself looking at his wife for the first time in years. Enid was altogether more pleasing to him than the younger woman.

"That's solved," he told her now. "Italian food is on the way." He withheld the information as to who was fetching it, expecting her naturally to ask.

Instead she clapped her hands and said: "Gee, that's perfect. Antipasto and chicken cacciatore is my vote. What a great idea!"

"Sorry," said Keese, "it's already on its way and is merely spaghetti and meatballs, I'm afraid."

She made a hideous face at an oval scatter rug. She said: "Carbohydrates are precisely what I don't need. I think I'll take this opportunity to diet. I'll go to bed without my supper."

"Enid," he said, but she was already on the bottom stair. He shouted: "Enid. I have to explain! This is very strange, but— You see, it's— Look, why don't I call the restaurant and tell them to include antipasto and cacciatore in the order? What could be simpler?" He had been too rattled to think of that immediately. In fact, the idea of spaghetti was suddenly loathsome to him. He would change the entire order. Beneath this resolution was something he had repressed: a suspicion that

Harry had not gone to the restaurant, but had rather stolen his car. Actually, Keese had not wanted to determine that as yet. Obviously it must be accepted at some time, if true, but this moment would have been too soon had not Enid rejected the existing menu.

He had now got the nerve he required, and he went to the nearest telephone, that which was to be found in the understairs niche in the hallway, dialed what he still knew as Information though the telephone company had given it a new designation, and asked for the number of Caesar's Garlic Wars, feeling preposterous as he pronounced the name though he was certainly not to be blamed for it.

His fears here were needless. The operator had a heavy accent, probably Hispanic ("Seize Her Golliwogs?"), and it was doubtful that she detected the pun, and anyway the natural sullenness of her voice suggested the kind of solipsism that would be impervious to elements that were beside the point.

She was back in a few seconds with the announcement that if such an establishment existed it was without a telephone.

"Might it be," asked Keese, "on a separate list of new numbers kept apart from the main one? Not yet added to the general index? It is very new."

"Barry New?" said the operator.

Keese thanked her kindly and hung up. Confessing to Enid that he had no means by which to supply her order was worse for him than reflecting on the theft of his car, which after all was insured. And Enid was still standing at the bottom of the stairs. He wondered where to send her; not to the second floor, certainly. Nor did he want her to stay here and listen to his subsequent phone calls: he had a bright idea and intended to re-ring Information; if that didn't work, he would dial the police and report his stolen car.

It was Enid herself who solved his problem. Though having apparently listened to his side of the dialogue with the operator, she assumed he had been successful in his quest.

"Fine," said she and turned into the route towards the kitchen. "I'll set the table." She set off briskly.

Keese believed it likely that she was still not aware that other persons had been in the house; and now she assumed that the food would be delivered by the restaurant for just the two of them and they would eat it together at the kitchen table. All the same he found himself in a kind of paralytic state as to disabusing her, though he could function efficiently enough in all other areas.

As soon as she disappeared he dialed Information again, having got the suspicion that the señorita might have looked up "Caesar's" under S.

And it seemed he was not wrong to try again. The new operator, a flat-voiced soprano, found the number quickly.

Keese dialed it. Another neutral voice, male, came on the wire and identified the restaurant.

"Uh-huh," said Keese, and he apologized in advance for what he must ask. Then he described Harry and said that if he were not there already he would arrive soon, and gave the corrected order.

"Please," said the voice of Caesar's, "we will open next week. We're still closed."

Keese refused to despair. "But my friend doesn't know that. He'll try to get in now, because he thinks you're open for business. When he gets there, please tell him—" But what? If the place was closed, then no talk of its menu would be meaningful. "Tell him, tell him to come on back, and we'll think up something else."

"I won't see him, sir," said the voice. "I'm alone here, upstairs in the back, and I won't even hear him if he comes." With gracious regrets he hung up.

Now Keese was in a quandary. It was certainly too soon to call the police. Harry might be at Caesar's, fruitlessly pounding on the front door. On the other hand, with full knowledge of the restaurant's schedule he might have stolen the car, counting on Keese's being in a state of confusion at this point and so gaining a head start on his escape. By the time it was established that he had stolen the vehicle, he would be miles away. But how rotten if, deciding that Harry had hoodwinked him, Keese sent the police in pursuit: were he in error in believing his new neighbor a car thief, he would never live it down, with Harry just next door.

He now thought about the situation in this new way: if Harry *were* truly his neighbor he would scarcely steal the car —unless of course he were insane. Perhaps he was an impostor —and if Harry was one, then it followed that Ramona must be one too, for Harry had mentioned her. And though she had not mentioned Harry, Keese had told her that Harry was downstairs and she had not asked for an identification. Therefore they were, Ramona and the tall blond fellow, in this together. So much was established. It would be useless then to go upstairs and question Ramona about Harry: they would necessarily be in cahoots on any kind of mischief.

But *someone* had newly moved in next door: Enid had seen the van being unloaded, a process that had taken most of the day.

Keese decided on a bold stroke. He would walk across to the house next door and see whether anyone was there at the moment. If they were not, he believed that he might gain entrance in some fashion and search for something that would identify the new tenants. If they were Harry and Ramona, then no harm would be done. Harry had his car and Ramona was in possession of his bedroom: examining their house would seem no more than that. If on the other hand someone else had taken the place and was in residence at the moment, Keese pretty much had the goods on Harry. If the new people had gone out to eat somewhere, he had a stickier problem: he must find, amidst their lately deposited possessions, evidence of their identity. And of course it would be dreadful if he were caught at it: he might be taken for a common burglar and brained by an enraged householder wielding some domestic object drafted into service as a makeshift bludgeon. (Again by means of extravagant fancies he was trying to forestall disaster.)

He let himself quietly out the front door. The evening was now going decisively towards night, as if to compensate for its hesitancy at the outset: Keese was always sensible of that effect. He stole around the side of his house. He saw a ghostly blur and heard the muffled sound of a running soft-footed quadruped: that damned wolfhound again! Why did it persistently lurk there? The idea of stepping on its stool in the growing darkness was repulsive to him. He decided to give it a scare. Dogs remembered to avoid places where they had been given disagreeable impressions. Keese was not cruel to animals. He planned merely to wave his arms and hoot, at most to shy a stone with purposely bad aim; sometimes a beast got the idea by merely seeing a hand reaching towards the ground.

He turned another corner and saw the rear of his house. The wolfhound was waiting at the back door, and as Keese watched, Enid came to the door and flung to it what looked very like a large piece of meat! He shrank back into the shadows. This was bizarre. Only frozen succotash in the larder, eh? It was almost as if he had seen his wife in an intimate situation with another man—not in bed, perhaps, but sitting *en famille* in the living room, the fellow in his shirt sleeves and socks.

Ramona had not admitted owning the dog. Did it then belong to Enid? If so, why had she concealed the fact? He was by no means averse in principle to keeping pets. In practice the matter had never come up between the two of them since they had been alone and Elaine had taken her cat to college with her, where she managed illegally to maintain it throughout three years of dormitories before it died of natural causes.

Keese decided to find the proper moment to speak to Enid of this matter, and now he turned towards the house next door, which had manifestly been designed by an architect of the eclectic school some fifty years before, at which time it had been surrounded by true "country," and if the owner had believed himself something of a squire he was given some justification by the absence of any other dwellings throughout the two miles from the center of the village. This state of affairs had changed, though the neighborhood was far from becoming a "development," as it was unjustly called sometimes by those who lived there longer than the latest comer.

There were in fact only some two dozen houses out that way (*du côté de chez Keese,* as Elaine had named it on her latest vacation), and only two of them, counting the château Keese, were on what was officially called Burt Street, an ugly name rarely used by either the Keeses or their late neighbors the Walkers.

Keese had now left his property and was traversing the generous side yard of what he had no choice as yet but to call the Walker place, a capriciously designed structure with little corner towers and a roof lined with false battlements. Yet the lower stories were, by contrast, exquisitely humdrum, shingled in poopoo brown and peepee yellow (again Elaine's bon mot: the latter color was actually a smudged sort of cream).

The house was dark, a condition which would support Harry & Ramona's claim to be the new tenants, because obviously they were elsewhere. But it was only negative evidence, and Keese pressed on. He soon arrived at an angle, with respect to the rear windows, from which he could see not only a light in the kitchen but also a figure moving within it.

Keese went right up to the glass. The figure was Harry's. He was stirring something in a large pot. The kitchen was stacked with cardboard cartons, some of which were imprinted with the name of a well-known national moving company; but others had obviously been packed by amateur hands and bore the disparate designations of sanitary napkins, fancy chocolates, and a blended whiskey. Harry had apparently opened certain boxes to get what he needed. He held a long-handled wooden spatula of a special sort: from the face of its oval blade rose a cluster of pegs. Keese could associate no function with this peculiar design until he watched Harry plunge the instrument into the pot, draw it up dripping, and display a hank of spaghetti.

Keese drew back from the window, his face as hot as if it had been slapped. He could not begin to understand the pretext for Harry's hoax. He tried desperately to think of a suitable piece of revenge: best would be locking the door, to go out to dinner with Enid before Harry returned. But Ramona was there. If he threw her out she would go home and tell Harry, ruining the plan to discomfit him. If she remained—but Keese would not leave her alone in his house.

Also he suddenly remembered that Harry had his car. Well, that could be a beginning: he would quietly take back his own automobile! Even Harry, who was none too sensitive, might be embarrassed to come out with his load of spaghetti and find that the borrowed car had been stolen—explain *that* to your new neighbor! Keese chuckled into his hand. He made it around the back of the house without mishap. He knew of old where the well cover was situated, and there was just enough light, when one's eyes had become habituated to the evening, to see the silhouette of iron garden furniture that could have disabled the unwary.

But of course when he reached his car and discreetly sought to open the driver's door he had to abandon the plan altogether. He had been prepared to find that Harry had removed the ignition key. Were this the case, he intended at least to try jumping the ignition wires beneath the dashboard.

But in point of fact Harry had locked all four doors!

Keese walked sullenly down the driveway. When he reached the street and turned towards his own house he saw another car, parked at the curb. Obviously this was Harry's own automobile, out of commission because of an ailing fuel pump. Keese in fantasy projected a better revenge than he had originally planned: what a joke to drive Harry's car into the Keese driveway! The only trouble was, if Harry had locked Keese's car, he must surely have secured the doors of his own vehicle, parked out in the street.

Keese anyway tried the driver's door—and it opened! The ignition, though, was locked, and tampering with the wires on a car not his own was of course out of the question. Yet the slope of the street, if he could once get the vehicle in motion, would probably be sufficient for the rolling of the car to his own curb, and perhaps there would be even enough momentum by then to make the left turn and penetrate the driveway for some distance.

Chortling *sotto voce*, he climbed into the seat. The car had a stick shift, but Keese could well remember, despite his years of automatic transmission, where neutral could be found: he had got his first license at sixteen. He released the hand brake. Though parked on a slight declivity Harry had spurned the advice of the Motor Vehicle Bureau (dispensed among other places on late-night TV when the commercials ran out) to turn the wheels towards the curb. And lucky for Keese that he had not so done, because his steering wheel would have locked in that position.

The car ignored Keese's wishes and the agitation of his body on the seat and refused to move. Nor did the opening of the door and the extending of his left foot to the roadway, there to apply a backwards pressure of the sole, overcome the massive inertia of the vehicle. There was but one answer to his problem: to remove himself altogether from the car, to push with all his strength against the foremost portion of the window frame while keeping the right hand upon the handle of the door, so that when momentum was established he might rip it open and leap in.

But Keese had not done anything of this sort for two decades. He was not as deft of hand as of old, and he had never been notable for agility of leg. The application of his bulk to the pushing hand forced the car finally to move, and once in motion the wheels were lured by gravity into quickening their revolutions. Even a faster man would have been nearing his limits by the time that Keese attempted to re-enter the vehicle. Worse, he could not find the proper angle of hand at which to trip the latch, which was subtly different from that of his own car, a major difference when rolling.

He fell out of the race before reaching his own house. Harry's car continued on, jumped the unpaved curb at the end of the street, easily flattened the guard rail and the DEAD END sign it bore (the posts being rotten), and vanished with rather less noise than one would have thought, but in point of fact there were no trees there and but a soft undergrowth, and the slope was such that a wheeled thing would continue rolling to the low bank of the creek and slip into the water with ease.

Keese assumed that it was now too dark to see much down there. In any event, he didn't try. His joke had failed: that was evident and good enough for him. He strolled up his walk and sidled into his house. His persistent conviction that he had been mocked by Harry relieved him from the claims of decency.

CHAPTER **3**

OF course hardly had he got inside when he was struck violently with the understanding that he *had destroyed Harry's car.* While participating in the incident itself he had seen it as a kind of dream. What terrified him especially was that Enid would be disdainful: he still had no great sympathy with Harry. No doubt the car was insured. In his brief experience of it, the vehicle had not seemed in any way special. It had surely been a standard model, partaking of few "options," e.g., not even an automatic clutch.

Keese's own car was something of a gas-guzzler, with power-assisted brakes and steering, white-striped tires, and a special kind of wheel cover which the manufacturer had pretended to be of extra value—all of this included in the one-of-a-kind deal. Keese was never taken in by such near-charlatanism: it had simply been the model desired by Enid. Actually, it was now four years old and what had seemed fairly luxurious in the first few months (though never approaching the degree of the advertisements) now was probably a bit tackier in tone than a more modest automobile would have been at a similar age.

He had given up smoking three years before, but he knew where an old pack of cigarettes was hidden, in an end-table drawer, behind a box of poker chips, some lacquered coasters, and a miniature parasol from a mixed drink served at a Polynesian restaurant: each of these souvenirs could tell a story, but their only value to Keese at the moment was in impeding his discovery of the little paper tubes stuffed with dried weed—he had kicked the habit after reading, in some self-help article, the advice to think of cigarettes as cylinders of smoldering filth. He was living proof that the theory worked. Should he discredit it by lighting up now?

He slammed the drawer shut. He remembered the wolfhound. He was not without weapons. So a joke had got out of hand? No person had been damaged, and the insurance would cover Harry's loss. But none of this would have happened had Enid not given a piece of meat, large enough to have fed them all, to that dog.

On the route to the kitchen this argument seemed feebler with every step, and by the time he reached that room he had decided to say nothing of either car or wolfhound.

His decision proved beside the point: Enid was not there. While he had been on his disastrous mission next door she had probably gone upstairs, found Ramona in bed, stabbed her to death with a pair of shears, and was waiting for him to return so that she could murder him by like means. Therefore he was in none too great a hurry to encounter her.

He returned to the front hallway and, having looked upstairs dubiously, went into the living room. There sat Enid under a lamp, leafing through a tabloid newspaper. For reading only, she employed a pair of half-glasses.

"You've brought the food?" she asked brightly.

"Unfortunately I haven't," said Keese. "But it won't be long now. Say, do you mind my asking? Have you been upstairs recently?" He had decided he must force the issue.

"Of course I have," she replied vaguely, returning to her reading.

But her air of indifference might well be a ruse. Keese

decided on another approach. "I've given this some thought. Now that Elaine's away at school, maybe you should have a pet to give you some company during the day."

"Earl," said Enid, though still staring into her paper, "Elaine has been away at school four years."

"But isn't the point still valid?"

"The biggest obstacle to owning a pet, as I see it," said Enid, closing the paper and rising to deposit it on the coffee table, "is what to do with it when you travel." She removed her half-glasses.

"Board it," said Keese.

Enid made a face. "Kennels have a terrible reputation. I wouldn't want a dog of mine—"

"Do you have a dog?"

Enid persisted in completing her sentence: "—to go to a kennel. If I had a dog."

"Uh-huh," said Keese. "Well, I think I'll go and change my clothes. You don't mind? Don't need the bathroom for anything?" He caught sight of the newspaper on the coffee table: it was one of those scandalmongering, UFO-reporting tabloids sold near the check-out in supermarkets. "Ha," said he, going near it with extended forefinger, "a new phase in your reading?"

"Mine?" asked Enid. *You* brought it home."

He drew in a sufficiently large breath with which to protest ardently, but released it without a sound. Undoubtedly this was more work of their new neighbors, though he had seen neither Ramona nor Harry with the paper.

He slunk from the room and made each stair a separate effort. Having called into active service all his reserve of energy, he stepped briskly over the threshold of the master bedroom. In the darkness he found the switch of the lamp on Enid's dressing table.

Ramona was gone. He ascertained that the bedspread had

been smoothed to remove her impress. He hastened into the bathroom through the private entrance from the bedroom. The bathroom also communicated with the hall through another door. In fantasy he saw how the two women could have eluded one another; it was farfetched, like some sequence in a farce, but possible: Ramona going into bathroom just before Enid enters bedroom; next Enid goes to bathroom by inside door as Ramona leaves bathroom by hallway portal. Noise of faucet obscures such little sound as Ramona would produce on hallway runner or carpeted stairs.

But where was the younger woman now? That she had left the house altogether seemed too good to be believed. Losing a towel was a small price to pay—he could not find the one, rose-colored, in which she had been wrapped. He realized that to be on the safe side the other rooms on the floor must be searched. It would be insupportable if he found her in Elaine's. The thought made him tremble in fury.

He was moving along the hall, fists knotted, when he heard the sound of the doorbell downstairs. Undoubtedly that would be Harry, bringing the food. Keese believed that, having destroyed his car, the least he could do was to give him a hand now. He started down the stairs, but when he had descended only halfway Enid came out and opened the door.

"Don't tell me!" she said. "You're our new neighbor. Please come in, and won't you stay for dinner? We're expecting a delivery of Italian food at any moment. Antipasto and chicken cacciatore!"

She stepped aside, and Keese, reaching the bottom of the stairs, watched the entrance of Ramona, who either did not see or positively ignored him.

"I'm sorry to bother you," said Ramona to Enid, "but someone has stolen our car, and I wanted to phone the police. Our service hasn't been connected up yet."

"How terrible," said Enid, and she led the new neighbor to

the telephone niche under the stairs, passing Keese en route.

Ramona still had not looked at him. Was this some sort of bluff, or was she really so distracted by the loss of the car?

She seized the handpiece of the phone. "It is really worse than just the car theft," said she. "Baby was in the back seat of that automobile."

Keese felt as if kicked simultaneously behind each knee. He really teetered for a moment before whirling, hurling himself at the door, and plunging into the night.

On the walk outside he nearly collided with Harry, whose long arms embraced several paper bags.

"Earl!" cried Harry. "Here, take one of these off my hands." He thrust a stuffed bag at Keese and let it go: Keese therefore was compelled to accept it or watch it fall to the concrete.

"Please," he said, trying in vain to return it, "a terrible thing has—" He detested himself for being unable simply to hurl the bag away without explanation, but he could not. He was paralyzed by his social obligation.

"C'mon," said Harry, "while it's still hot." He headed for the door.

Gathering his powers, Keese finally managed to produce what seemed to him a hideous scream. What emerged must have been much vitiated, however, for it had little effect on Harry. Harry did stop before the door, for even though he had got rid of one bag his burdens were still too cumbersome to permit him to turn with impunity.

"C'mon, Earl," he shouted, "do your duty," nodding his blond poll at the knob.

Keese came up the walk, managing to gasp: "Your baby may be drowning."

"Huh?" Harry's expression could not be seen, though the two door-flanking carriage lamps had suddenly come on. But he sounded none too concerned. "Why don't we talk about that later," he said. "Meanwhile, let's get this grub inside."

Keese could not believe he would allow Harry to lure him into opening the door, but he found himself doing as much. Once they were both inside, however, he rested his bag upon the little table under the mirror, where junk mail sometimes remained for many days. (There was an envelope there at the moment, labeled Free Gift in red printing.) The women had gone from the hallway.

But before Keese could speak Harry said: "Oh, you mean the dog? Why should he be drowning? He's a great swimmer."

"Child?" Keese produced this one-word query.

"No child," said Harry, leaning towards him between the paper bags and speaking with exceptional clarity and at raised volume, as if to a foreigner or imbecile. "She calls the dog Baby. Nothing's wrong with him: he's out somewhere with her in the car."

Keese was blacking out in relief, sagging against the table. He remembered that the driver's window had been open: the dog would not have been trapped inside. Moreover, the creek was only two feet deep at that point. Even a helpless baby would probably not have been in mortal trouble, on a seat above the water-level—unless of course it rolled off. Even so, it was a narrow escape in an emotional sense.

Harry let his bags sag for a moment and then, breathing in, gave them a squeeze and a boost and headed for the rear of the house. Keese, recovering, came along behind. When they arrived in the kitchen only Enid was there.

Keese put his bag on the nearest section of the counter and introduced his wife. "Enid Keese," he said pompously, not having quite recovered from his terror, "Harry uh—" He laughed in dramatized embarrassment. "Do you know, I don't yet know your last name?"

Nor did Harry furnish it now. He deposited his bags on the counter, waved his large hand, and said: "Hi again, Enid."

Keese looked questioningly at his wife.

"We met hours ago," said Enid, and perhaps it was a hallucination, but Keese thought he saw her peer fixedly, rudely, at Harry's crotch as if his fly were undone. Harry seemed to be her junior by a dozen years, whereas he, Keese, was about two decades older than Ramona.

"Where's Ramona?" Keese asked quickly now.

"She went out to try and find Baby," said Enid.

"You see?" Harry pointed a finger at the level of Keese's belly button.

He explained to Enid: "Earl was worried about Baby too."

"I didn't know you were acquainted with him," Enid said with an apparent hint of jealousy. "*I* looked after him *all day* while they were moving in."

"I wish you had told me," Keese said in a severe tone.

Enid simpered at Harry. "They spoil him awfully." She used that affectionately chiding tone which was the favorite style of certain women associated with Keese in his childhood, though not his own mother.

Harry responded in such a solemn voice that his joke was not instantly apparent. "I want him to have every advantage I was denied as a young dog." He then silently showed his teeth to Keese: they were in proportion to the rest of him, i.e., large. "Well," he said then, rubbing his palms together with the sound of sandpaper on cinder block, "let's tie into this food before the sauce congeals."

Keese began to worry about Ramona. He wanted to get his meal put away before the matter of the car intruded. "Should I look for your wife?" he asked Harry.

"If you want to," Harry said, sinking his hands merrily into the first of the bags, "but you'll have more to eat if you don't!"

Given Ramona's slenderness, this seemed an empty threat. Keese hahaed politely and let himself out the back door.

Even before his eyes adjusted to the darkness he saw Baby coursing through the back yard: its white fur caught the illumination from the kitchen windows. Therefore he had damaged nothing but Harry's car, which was enough, perhaps, but at least it was not a thing of flesh and blood. Wolfhounds, however, gave Keese the creeps: it was that weird curve made by their back and hind legs.

"Earl." It was Ramona's voice, at his elbow. "Baby survived."

"That's fine," said Keese. "I'm glad he's O.K."

"Mum's the word on the car."

"Excuse me?" He could hardly see her; her olive skin and the lilac turban did not reflect much light.

"I realize it was an accident," said she.

"Then you saw it?"

She pressed against him, but not with any intimate part that he could feel. She seemed to be enlisting him as a coconspirator. "Happen to anybody."

She was certainly being good about it. "Look here," said Keese, "I'll take care of it. Least I can do. It's awful of me, but I'm afraid I was actually too embarrassed to confess. Isn't that terrible? It wasn't the money or anything—I want to pay the damages now. It was pride, I suppose. Do something so stupid —well, it's hard for me to admit it before other people, especially ones I have just met."

"It seems to bother you much more than it does me," Ramona assured him. "But, if you insist, I'll accept your kind offer. Fifteen hundred should take care of it."

"Fifteen hundred!"

"Look here," said she, "I think I am safe in saying that fifteen hundred is a conservative estimate."

He saw the time had come to be completely literal. "The fact is, I'm sure that your comprehensive insurance will cover most of it. What I meant was that I would pick up the 'deductible,' which is probably a hundred dollars or so."

Ramona smiled at him. "You're speaking of the car, I think.

What I mean is your own trouble. What was that, vandalism, malicious mischief? I won't go into the motive why a man would push someone else's car down a hill."

"Do you mean . . ." Keese forced the words through almost closed teeth. He was both furious and frightened, and he would not have been able to say which emotion was foremost.

"I can't believe it," he said. "You're *blackmailing* me?" He had never expected to use that word in real life: it seemed too cinematic.

"Well, wouldn't you, if you had somebody cold?"

Despite his anger he believed her question to be authentically ingenuous. She was a terrible young woman, but he could not find it in himself to declare her evil in a positive sense. He decided to explain himself. He told her of Harry's trick in borrowing the car and pretending to get the food from a restaurant when actually he cooked it himself, and how rolling the car into the Keese driveway was supposed to pay Harry back in the same coin. "So you see," he concluded, "there was no criminal intent, nor am I a maniac who ruins valuable property willfully."

She peered at him for a long moment. "How far would you go to avoid humiliation? That's what I always think when I look at somebody like you." Again, detestably, she tweaked him in the rump, snorted, turned, and went indoors.

He found it impossible to follow hard upon her heels. Instead he called to Baby, but though the wolfhound approached him immediately it soon skittered away. He preferred cats because with them there was never any pretense that they would come on call.

When he entered the kitchen at last the three of them were seated at the table, tucking into the spaghetti. It amazed him that Enid had not emptied into a decent bowl Harry's paper bucket, which bore the printed name of a takeout-chicken business; nor had she provided proper glasses for the red wine from the jug he had brought along. The trio were drinking from Styrofoam cups.

Alcohol was what Keese badly needed at the moment, so badly that he abandoned his plan to go as far as the dining room and get a wine goblet from the cabinet there. He seized a spongy white cup and splashed it almost full of wine. He drank it all in one lifting of the hand, three swallows. He was no connoisseur; wine for him was merely a less damaging source of alcohol than spirits, less fattening and in general less obnoxious than beer.

"Help yourself, Earl," said Harry, coarsely shoving the spaghetti bucket towards him. He had tomato sauce at the corners of his mouth. More than one strand of pasta had strayed from bucket or plates onto the usually spotless lemon-yellow tablecloth. There were wine stains as well. It was, in truth, a loathsome place, and they were, all three of them, including Enid, feeding like beasts.

It disgusted him to watch them, but suddenly he was overcome by a violent hunger, and he seized a plate and, from a standing position, heaped it with a cargo of spaghetti. He would have eaten it while erect, but all three of them lowered their cutlery at this point and he was brought to his senses by their disapproving stares. Depraved as they were, they evidently had some values they would preserve.

He hooked a chair leg with his toe, pulled it from the table, and sat down, all without the use of his hands, which held the plate high and level, as if it were some sort of offering he was taking to an altar. He lowered his face and forked into his mouth the slippery ends of a clump of pasta and then ingested them by suction: a style he had not used since boyhood and not then with impunity if his parents were near.

He was being deliberately provocative. He washed the spaghetti down with a draught of wine from the new cupful to which he had helped himself. He could hardly bear to look at

Enid, who usually was an impeccable diner and ate like some-one in a movie, i.e., as if contemplating the Platonic idea of food and not actually filling the belly. Now her mouth was encarmined with tomato sauce, and as if in sympathy her eyes were bloodshot. There was a wine stain on the collar of her beige blouse at its bustiest protrusion.

"I see your appetite is good," said he, "despite the absence of chicken or antipasto." He turned to Harry, to deliver the telling thrust: "I must call up Caesar's and commend the chef."

Ramona swallowed and said: "That's a mob place if I ever saw one. You know how you can tell? Look at the name on the laundry-service trucks and the deliveries of soda."

"Naw," said Harry, "that's not a good way."

"Yes it is!" cried Ramona.

"You're full of shit," Harry said quietly.

Ramona quailed, though he had not suggested physically that he would touch her. "O.K., O.K.," she whined, putting up her hands as if to fend him off, "I don't want to lose my teeth over it."

Keese looked to see how Enid was taking this, and was interested to note that she seemed oblivious to all but her spaghetti.

He tried again with Harry: "Were they crowded this eve-ning?"

"What?" Harry wrinkled his nose and resumed chewing.

"Caesar's!" shouted Keese, who now could smell blood. "Friday night, the only place in town. I imagine they're turning them away in droves."

Harry's eyelids became heavy and fell. "Earl," said he, "knock off this line. You probably called them and found out they haven't opened for business yet. But does that give you something on me?"

"I think it does," said Keese, glad that the matter was in the open at last. He took another pull at the wine, which he had begun to feel by now.

"All right," Harry said, leaning back from the table, his arms thrown wide. "You've nailed me. By your lights I'm a liar, is that it?" He pointed. "But with a little charity towards the human race, you might not be so quick to condemn. Maybe in all good faith I went down to Caesar's and found they were closed. So I got a bright idea: I bought some spaghetti and a jar of meat sauce and cooked them up myself."

"Where?" asked Keese. "Everything's shut at this hour. And where'd the wine come from?"

Enid spoke at last. "Earl, this is disgraceful! You let a new neighbor provide us with dinner, and if that isn't enough you insult him while wolfing it down. Have you no decency whatever?"

"No, Enid," Harry said protectively, "I don't mind confessing to Mr. District Attorney. You know that little Mom 'n' Pop deli? Across from the movie theater and next to the Singer Sewing Center?"

Keese took his time, sucking in spaghetti, and he polluted his napkin further: these serviettes would have to be discarded when the meal was done; never could they be washed clean. Then he said: "Harry, I don't say this lightly. But there is no deli in the village. There is a proper grocery or market, self-service. But even if your terms were badly chosen—two young-ish Italian-American brothers own this place—the establishment is not situated where you say, because—and I'm afraid this is devastating—*there is no movie theater and there is no Singer Sewing Center in the village.*"

Harry smirked and said: "You wouldn't want to put money on it?"

"No," Keese said wearily, "I wouldn't, because it's too ridiculous. I've lived here for more than twenty years, and I know that village absolutely. You might be thinking of Allenby, except that I know of no such arrangement over there either. They certainly don't have a movie, for one, and for another, a round trip of nine miles is too much for you to have made just now and also have time to cook the spaghetti."

"What do you expect me to do, then?" asked Harry. "Beg your pardon, as if I'm guilty of some horrible crime? Has anybody been hurt? Isn't this meal just about as good as any you've had in the routine wop restaurant, if it comes to that? So what's the difference?"

"That, Harry," said Enid, with an affectionate look at the large blond man, "is precisely my point."

"Anyway," Harry added, "it's just your word against mine."

Keese now came to suspect that it was all an elaborate joke on Harry's part. His own sense of humor was rather too keen to appreciate such foolishness, but neither was there reason to make an ugly thing of it. The spaghetti was O.K., and the jug wine was ideal for such swilling. He and Enid had had no rousing plans for a Friday evening in many a year. If they had dinner guests, or were entertained, it was invariably on Saturday night. They had a small, fixed corps of local friends, and except during the winter holidays nobody participated in more than one social event per weekend since reaching, most of them, their mid-forties.

Thus it might be inspiriting to forget the petty occasions for annoyance and have a bit of gala now with younger companions.

"My gosh," said Keese, "aren't we serious?" He chose Enid to ask: "Where's your sense of humor?" To Harry: "I'm ribbing you. . . . Listen, I'm sincere now, welcome to the neighborhood, if it can be called that, but we do have garbage pickup." He felt slightly drunk.

"Why did you say that?" asked Ramona, who was to his right.

"To show you that we aren't exactly in the wilderness," he

answered. "And there are a few people worth knowing here-abouts. We have a little circle of kindred souls, and generally eat dinner at one house each Saturday. Tomorrow night it's at Marge and Chic Abernathy's: I'm sure we could haul you along." It was an unfortunate phrase; he understood that the moment it emerged. He was usually more careful, and he didn't know why he was not now.

Harry closed his eyes and shook his head from left to right. Ramona said: "*Yuhkkk*. It sounds awful."

Enid smiled across the table and said: "It *is* awful, dear."

Trying to fit in, Keese said: "It can be painful if too much coconut and banana come into play, in some South Seas concoction, but fortunately that's rare enough. But if the food is good, I enjoy myself and I don't mind admit-ting that I do."

Harry appeared to be offended by this. "Well, *I* don't," he said, flushing angrily. "Your suggestion stinks, Earl. Forget it. We don't want to know any of your boring friends. The people who live in areas like this are deadly."

Keese made mild objection: "Of course, *you've* just moved here, haven't you?"

"I may be *in* the country," said Harry, "but I'm not of it."

"Do they have any fairs around here?" asked Ramona. "Where they do things like see which bull has the biggest balls?"

Keese couldn't help flinching. "This isn't the real country," he explained. "This is mainly commuting territory. The locals are small trades- and service-people, not farmers."

Enid, holding a sagging forkful above her plate, spoke sol-emnly to her husband: "Can't you see how offensive it is to our new friends to persist on this subject?"

"O.K., O.K." Keese grinned, though in fact he felt ill used. He was amazed to see that Enid continued to stare reprovingly at him, and he watched helplessly as a thick droop of spaghetti developed from the underside of her fork and got heavier, heavier . . . yet did not fall.

"Well," said she at last, speaking through pursed lips, "we're waiting."

"Waiting?" He had no sense of her aim.

"For an apology, Earl." Now, when in anger he looked away for part of a second, the spaghetti fell onto the tablecloth with a loathsome plop, and the excess of tomato sauce in which it was swathed burst in droplets and one or two reached the back of his hand.

"I should apologize for inviting somebody to dinner?" Keese shook his head. "Come on, Enid." He turned to Harry and Ramona. "Excuse us, folks. Must be embarrassing for you. Suffice it to say that if you were insulted, I regret having been the cause of it. I certainly had no evil intention." He looked into the middle distance and really addressed himself: "This is crazy."

Harry shouted: "That does it!" and pushed his chair away from the table. He stood up. "I don't have to take this, Keese. Let's go outside and settle it man-to-man."

Keese was frightened by the irrationality of it: that was far worse than the threat of taking a beating from Harry, large as he was.

"Please calm down," he said. "I don't quite understand what it was I did, but I apologize for it, Harry. I apologize for everything." He tried to keep his mind off the prospect of having these wretched people as neighbors, if they were so terrible on first meeting. He was aware that most men could be placated by being flattered on their size and strength, and therefore he proceeded to do this with Harry and furthermore denigrated himself in a lighthearted style. "Do you think I would take you on, anyway? I'm no fool. You look like a professional athlete. I haven't touched my toes in twenty years, you know." He waited for Harry's cold expression to change, and when it did not he was irked. The man was fifteen years younger than he, a head taller. It was monstrously unfair of him to challenge a man like Keese. In fact it was a kind of cowardice.

In despair Keese finally said it: "Why don't you pick on somebody your own size?"

Of all things (Keese thought it possible that Harry would be further enraged), Harry winced as if he had been slapped in the face. "Wow," said he, breathing heavily, "you don't call your punches, do you? I think you suckered me with that one. I guess I *do* seem like a skunk, leaning on a little old fat guy. O.K., I'll ask your pardon. Gee, you're old enough to be my dad."

Keese smiled in the bitterest irony. Apparently if he fought back in any way he would be punished severely. Nevertheless he could not forbear from saying, "You mean, your grandfather!"

Harry winked at him and silently mouthed some words, which to Keese looked like: *I'll get you for that.* But he couldn't be certain, nor could he understand why Harry wanted revenge on him. . . . Until he remembered destroying the car. But Harry didn't yet know about that, did he?

He decided to lance the boil, if it was the right one; he couldn't stand a continuation of this bad feeling. "Look," he said, "it isn't easy to say this, but about the car—"

Harry's wide shoulders slumped, and he sat down violently. "Insurance will cover that," said he. "But even so, it was my fault and I feel lousy about it."

Keese put out his hand. "Just a moment. *Your* fault? Hardly."

"See, I thought it was in gear," Harry said. "The grade isn't that much, either. So I didn't set the brake."

Keese smiled and shook his head. "No, no, Harry, you see—"

"But it's a heavy car, Earl. Its weight was enough so that mere gravity got it going."

"That may be, Harry, but it's no excuse. It didn't start off by itself. It was helped."

Harry frowned. "No, I'm sorry, but I'm not going to admit to something I didn't do, Earl."

Enid and Ramona were serenely, doggedly eating.

"You certainly didn't do it, Harry," Keese said. "*I* did."

Harry shook his head. "I think we've got our wires crossed in some way that I for one don't understand. Here's my point, as simply as I can make it: when I came back from the village I pulled your car up in my driveway. I *thought* I left it in gear. I definitely didn't set the parking brake. Now, when I come out, having made the spaghetti, the car isn't there. My first assumption was that it had been stolen. But when I come down the street I see the guardrail at the end of the road has been busted out and the bushes there are crushed. What happened was, your car rolled down the drive, hit that stone at the edge, which turned the wheels left, so it proceeded down the street, jumped the curb, went through the fence, and on into—what is it, a gully there?"

Ramona whinnied with laughter and Enid said, chuckling: "The little comedies of everyday life."

"I know I should have told you earlier," said Harry, "but why spoil our dinner together? The first of many such, I trust."

Keese prayed to his barbarous gods that it not prove so. Now he was faced with the sticky matter of deciding whether it had indeed been an accident or Harry had destroyed the car in revenge for the destruction of his own. He would love to beat a confession out of the man, striking his huge body with a stout truncheon until, falling whimpering to his knees, Harry would implore him to hear a full account of his malefactions.

However, what Keese said now was: "My gosh."

Harry said: "I knew you'd take it like a man. Then we're still buddies?" He dropped his fork and put his hand across the table. Keese was constrained to take it. Harry's handshake had been flabby on their first meeting, but now it could have crushed metal. Keese pulled out of it as soon as he could, but he feared permanent disability. But one thing had been established: he was certain now that Harry knew about his own car, and how could he *not* have known? Keese was disgusted with himself for conceiving such ludicrous doubts about things that were self-evident.

He had difficulty in retrieving his fork with his maimed hand. He had lost his appetite anyway. He drank more wine.

Ramona turned to him and asked: "Isn't it time, Earl, for a little confessing of your own?"

Ordinarily the fairest of men, Keese felt he was being manipulated by these loathsome people (to what end he could not have said, for he was alternately both victim and victimizer), and he decided now to be stubborn. He had a moral advantage over Harry at the moment, or at least the appearance of one. Why should he voluntarily give it up?

"Confess?" he asked disingenuously. "To what? To living in my own house? To breathing air?"

Ramona sneered. "Here Harry has been decent enough, honest enough, to admit that because of his negligence your car has been wrecked. And what do you have to say? Nothing."

"Earl," said Enid, lowering her fork and still chewing, "you are really humiliating me. What you did was bad enough, but your silence is obscene."

Keese was shocked by this assault from his wife—he had been conscious of her previous malice, but he assumed it was her way of being hospitable to their guests—but still he held his ground: if anything, more defiantly than before.

"So you're ganging up on me, eh?" he said, drawing himself up in the fashion which conventionally suggested indignation. Keese performed this as a conscious parody, subtly to indicate his contempt for them and also for the gesture. He was not sure he succeeded with this overload of significance: at any rate, no one appeared to be bluffed by it.

Harry scowled across the table: a blond curl had drooped onto his forehead. If he knew about it and let it stay he was excessively vain. But soon enough he swept it back with the flat of his hand, denying Keese the use of it against him. He was no mean opponent!

"We're waiting," Harry said then. "Or do I have to pound it out of you?" He displayed a large fist.

Keese did a thing by which he astonished himself. He rose quickly and went around the table to Harry's side. "Don't speak like that to me in my own house," he said quietly, but he seemed to hear a deafening ovation thereafter: this was utterly imaginary. Enid pretended to be embarrassed and turned her flushing face away. Ramona hissed venomously.

Harry however was impressed. "I meant no offense, Earl. It's just the sort of thing a fellow says."

"Why?" asked Keese, standing over him.

"I don't know. It's ridiculous, really. I've made an ass of myself, I guess." Harry displayed a sickly grin.

Keese however did not trust him; this knuckling under seemed more than a little bogus. "Well," he said, leaving, "too much could be made of it. Let's drop the subject."

"You don't really think you'll get away with it, do you?" asked Ramona as he passed her. "Oh, you're the cool one, aren't you?"

Enid said: "Earl, this is insufferable."

How in the world had he got into this mess on a Friday evening when he had stayed at home? Much of Keese's trouble lay in his inability to accept the situation as a real one and not a masochist hallucination. But perhaps he was being too stubborn.

"All right, you win," he told Ramona. "I confess." He looked at Harry. "About your car—"

Ramona interrupted with a scream. "No, no!"

"Please," said Keese, "you wanted me to admit committing my little crime, if such it was, and now that I start to do so you stop me."

"You filthy pervert," cried Ramona.

Harry put both his hands out as if he were calming the waters. It was a pretentious gesture, and it was matched by his speech. "Now, now," he said, "let's not have an altercation."

Keese was stunned by Ramona's choice of terms. He had had quite enough of this wretched pair. He would throw them out immediately, regardless of their threats, despite the strong possibility that in revenge they could make of the dead-end street a perfect hell.

But before he could put his decision into effective words (he did not wish to dissipate its force by expressing it badly), Ramona turned to Harry.

"He tried to rape me," said she.

CHAPTER 4 /

WHO could have predicted that in a time of true stress Harry would act responsibly?

"Earl," he said in a judicial sort of voice, "you'll get your opportunity for self-defense. I'm aware that such accusations are flung about wholesale these days. Still, it's a serious charge. In wartime the old Army used to execute those convicted of the crime."

Keese felt very grateful to Harry for this reassurance. For that matter he agreed with him that the crime was despicable. He had brooded about Elaine's being a victim, and he had sworn he would kill the perpetrator if he could find him. He had never worried about Enid in that regard: she didn't seem the type who could easily be brutalized, and it was a fact that fiends, like water, sought the line of least resistance.

But of course Ramona was clearly demented. If Harry was at all reasonable, and he seemed so now, he must understand that his wife needed special care. No doubt he would be obliged by the requirements of familial loyalty to pretend to take her accusation seriously, but was it being sentimental to believe that he would soon dispose of it, clear Keese of all charges, and leave with a certain sheepishness? Keese had not liked Harry until this moment, no doubt because he had not understood him.

Harry peered sharply at him. "I tell you for your own good, Earl, that you'd better wipe that smirk off your face: it will hurt your case, make you look like a cynic."

Keese had been sure he wasn't smiling, let alone wearing a derisive expression. "Sorry," he said. "Must be the strain I'm under. It isn't pleasant to be accused of such a thing under one's roof, in front of one's wife. And there's as good a defense as any: what a place and time to pick, if I were thinking of rape!"

Harry put his finger out. "I doubt that you were *thinking* of it, Earl. You're not the premeditative type. You're the sort of fellow who would be overcome suddenly by a feeling of lust— I can see that. But whether you'd try to put your yearnings into action is what we're trying to determine here. Now I might say that Ramona, in my experience, is not a reckless person. In fact, call this prejudiced if you will, but she's the most level-headed woman I've ever known."

This could of course still be a necessary buttering-up, but Keese's feet had begun to grow ominously cold in his comfortable old house-shoes. His only hope was that Harry would be well versed in Ramona's hysterical transports. If he truly believed her to be of equable temperament and capable of good judgment, then Keese was under a threat. If it was her word against his, and if those words were considered of equal weight, his chances to get justice were poor—for the obvious reason: why would an altogether sane woman accuse an absolutely guiltless man of sexual assault?

"With all respect," Keese nevertheless said to Ramona, "just why do you maintain that I tried to, that I attempted . . ." He was having the most damnable difficulty in mouthing the word: no doubt suppressed rage was the cause of this impediment.

Harry slapped the tabletop with both hands and stood up, moving the chair back with his legs. He spoke in a voice that was sad, not angry.

"Enid, I think you can see why we have to leave. This is not the time for a sermon, so just let me thank you for your hospitality. It could have made a great friendship, but then how many things go right in life?"

Keese got up too. "I thought I was going to get the opportunity to defend myself!"

"Don't you raise your voice at me, Earl," Harry said threateningly. "It's all I can do to hold myself in as it is."

"Goddammit!" Keese was getting louder: it was his house. "I said *I thought I was supposed to be able to defend myself.*"

"You already said that. But I have decided against taking you to court. That kind of thing makes for permanent bad blood, and we may be neighbors for the rest of our lives."

Keese shuddered. He believed he might be on the point of seizing the enormous chef's knife from the wall rack nearby and carving out Harry's guts.

Instead he put his head back as far as it would go and shouted at the ceiling: "Get out of my house, you sons of bitches!" When he brought his eyes back down Harry was at the back door and Ramona was at her husband's heels.

Crying more abuse, Keese hastened them on their way, literally chased them over the threshold and into the night. He returned to the kitchen, gasping. High blood pressure was routine for him in the best of times.

Only now did Enid stop eating. "That was quite a performance," she said. "I can't remember seeing you like that before."

"I have been known to lose my temper," Keese said, "but not usually in front of other people. But this was too much. Those two are a real menace. The thought of them living next door is unbearable. I say this seriously, Enid: we may have to move. Did you ever see anything like them?"

"*You* were the strange one," said she. "They seemed to bring out the worst in you."

This stung him. "Listen here: *you* supported them, you agreed with them, everything you said and did was on their side and not mine."

"Earl, I was being hospitable. Did you not just now hear Harry thank me? I can't forsake my manners simply because you get yourself into some squabble."

He went to the sink to throw cold water on his face. But first he said: "Squabble? They accused me of rape. Me, for God's sake, Earl Keese." It did not seem absurd to him to identify himself formally. "Even yet I can't believe it." He opened the tap and took the splash of cool water on his hands. "And why didn't you defend me? You were here all the while. How could I have raped anybody?" He threw water into his eyes. "*Court.* He was apparently thinking of having me arrested and tried! No matter that they wouldn't be able to prove it. My name could never be cleared. Sex charges are always believed. You can destroy anybody by that means, if you are ruthless enough to lie with a straight face."

Enid rose and took her plate to the sink. "Hadn't you better do something about the car?"

God, he had forgotten about that altogether—and the matter of *their* car as well.

The kitchen telephone hung on the wall. In the directory he looked up the number of the local garage. He had inserted his finger into the first of the appropriate orifices in the dial when the back door burst open and Harry & Ramona entered, howling and hooting like savages at a blood-ritual. Finally he was able to identify their commotion as being good-humored, at least in intention. The abominable noise was their laughter.

"I think we had you going, Earl," cried Harry.

"I'm sure we did," said Ramona. "Now admit it!"

"You did," said Enid, "you really did. I can certify that. He admitted losing all control."

Keese was furious with that one word. "I did *not* say 'all'!"

But it was Enid's way never to admit correction. She smiled all the wider. "Never," she said, "have I seen him more devastated."

Keese produced a stage-laugh. "O.K., have your fun at my expense. I'm not ashamed of reacting strongly to that accusation."

"You made a complete ass of yourself," said Harry. "Don't try to retrieve anything from that hopeless performance, Earl."

"I've already admitted being taken in," Keese said. "What more do you want? I'm simply saying that I don't really regret it. Better to err on the positive side than on the negative."

"Just a minute." Harry apparently wished to pursue some moral but was stopped by Ramona.

"Now don't get dreary, Harry. The joke worked. That's what matters, not *why* it worked." She giggled desperately.

"The thing about your car was *my* idea," said Harry, claiming his former seat at the table, and Ramona took her own. "Obviously it was pretty lame. I'm not very good at these hoaxes." He pointed. *"She's* the genius."

"Yes," said Keese, sitting down. "But I must make a genuine confession, I'm afraid: by accident I really did send your car down into the hollow and no doubt into the creek, though it's too dark to see out there now."

"I'm disappointed in you, Earl. You're just trying to top my story," said Harry. Interested in the proceedings, Enid had come towards the table on his side. As if it were the most natural thing in the world, Harry put his arm around her waist. This action brought her hip against his shoulder. Bone-to-bone contact could hardly be objected to, but Keese was unsettled by the insouciance of—well, really all three of them, for Enid seemed perfectly comfortable and Ramona was smiling lazily at the pair. Actually they made an appropriate-looking couple, large as they both were: a brother and an older sister from some big-boned family.

Keese felt as though he were defending his right to damage Harry's property, whereas at the outset all he had wanted to do was come clean. "I'm not joking," he said. "What you told me you did to my car, in your hoax, I actually did to *your* car a bit earlier."

"How about it, Enid," said Harry, pulling her robust middle body against him and inclining his large blond head against her left breast. "Do you think this little hubby of yours is capable of that sort of thing?"

Enid smiled down upon his curls. "Don't let him dupe you, Harry."

"There you are," said Harry. Abruptly he let Enid go and refilled his glass from the wine jug. "Well, we've provided the dinner and the first act of the entertainment, Earl. Isn't it time you did something?"

Keese had not forgotten that he had given Harry thirty-two dollars, which seemed adequate compensation for these services. The destruction of the car was quite another thing: he must, before any more foolishness occurred, get Harry to accept the fact.

He rose, saying: "I'm going to prove it to you." In a cabinet over the refrigerator he found an electric lantern. "Come on, we'll take a look." Impatiently he punched the lantern's switch. The beam was invisible from his end in the lighted kitchen, but Ramona winced and looked away as if he had got her in the eyes with that one precise focus which would be effective.

Harry got up, groaning. "I never knew you'd take it this far, but I'll call your bluff!" He saluted the table. "To the ladies, God bless 'em." Then he slapped Keese on the rump and sauntered to the door.

It occurred to Keese that Harry might be drunk. Or had he

been thrown into such high spirits merely by the rape-hoax? There were such persons, whose taste in comedy required someone's embarrassment. For them a joke was not a thing-in-itself but must have a butt to complete it.

With his light he led Harry through the side yard and to the brink of the hollow, at a point where the descent was not so steep as that which the car had gone down in its headlong rush. In fact, there was an old path there, probably made by bygone boys, and current lads came there now and again after fording the creek from the other bank, which was at the edge of the village proper, only a hundred yards from Keese's house to a bird, but a mile and a half by car. Keese did not forbid the use of this shortcut, because it was not often used, but neither did he see such youthful trespassers with pleasure, for years ago he had one night caught three boys watching fourteen-year-old Elaine take off her first brassiere behind her unshaded bedroom window.

Keese pointed his lantern beam into the hollow. Before the light got far it was absorbed by the darkness, as water by dry sand. He turned it towards his face and saw the light was jaundiced: the battery was petering out as he watched. He struck it sharply, either to stimulate or to punish it, and he was all but blinded by the sudden radiance. He dropped the lantern.

"Sorry!" It tumbled down the path. "Damn!" He pursued it, but soon he no longer had a guide: the light went out. Suddenly he was impelled from behind. In his involuntary haste he hooked his foot in an arch of root which fate had cunningly thrown across the path to impede fat men who desperately went after dropped lanterns: the remainder of this arrangement comprised clusters of sharp stones at just the places where such a man, falling, would deploy his hand to catch himself.

He had been pushed. That Harry should do such a thing in

a dark night and upon a descending dirt path seemed criminal: there was nothing funny about it. He found the lantern and pressed the switch. The light came on, perhaps even a bit stronger than before its tumble. He turned and played the light on Harry, but was careful to keep it from the man's eyes: pretty decent in view of what had happened.

"That was a rotten thing to do," he said. "I could have been killed in the dark."

"Better be more careful from now on," brazenly said Harry. The bush of hair which clogged the vee of his knitted shirt was offensive to Keese.

"Push me again," said Keese, "and you'll be sorry."

"Huh?"

"You know what I mean."

"Search me!" Harry almost wailed. He was truly shameless.

"I'll show you, then," Keese said, and bulky as he was he found enough room on the beaten part of the path to stand aside. He then gestured, with sweeping hand, for Harry to precede him and gave him plenty of light. When Harry gullibly obeyed, Keese struck him in the small of the back. The larger man lost control of his stride and went hurtling down the path. Suddenly, horribly, he vanished from view, as if a precipice had opened before him and he had gone helplessly over its edge. A brief and terrible cry was heard, which faded away below Keese's feet, and then the utter silence of vegetable nature on a windless night.

As if destroying Harry's car had not been enough, he had now killed the man! It was new in Keese's experience (of almost fifty years) for things to get so completely out-of-hand. His instinct was to turn and escape, hasten to the city, buy a ticket to some remote part of the world, and hide out there forever, living by the proceeds of some depraved trade in flesh or drugs. He hoped to diminish his horror by conceiving such a fantasy of romantic farce. What he did in practice, however, was to trudge carefully down the path, which did become progressively more steep, but when he reached the point at which Harry had apparently fallen he saw no precipice whatever. In fact, just here the hill gave way to level bottom land. He was all the way down, as surely was the unhurt Harry, who however could not be seen.

"Harry! Better stay close to the light," Keese cried. He was pleased to have done nothing to betray his initial belief that he had killed his neighbor.

He heard no response to this advice. He took a few paces, sank into a soft surface, and felt his shoes fill with water: after the recent rains this place was a marsh. He played his light about. Harry's automobile could not have gone far then, surely not as far as the creek, rolling in this resistant medium. It was probably embedded to the axles somewhere close by: some job for even a wrecker to pull it out of this glue. Keese's shoes made great sucking sounds as he plodded about. He was already soaked. He might as well do what he had come for—but that had been to prove to Harry that his car was down here, and where *was* Harry?

That question was answered by a savage blow to Keese's nape, the rabbit punch of legend but rarely of actual experience, at least not when it was delivered with force, as now. For an instant Keese felt as though he had been beheaded, and then he fell prone into the swamp. His nose and mouth were in slime: the blow had surely paralyzed him; he would drown miserably.

He found, when he tried to get up, that the prognosis was inaccurate. He was not paralyzed, but someone's large foot was planted in the middle of his back. Owing to this impediment he could not rise. He could, by lifting his chin, raise his nostrils high enough above the mire to breathe, but it was painful, owing to his sore back-of-neck. He now greatly regretted not having killed Harry. It was clear that Harry was not beyond killing *him*. Obviously the man was mad, to take this sort of reprisal. He must appeal to him with some materialistic argument.

"Don't you want to look for your car?" he asked, with great difficulty.

In answer Harry leaned down, put his hand against the back of Keese's head, and pushed his face into the slime. But when Keese was once again certain he was a goner Harry took away both hand and foot, and next, surprising as always, he helped Keese get up.

The lantern was in the mire, but Harry seemed to have adequate night vision. To Keese he was a tall murky image, and Keese hated him so much in that indistinct form that he could not imagine seeing him in the light without assaulting him murderously. But having felt the ruthless strength of his foot and his hand, he feared him as well, and he determined to attack him only when Harry was off guard.

Meanwhile Keese had a façade of muck. Luckily he was wearing old corduroys and a sports shirt. Popping the clothes in the washer and himself in the shower would be simple enough, and neither had sustained permanent damage from the abuse. He tried to make the best of the situation, because he feared what he might do if he were forced to see the worst before he had the proper opportunity to pay Harry back.

"I found my car," Harry said now. "It's about thirty feet to the right, and sunk halfway up the hubcaps."

It could have been far worse.

Harry added: "You really did a job on me."

But Keese was not displeased to hear this, because it made some sense of Harry's most recent assault on him: revenge for wrecking the car. Not even being pressed face down in the swamp was the equivalent in damage. Could he expect more vengeance until Harry considered the debt to be paid in full?

"It was certainly an accident," said he, "but what matters is only the result, I know that."

"No," said Harry, "the motive is all that ever matters, Earl. Anything material can be replaced." Without warning he became sententious: "By golly, if we can't get along on this planet as it sails through cold space, then we deserve to lose it."

Keese was not sure whether he should be taken in by this sentiment, which could be rank charlatanism. "I guess that's what we came for then," he said, with reference to the car. "We'd better go on back up and call the wrecker." He looked about for the lantern, but it had now either gone out or sunk so deeply into the mire that its beam could not be detected. They could anyway see well enough to get home.

He stepped aside when they reached the bottom of the path, hoping Harry would go on ahead, but Harry stopped too.

"Go on, Earl," said he. "I don't want to be tormented from behind."

Which was exactly Keese's own fear! Well, perhaps having said that, Harry would himself refrain from offending. But this, of course, proved too much to expect, and at the steepest stretch of the ascent, when Keese was virtually on all fours, Harry (who had apparently had no difficulty in climbing) equipped himself with a slender stick and punished Keese's buttocks with it. This did serve to quicken Keese's climb, and when the butt of the stick came in for a dead-center goose in the final six feet, he scrambled up to the yard with dispatch. And turned there, thinking he would be admirably positioned to give Harry a savage shoe in the crotch as he came into range, but he discarded this plan after projecting Harry's subsequent fall: Keese most certainly did not want to descend to that swamp again.

Therefore he allowed Harry to emerge without damage. He

was thanked by Harry's saying, when he reached his side: "I think I'd better sue you, Earl."

"Excuse me?"

"I think I'll have to."

Keese said: "I don't believe we have to bring the law into this, do we? I admit I was at fault, and my insurance company will simply pay off."

"But what kind of insurance would cover this?" asked Harry. "Certainly not the policy on your *car:* you were on foot. And hardly your homeowner's policy: you found the car in front of *my* house, and you willfully pushed it down the road past yours: your own property wasn't involved at all."

Keese felt his blood turn against him, pounding in his ears and refusing to heat his limbs. "Look, Harry, can't we make some kind of arrangement here?"

What he had to explain was a bit ticklish, and before he could begin, Harry spoke. "What sum did you have in mind? The car was in perfect shape."

Keese laughed politely. "What I actually meant was—well, could we let *your* insurance cover it? Here's what I mean: say it was stolen and the thieves drove down the hill, lost control, and it went into the swamp?"

"Fair enough," said Harry, "but then you'd have to identify yourself as the thief, wouldn't you? And would you really want to do that?"

"No, no. The idea would be that the car thieves, young kids, ran away before they could be identified."

Keese's eyes had now become sufficiently adjusted to the darkness so that he could see Harry's change of expression: a grimace of puzzlement.

"You didn't mention these kids before. If they did it, then why did you take the blame? To make the neighborhood seem more respectable? But can't you see that I'd find out anyway soon enough?"

Keese said: "No, please, Harry, wait a minute. The kids were hypothetical. *I* was the culprit. But I don't relish admitting that to the authorities."

Harry's eyebrows rose. "You want me to lie, is that it? Also it would go on my insurance record, wouldn't it? You become none too popular with a company when you claim money from it, you know. The idea is for *them* to take money from you, not pay it back. They'll raise my premiums. And why should I do all of this? To protect you? And why should I protect you? Are you my dear friend?" He was working himself up. "Are you even a good neighbor? What have you done for me? You wrecked my car and ate my food and drank my wine. You made a pass at my wife. You've been sarcastic with me ever since I introduced myself, insulting, arrogant, and disagreeable."

Keese could not believe he heard this. Of the many accusations, grand and petty, all detestably false, he chose the most outrageous: "Your wife! Did you—and she—not admit that the rape charge was a hoax of your own invention?"

"You cheap crook," said Harry. "God almighty, what a man to move next door to: it's a sort of a nightmare."

He was doing no more than echoing Keese's own sentiments. It was startling to Keese to hear that he himself inspired the same feeling in someone else, someone who had offended him from the first: had he returned the favor with Harry? But what, aside from the car, had *he* done that was so awful?

Keese had all of his life behaved justly: he could easily enough envision himself as the Hon. Earl Keese, in black robes and on some bench beneath the blindfolded goddess. The image came in handy at such a time as this.

"Let's both calm down, Harry. We *are* neighbors and I hope we can be friends. I beg your forgiveness for all the things I've done that have offended you. Foremost among them is of course ruining your car. I don't admit to any of the others. I haven't meant to be sarcastic, however it's seemed, believe me. And maybe it's a bit crude to mention it, but you did take thirty-two dollars from me for the food and drink, if you remember. The thing about your wife is absolutely untrue, and I don't mind saying that it is an infamous charge to make even in jest."

Harry spread his legs and put his hands on his hips. "Do you deny entering the bedroom when she was lying on the bed, naked under a towel?"

"But it was *my own* bedroom," cried Keese, "and I didn't know she was there. She helped herself to a shower without my knowledge, simply went upstairs in our house without asking anybody!"

"You're cool, I'll say that," Harry stated. "O.K., you've got your story, she's got hers."

"Oh, shit," Keese shouted, forsaking all hope of being judicious, "what's the use of trying to be rational with you? The both of you should be put in a cage!"

"Now you're showing your true colors," said Harry in a jeering tone. "The truth is that you think you're better than us. You don't think we belong in this neighborhood. Admit it."

The accusation took Keese totally by surprise. He had no sense of what Harry's implication could be, and he told him so.

"Come *on.*" Harry sneered knowingly. "What a hypocrite you are. I hate that trait more than outright bigotry."

"I'm not going to let you get away with this, Harry," Keese said. "First, I'm not a bigot of any sort, but moreover I haven't any idea of what, if I were one, there would be about you that's objectionable."

"For your information," Harry said defiantly, "Ramona's not one of *them.* So you can stop worrying."

Keese emitted a laughing sigh. "God, how wrong can a man be!"

"At least you have the decency to admit it," said Harry.

"Not *me,*" Keese cried. "*You.* It never occurred to me to

consider what she was or was not. I had absolutely no reason to think of the subject, in fact."

"Relax, Earl. Your worst fears haven't been confirmed."

They were still outdoors in the night, everything as before, Harry's car in the swamp, Keese covered with muck, his shoes oozing.

He made a weary effort. "Harry," he said, "I don't care what Ramona's extraction is, I assure you."

Harry persisted. "As long as she's your kind, eh?" But when Keese walked away in disgust Harry followed him with what was apparently intended as placation. "Look, I don't blame you. I'm not criticizing. It makes perfect sense to me."

Keese made no response. Which turned out to be the right way to deal with Harry, but by this point Keese would have preferred to have nothing further to do with him—which might have been possible had he not done that stupid thing with the car! It was essential that he never again contemplate taking revenge on Harry: this was a fervent promise to himself.

"Hell," said Harry to his back, "I didn't really think you were prejudiced, Earl. I realized you were just being sarcastic as usual, and that always gets my back up."

Keese could remember not one instance in which he had been sarcastic, and it annoyed him to be so characterized again, but he had himself under firm government now, as he squished across the lawn, and he made no reply.

"You're right about that thirty-two dollars," Harry said, pleading. "You don't owe me anything for the spaghetti and wine."

Good of him to admit that, but obviously he wasn't so desperate now that he would return it! Oh, he was a beauty, that Harry. Keese had now reached the back door. But he shouldn't go as he was, dripping with filth, into the kitchen. He continued, therefore, to the outside door to the basement, went down the concrete steps, and let himself in. It was with the greatest relief that he saw he had shaken off Harry, who had presumably entered the kitchen.

Keese felt somewhat better, having everything he needed down there. There was a metal stall shower in a corner, and a full outfit of work clothes—pants, shirts, and shabby sneakers —hanging from a nail, the sneakers by their tied laces. This ensemble was flecked with green paint, but signifying honest labor as it did, was not shameful. When the light was on he saw that what had soaked him was principally water and not the slime he had assumed it to be: here and there were strands of brown weed.

He stripped and took a successful shower (the downstairs facility could not always be counted on: the proper mix of hot and cold was often difficult to compound). He took the final burst of water onto his face and then stepped blindly from the doorless enclosure onto the square of carpeting on the concrete floor outside. He seized the towel from the hook on the outer surface of the stall and, having dried his head first, stretched its terry-cloth length across his back.

"Is that what naturally happens to a man?"

It was Ramona, whom he had not heard arrive, owing to the sound of the shower. She was looking at his body, and her upper lip was rising towards her nostrils.

CHAPTER 5/

THERE had been a time, when he was younger, that in such a situation Keese would have clasped his hands across his groin. Why? How could his privates be shameful if he had been born with them willy-nilly?

"Of course," said Ramona, "we're all in this together."

For a moment Keese believed she was admitting to her involvement in some mass conspiracy against him, but the statement which followed disclosed that its predecessor had been merely more of the show-biz kind of humanism to which Harry had given voice: "I mean, it happens to us all. We're all mortal, aren't we?" She stuck a fingertip into the corner of her cheek.

He flung the towel around his waist and sought to tie the ends at his far hip, but in point of fact they barely touched.

Holding the terry-cloth points with one hand, then, he said: "May I have some privacy in my own basement?"

"Ownership means everything to you, doesn't it?" Ramona asked, not disapprovingly. Indeed, she seemed almost wistful. "Pride of possession." She enunciated this as a thing-in-itself, as a term to be displayed on a license plate by way of state motto or tourist-exhortation.

"I don't know that it does, especially," said Keese, surlily deciding to challenge this too easily assumed judgment. "Did you come here for a particular purpose?" He snorted. "I doubt that you bargained for seeing me in the shower."

"I opened the wrong door, I guess," said Ramona. "I was looking for Baby. You haven't seen him, have you? He kills chickens."

There really was no good way of dealing with Ramona, who was obviously unbalanced. But no sooner had he arrived at that conclusion than she made perfect sense of her latest speech.

"Does anybody keep chickens around here? Or ducks or geese, for that matter? Baby will kill them if he can. He thinks they are toys, soft stuffed things that he can tear up for fun."

"No," said Keese, "not to my knowledge."

"He means no harm," Ramona said. "He doesn't know they're alive."

"I don't believe that," Keese said with stubborn conviction. "It's undoubtedly some natural instinct, but I don't believe that he, an animal, can't tell the difference between a toy and a living thing!" Keese had never subscribed to the sort of ethics which granted immunity to the innocent of heart. Murder, for example, was just as much murder when committed by a maniac—well, of course, it wasn't really, but he was fed up with the philosophies which disregarded the problem of guilt.

"Don't get high and mighty about my dog!" cried Ramona.

Keese shrugged. "Would you mind?" he asked significantly, meaning that he wanted to dry himself and get dressed. "Baby is not down here. You can go up to the yard by that door over there."

But she turned and went in the other direction. The lights were not on, and while he had no benevolent interest in furthering her prowl, he didn't want her to fall and hurt herself on his property. He told her how to find the switch.

"You've got a game room?" she said rhetorically, crossing the threshold of that to which she referred. "Ah, pool!"

Keese took advantage of her absence and dried himself, and

then, as he heard the balls clicking one against the other, donned the set of "work" clothing. He was the sort of fellow who looked as if he belonged in whatever he wore, so long as his costume had no particular style. But the incongruity would have been striking had he been attired in military uniform, dinner clothes, or, say, a hacking jacket, though as a stripling he had worn all of these, not without advantage.

When attired he looked in at the game room. Ramona continued to slam pool balls against one another indiscriminately, her stroke looking very strong for a woman's.

"Take you on?" she asked when she noticed him.

In itself this was a reasonable invitation, but he still resisted her whenever she treated him as a guest in his own house. He believed that she and Harry worked by attrition. God knows what would happen if one let them abrade him to the point of surrender!

"No, I don't want to play pool," he said decisively, his hand on the light switch. He was obviously suggesting that they return upstairs, but he was not astonished when Ramona ignored him. In fact, in anticipation of the difficulty he would have in getting her out of the basement he had formulated a plan to use the situation against her.

Without saying another word he stole away and having locked the door to the outside and taken the key, he climbed the stairs to the kitchen, where Harry was seated at the table again, eating what remained of his spaghetti, which was surely quite cold now. Enid was not in evidence.

"Say, Harry," Keese said aggressively towards the man's back, before reaching a position in which he could see his face, "I've got a pool table downstairs."

Harry was chewing when his face came into view. "So?" he asked when he could speak.

"I thought you might like the game," said Keese.

Harry emptied his wineglass and poured himself more from

the jug. The latter, Keese saw, was almost empty, but as yet he had no means of gauging how much had been drunk by whom.

Finally Harry said: "I was waiting for the hustle, Earl. I knew it would come, though what I expected was cards."

"What?" asked Keese. "I'm talking about pool, Harry. If you'd like to fool around with it, go on downstairs. Ramona's there."

Harry made his eyes small and mean. "Stay away from her, Earl!"

"I'm not going to get into an argument on that subject," Keese said. "It should be obvious who came down there without an invitation. I was with you until the moment I entered the basement from outside. What I am talking about here is my pool table." Because of his irritation Keese suddenly became authoritative. "I want you to go down there, Harry, and play pool."

Harry looked up at him with astonishment. "Heil Hitler," he said. Nevertheless he put down his fork and he rose. He peered at Keese and scratched his ear with his little finger. "I hope you're ready for this," he said. "It could cost you some money."

"Sure, sure," said Keese, patting him on the back and none too gently impelling him towards the stair to the basement. Harry accepted this. He always seemed compliant once the initiative was claimed by someone else. He was much easier to handle than Ramona, over whom Keese had not once had even the beginning of an advantage.

Unless it could be said that he had one now. When Harry had taken two steps down, Keese, still in the kitchen, closed and locked the door and took the key. The neighbors were now confined in his basement. They had been deactivated for the moment. Keese felt the sort of emotion that must come to a member of a bomb-disposal unit when the last wire has been cut and the ticking stopped.

He let out a suppressed breath and sat down on the chair lately vacated by Harry. There was still some spaghetti in the bowl and wine in the jug. Keese really had eaten only a mouthful or two of what had turned out to be dinner. In effect the new neighbors had done their best to deprive him of his daily bread. He moved Harry's plate and reached over to get the one he had himself used earlier.

He had just mounted a heap of spaghetti on his plate and forked up a mouthful, which was cold and slimy, when Enid came in through the door to the yard. She pretended to be shocked when she saw him, uttering a small cry and lifting her hands at the wrists.

"I didn't recognize you!"

"In these clothes?" he asked, dropping his fork and its burden. "There's a tale in that, but I won't bother you with it at this time. The important thing is that I've taken control."

"Is that what you wanted?" Enid asked idly. She went to the sink and rinsed her hands.

"It's a thing I found necessary to take," Keese said. "That's a better way to put it. I was being forced into a corner by those people—not that I blame them entirely: they found what seemed to be an ideal victim in me. No doubt I encouraged them by my friendly manner. That brings out the worst in some types."

Now Enid acquired at least a mild interest in the subject. While drying her hands on a paper towel she said: "I'd hardly call your manner friendly. Whenever I looked at you you were baring your teeth at them. And I wouldn't be surprised now to find that you have driven them out of the house. I have never seen you like this, Earl, in all the years I've known you."

Keese stared at her. "Now, Enid," he said, "you're pulling my leg. You don't mean to say that you found them unobjectionable? What about that awful Ramona?"

Enid shook her head. "I think I know what you're trying to

do, Earl, but I'm afraid I am rather more aware of the situation than you think."

Keese had taken a sip of wine and now he almost expelled it in a spray. Instead he suppressed the cough and the wine went acridly up his nose through the interior passages. He took a moment to recover from this unpleasant effect.

"What do you think you know?" he asked.

Enid leaned her substantial body against the lip of the sink and crossed her arms. "I wouldn't try to bluff it out if I were you, Earl. Let's just forget it. But by the same token let's try to get along with our new neighbors. They're all right. Your grievances against them are imaginary, and I'm afraid your motivation is not in good conscience."

Keese chewed his lip. He had the terrible feeling that he would never get a proper dinner this night.

"Enid," he said slowly, "I demand that you explain your allusions. If you mean that I am responsible for their car being down in the swamp, I admit it. But it probably wouldn't have happened if they hadn't made me so nervous. That Ramona!"

"No, no, Earl, you leave Ramona alone. She's behaved like a saint." Nor was Enid apparently saying this tongue in cheek: her lips were in a sanctimonious configuration of the sort she had worn when correcting Elaine as a child. "But for her restraining him, Harry would have beaten you savagely."

"What?" cried Keese. "For wrecking his car? Don't be ridiculous. He wasn't bothered that much. Besides, he got his revenge. He pushed me in the water. Frankly, I thought it was childish, but then I guess he saw it as tit for tat."

"We could skirt the real issue all night if you want," said Enid, "but it is painful to me to prolong this ordeal. It had nothing to do with the car, as you very well know."

Keese looked disgustedly at the overhead light. "Now, you're not going to take that madwoman's accusation seriously, are you? Can you actually imagine me making advances to her?

That's what I mean, Enid. She's sick in some way. She gives me the creeps, if you want to know. Harry's not exactly a great guy, but he's some improvement over her."

"That's pretty lukewarm, isn't it?" asked Enid, with a bitter smirk. "For a man towards whom you feel the great passion of your life?"

Keese drank some wine. He did not understand what was going on here.

"Isn't the truth really," said Enid, "that your overtures to him grew so violent that he was forced to overpower you, knock you down in the swamp, and hold you underwater until you came to your senses?"

"The truth?" Keese asked numbly.

"To humiliate yourself in such a fashion! What did you intend to do—rape him? A man so much larger than you?"

Keese kept his eyes on his plate. "Enid," he said, "I want you to listen to me. You know very well that I'm not homosexual, for one. But I grant you for the sake of argument that one might suppress such desires for many years and then be overcome by them—actually, mind you, I don't really believe that, but I'm trying to be fair to your side of the argument. But if this did happen, such a fellow would not try to impose his attentions by force on anyone, because that would be at odds with his personality."

"I grant you that it was bizarre enough," Enid said, "because you were desperate, I suppose. But who am I to tell you what you feel?"

"Now, no bogus sympathy, please," Keese said, his voice rising. "Can't you see that the accusation is the work of a warped mind? There's no point in our arguing or discussing what happened: it's an absolute lie, as you should very well know. I've never in my life made a sexual advance towards a man, but when I was a young fellow and slender and not the worst-looking guy, I had a few passes made at me, and I assure you that nobody tried any strong-arm stuff. That simply would not be done. It is different from the relations between different sexes, though for that matter it is rare enough even when a man forces himself upon a woman. Rape is not exactly routine, is it?"

Enid made no response to this question, which was admittedly rhetorical.

"Earl," she said sympathetically, "I've never pried into your secret recesses, which you undoubtedly have, as we all do. But what I do feel responsible for is how guests are treated in this house. I can't stand by and watch them being threatened, abused, insulted, perhaps even put in danger of their lives if the truth be known."

"Oh, come on!" Keese cried. He pushed away his dish. Quite clearly he was to be denied all nourishment this night. He was not to be allowed even the basics of human life! Would they even find some way to prevent the air from reaching his lungs? "Why can't you understand that *I'm* their victim— they're not mine!" He pointed to the cold, red-streaked debris of the spaghetti. "I paid thirty-two bucks for that wretched meal." And then didn't even get to eat it! He felt like bursting into tears for the first time in forty years or more.

He resisted his weakness. "That is, they *want* to make me their victim. But I've defanged them, rendered them harmless."

Enid's large blue eyes grew larger but turned almost gray. "I was afraid of this," she said, putting a hand to her mouth. "You've murdered them."

"Murder?" asked Keese. "Get hold of your imagination, Enid. I don't go around killing people, for God's sake. What a thing to say. I've never harmed anyone in my life." But he realized that he was sounding feeble again. "All right, then, maybe I *have* killed them. So what? Were they your friends? Would you miss them? You never laid eyes on them before a couple of hours ago."

In the face of this challenge Enid seemed callous about the

neighbors' dire fate. "You're right," she said. "I couldn't care less. They would hardly have worked out as friends anyway."

"I wonder why not?" Keese asked speculatively. "Their age, maybe? But they're not that young. Anyway, Harry isn't. He's well into his thirties, wouldn't you think? I'd say he's much too old to have had me as a father, and certainly he must be within about ten-twelve years of you."

Enid shrugged and came away from the sink at last. "I don't think you've murdered them, after all, else you wouldn't use the present tense."

"What's happened to you, Enid? Did you really think I was serious? They're both down in the game room at this moment, playing pool, I guess."

Enid marched to the door to the basement and tried to open it. She seemed not to consider that it was locked, but rather assumed that it was merely stuck, and she braced herself against the jamb and struggled with the knob.

"You won't get that open without a key," said her husband. "That's what I meant when I said I had taken care of them; not that I had committed murder but merely that I locked them in the basement."

"That's pathological," Enid said. She came to where Keese sat and loomed over him. "Let's have it." She put her hand near his chin.

"Certainly not," said Keese. "I've got them where I want them now. You ask what am I going to do next? Frankly, I don't know. I'm playing for time, you see. I've got to work this out. At the moment the outside basement door is locked too, but what I thought I might do is to open that outside door, and they might get the idea to take the line of least resistance and leave. Remember the time that the starling got into the cellar? We opened the door and opened the windows and took all the screens out of them, and eventually the bird got the idea and left. But given his birdbrain, it took a great deal of work on our part to prepare the ground. Perhaps Harry will be a bit more intelligent."

Enid went around to the other side of the table and sat in Keese's former chair there. She leaned into the table: her breasts were almost as large as her face in this perspective. Keese had begun to find her tenseness repugnant.

She said: "Now look here, Earl. This is going too far. You can't deprive people of their freedom of movement. You can't lock them in your house!"

"Didn't I say just now that I was going to unlock the outside door?"

Enid put her hand across the table, between the spaghetti bucket and his dish. "Don't bother about that," she said. "Give me the key to this door and we'll forget about the problem. No one will know."

Before Keese had an opportunity to respond (which he would certainly have done in the negative) a noise was heard from behind the door in reference—the knob was twisted, the panel was pounded, and Harry's voice, hardly dampened by the thin door, said: "Earl, are you there? Open up!"

Enid leaned farther across the table. "Do it quickly," she whispered. "It's still not too late if you pretend the key was turned by accident."

Keese was certain he could smell hard liquor on her breath. He rose quickly and went to the basement door. "Go to hell, Harry," said he. "You're not getting back in here."

"All right, Earl, ver-ry fun-ny. Now open up."

Keese fancied that he could see Harry through the wood. Harry was probably one step down: unless the door was open there was really not room comfortably to stand on the very top step. Therefore their height was more or less equal.

"Harry," said he, "forget about it. Go to the outside door. I'll come out and open it."

Harry sounded baffled, not angry at all. "Would you mind

giving me an explanation? Is the door stuck? Did it get locked by accident and then you lost the key? Or has some catastrophe occurred in the kitchen that it would embarrass you for me to see? You get my point, Earl? Without some explanation it would seem that you are being damned rude to your guests for no reason at all."

"*For no reason?*" cried Keese.

And as if he had not heard this, Harry completed his plea: "And you're not that type of guy."

"Oh, no?" Keese asked sardonically. "Maybe you've got me wrong."

Harry said no more. In a moment his feet could be heard descending the basement stairs.

Enid said, behind Keese: "You're perilously close to committing a crime."

Keese whirled on her. "Is it a crime to drive someone out of your house? I'm not confining him. I'm merely simplifying his exit. I was telling the truth, Enid. I'm going right now to open the outside door."

His wife laughed bitterly. "What a welcome you've given them to our neighborhood!"

It annoyed Keese to have her persistently ignore his side of the matter, but he was worried now that until he unlocked the outside basement door the situation could be considered— well, what? Illegal restraint? Perhaps even kidnaping?

He left his chair and went towards the door to the yard, feeling in his pocket for the key to the outside entrance to the basement. He failed to locate it immediately, and he continued to search as he let himself out and went around the house to the cellar door. He suspected that Enid had come in from tending to the wolfhound again, of whom she had apparently become an addict, but he neither heard nor saw the animal.

He had arrived at the concrete steps leading down to the basement door, but the key was not to be found on his person:

he had ransacked his clothing and while doing so had discovered the enormous hole in the right-hand pocket of his "work" pants. The key had undoubtedly been lost through this hole, but where had he been at that moment? Probably on the stairs between the basement and the kitchen. Perhaps Harry even found it: if so, then he was merely pretending to be a prisoner, for the purpose of mocking Keese. Another marvelous scheme had gone awry!

But perhaps he was giving up too soon. He found sufficient energy to trudge around the corner of the house and kneel in the strip flowerbed against the foundation and peer through the narrow window into the game room.

Harry and Ramona were nonchalantly playing pool. How he wished he could hear what they were saying, for they were undoubtedly plotting more mischief—or at least gloating over that which they had perpetrated against him. Of course they had already overreached themselves by any reasonable standard: who in the world would actually believe that he had made aggressive sexual advances to both of them? Watching Ramona confidently manipulate her cue, he understood that he disliked her sort of young woman, the sort who were forceful with the wrong matters and consequently squandered their spirit meaninglessly. Elaine could be willful, sometimes tiresomely so, but her main thrust was always towards the positive. On the other hand, Enid in her twenties had been almost recessive, at least in the character she revealed to others. Keese could well remember how chagrining it had been for him to hear her evade a hostess' inquiry as to what she would like to drink. It had taken him years to understand that this was not indecisiveness but rather a purposeful means to establish her existence as one that could not be disposed of by the mere provision of refreshment. Keese could not really understand how Enid had any friends. He admired her, but found her to be without charm. But in point of fact she had a great number of what seemed dear friends, whereas he, a much more likable person by any measurement, had no intimates whatever.

He thought of that state of affairs now, as he crouched spying into the basement. Who apart from a few relatives, who had so to speak an obligatory interest, would miss him when he was gone? Perhaps that very plain girl at the office, the one with the unusually large nostrils and the skin problem—or was her sweet sad smile given so freely to everyone?

Something stirred in the corner of his eye and he turned and found himself face to face with the wolfhound. They stared neutrally at each other for a second or two, and then it was Keese who gave way. He got to his feet. He had no feeling whatever about Baby, who obviously returned the favor and had come to the window only to look in upon its owners and whimper faintly.

Well, Keese thought, they can scarcely feel they are prisoners if they are so blithely playing pool. But without the key his plan to induce them to leave by the outside basement door was useless. And he had nobody to blame but himself: he should have tested his pocket for soundness before dropping in the key. He added another promise to the earlier one by which he vowed not to seek revenge on Harry again; this one imposed a ban on all careless procedure.

He returned to the kitchen, where oddly enough Enid had remained, and not only that but had stayed in precisely the same position, elbow on table, left forefinger mustached under her nose.

"You can relax," he said. "They are happily playing pool, not writhing in their chains."

She took the finger from beneath the nostrils and pointed it at him. "All the same . . ."

"I know! I don't want to keep them here. I'm trying to formulate a plan by which to get rid of them, but it's far from easy." He saw her look of horror before it developed. "By 'rid of' of course I mean that literally and not figuratively. I don't intend to murder them, for your information."

Enid was hardly appeased. "Little did I think yesterday that today I'd need such an assurance. This monstrousness seems to have come from nowhere."

"No," said Keese, "it came only from next door."

"Maybe I should worry that, having disposed of them, you'll turn on me."

"Look here," Keese shot back, "I may be fighting the battle of my life and you are behaving like a sympathizer with the other side. Is not this your home as well as mine? Will you not defend its honor, its self-respect?" He pounded a fist into a palm. "And the pity is that you could do a far more effective job than I, if you wanted to."

"But as it happens I see no need for defense," said Enid. "I am not going to allow your sense of persecution to affect me. I am going to behave exactly as I always do, insofar as I am permitted."

"What does that mean? You act as if I would stop you. Don't you always do just what you want? Have you not been feeding that wretched dog? Did you not give it the meat that was supposed to be my dinner?"

"I think I see what you're getting at," said Enid. "You are implying that if I had not fed Baby you wouldn't have done any of these awful things."

Of course this had not been his point at all, but now that she had brought it up—but, just a minute!

"What do you mean, 'awful things'?"

"Earl, if you are so far gone that I have to explain," Enid said, standing up, "then you are too far gone to be saved." She pushed her chair neatly against the table and began deliberately to leave the room. At times there was something almost majestic in Enid's movements, and this was such an occasion.

He rose and followed her. "Where are you going now?"

"Do I need your permission?" She went stately through the dining room. At forty-five Enid seemed younger than she had five years earlier; at the same age Keese had felt he was really finished, irrespective of how long he would exist, and he had not since been rejuvenated.

"What I mean is," he said to her back, "are you going to be out of the way?"

They had now emerged into the front hallway, and Enid turned to go up the stairs. "Earl, I'll appeal to your reason once more. In all the years I've known you, there wasn't a better-balanced man in the world. I think you can limit this to a temporary aberration and make amends. Get the car hauled out of the swamp, release our neighbors from the cellar, and apologize to them. They're reasonable people, Earl. And—" She would have gone on, but Keese threw his head back, pointed his muzzle at the ceiling, and literally howled in cha-grin.

"Well," said Enid, shrugging, "there you see what I am up against." She mounted the stairs.

Keese sat down on the bottom step and put his face into his hands. Perhaps if Harry and Ramona continued to play pool he could quietly search the stairs to the kitchen, find the basement-door key where he had dropped it, steal around the house again, and unlock the door. Let's see: when they decide again to try to leave, Harry will come up and try the kitchen door. Locked. Then he'll go back down the stairs and try the door to the outside. Open! He and Ramona will exit. But what if instead of going on across to their own home they merely come around and re-enter one of the doors of this house? Certainly by this time a normal couple would have had enough, but obviously they weren't normal. Of course Keese could lock all the doors to the outside, but there would be something degraded in that measure. He and Enid had, years ago, moved to the country from the city precisely so that they "would not

have to keep the doors locked." Crime had since then extended
its tentacles far beyond the city limits, but the Keeses had not
been touched by it, and Keese felt that to turn a key was
somehow to lower one's flag.

He arrived at the conclusion now that his only effective
protection would lie in numbers. He went to the telephone in
the niche beneath the stairs. The instrument rested on the
phone book, which was covered in the yellow plastic wrapper,
imprinted with advertisements, that was provided gratis every
other year by the association of local merchants. Keese seized
the directory and looked up the Abernathys' number.

Hardly had the last digit been dialed when a raspy voice
answered. Keese said: "Chic? Earl."

"Earl?" asked Abernathy. *"Earl?"*

"Come on," said Keese, "no jokes, please. I was wondering
if you could come over."

"You mean to your house? Now?"

"Exactly."

"No."

Keese said harshly: "You don't mean no, Chic."

"Then what do I mean?" Abernathy asked coldly.

"Sorry. I'm overwrought. What I mean is, I'd like to see
both you and Marge over here, if possible. I could use some
company. I've got a problem."

Abernathy said: "No, I don't want to come over. But I'll ask
Marge if you'll wait a minute." He went away from the telephone. Keese had begun to feel angry at the abrupt and absolute refusal, without even a word of explanation, but he decided
to wait for Marge's verdict before giving vent to his feelings.

Marge came on herself rather than let Chic speak for her.
This seemed to Keese to be a pleasant courtesy. He had always
preferred her to Chic anyway. In point of fact he had never
liked Chic at all.

Marge said: "Earl?"

"I realize," said Keese, "that this is spur-of-the-moment, but I really need to see somebody."

"What's the nature of your problem?" asked Marge. She had a high, ingenuous-sounding voice that might have been produced by a ten-year-old girl.

"It can't be described on the phone," said Keese.

"Then can't it wait? You'll be over here for dinner tomorrow night. By the way, I was going to do Polynesian, but I've changed the menu to spaghetti and meatballs."

"Be that as it may," said Keese, "I can't wait. I've got the problem right now, and I can't come over there and leave my house unguarded."

"I don't want to," said Marge. "It would bore me, and I never do anything boring if I can help it. Life's too short."

"You mean you won't help me in an emergency?" Keese almost screamed.

"The police and fire departments are there for that sort of thing. Besides, you've got new neighbors who are a lot closer than us. Go over and ask Harry 'n' Ramona. They'll be glad to help."

"You know them?" asked Keese, panting.

"They're our dearest friends," Marge said. "That's why they moved here."

A surge of hatred went through Keese like a shot of some energizing, maddening narcotic. "You rotten bitch!" he cried and slammed the phone down.

There went a friendship of a good fifteen years! The Abernathys were the Keeses' oldest friends locally. Keese now told himself that he had never liked either of them: it had been an association of convenience and habit. All the same, he regretted this turn, and he dreaded the time when Enid would learn about the rupture.

Then he remembered that he had mentioned the Abernathys when they had all sat down to eat Harry's spaghetti, and the new neighbors' response had been only an ugly sneer. Not even an acknowledgment of acquaintance! Marge's "dearest friends"? Either they did not reciprocate her tender feelings or they had been playing some devious role for Keese's benefit.

Howie Johncock came to mind next. Shaken by the failure with the Abernathys, Keese now required a steady type. Howie was certainly that: bald, genial, and uxorious, he was slightly older than Keese.

Johncock answered only after many rings. Obviously he had been asleep, but he was one of those persons who could not admit having been awakened, believing it a flaw to be caught napping whatever the hour.

"Earl Keese. Look . . ." Keese went through the same preliminaries as with Chic Abernathy.

"I can't, Earl," said Johncock when he could speak. "Millie's sick."

Keese was determined not to repeat his error with the Abernathys and allow the situation to deteriorate to the point of no return.

"Gosh, I'm sorry. Anything I can do?"

" 'Fraid not," said Howie, "but thanks anyway. She's just got to sweat it out."

"Cold then, or flu? After she's warmly tucked in maybe you could just step around here for five minutes."

"Well, anyway, we'll see you tomorrow night at Chic 'n' Marge's," said Johncock. "Bye for now." He hung up.

Now Keese regretted having been so cautious. He should have given the bastard both barrels. In this mood he found and dialed the number of Gene Lacy, and when someone picked up the instrument Keese, in panicky anticipation of rejection, poured a stream of abuse into his end of the line, stunning the listener into silence.

Fortunately he had not given his name at the outset, and when he cooled somewhat he was quick to hang up. Of course, it was possible that his voice could be identified, but except in the rare event that Lacy had a tape recorder hooked up to his telephone and wanted to go to the trouble and expense of having voiceprints made, it would be difficult to prove. Yet the thought that he might be taken for a mere obscene telephoner rankled.

While he was deliberating on the choice of the next name —he was nearing the end of the list of couples who belonged to their social circle—the phone rang.

A jovial voice cried: "You old son of a bitch!" And proceeded to laugh heartily. "You really had me going, damn if you didn't!" It was Gene Lacy, who believed that Keese's call had been in the cause of high wit. He continued to roar happily for some time. Lacy was the soul of generosity; Keese wondered why he hadn't thought of him earlier. Lacy was just the man. For another, he was physically formidable, as tall as Harry and much more thickset.

Keese waited for the laughter to fade. Then he said: "I thought I ought to soften you up first, Gene old boy, because I have a favor to ask." He felt cautious once more. "You don't know the new couple who moved in next door to us, do you? Harry and Ramona?"

Lacy's reaction was markedly cool. "Naw, naw," he said. "You're losing me now."

"I guess I haven't made myself clear," said Keese. "I'll explain when you get here. Can you come over for a minute?"

"Can't you pull it on the phone?" Lacy asked.

"Oh, I get you," said Keese, to whom this role was altogether new, "you mean some kind of joke? No, no, I'm not kidding now, Gene. My home has been invaded, see."

"That's not funny at all, Earl." Lacy groaned. "Your stuff is getting worse by the minute. I'll do you a big favor and hang up." He did so.

Keese continued to hold the instrument across his face. He couldn't believe in the reality of what was happening.

When he heard, "It's hopeless, Earl. You're all alone," he might have believed it was his imagination had he not recognized the voice: Harry was manning the recreation-room extension.

Keese decided to bluff it out. "How's the pool game going?"

Harry answered ebulliently: "Ramona's beating my pants off."

"She wields a wicked cue," said Keese. "I noticed that."

"That's not some double-entendre, is it?" Harry asked, his tone going ominous.

"Not at all!" Keese assured him. "I admire her prowess."

Harry then asked stoically: "You're not going to let us out of here, are you? You're simply not going to listen to any argument of mine."

"That's not true," said Keese. "I've got nothing basically against you, Harry. It's just that you don't always act right."

"O.K.," Harry said with a groan. "I'll give you back your thirty-two bucks. I never intended to keep it in the first place. Just throwing a scare into you."

Keese hated to feel cheap. "That's not what bothered me," he said with feeling. "It was those crazy sexual accusations. First I was supposed to have made advances to Ramona, and then to you. Can't you see that's not funny? Suppose it got around and people heard it who took it seriously?"

"I'm sorry," said Harry. "Will you accept my apologies?"

Keese was not naturally a spiteful man, but whether he was ready to trust Harry was another matter.

"I don't know yet," he said.

Harry was incredulous. "Are you saying that you won't honor my apology? If so, I don't think you can continue to call yourself a gentleman, Earl, I'm sorry."

"You've got some nerve, Harry," Keese said heatedly, "considering the tricks you've pulled."

"Which have been so successful that my car is in the swamp and we are locked in your basement," said Harry. "Come on!"

Did he really see those as Keese's victories? Well, maybe he did. Keese sighed into the telephone.

"All right," he said, "you've convinced me." He hung up and trudged to the kitchen. He unlocked the door to the basement and opened it, expecting that Harry and Ramona would be waiting impatiently on the steps for their liberation. But they could not be seen. "It's open!" he shouted. Silence. "Hey! You wanted out!" He went down a few steps, far enough to lower his head and look across, beneath the pipes and ducts, to the door of the game room. It was closed.

What were they waiting for? Did they expect him to come and fetch them, conduct them upstairs as if they were royalty. Ha! He climbed back to the kitchen.

But after waiting there for a time which seemed as though it might extend, without straining itself, to the following morning, Keese found further suspense unbearable. He marched smartly down the steps and across the concrete to the door of the game room.

He rapped on the upper panel. "Come on," he cried. "You're free."

A rustle and a scraping sound came from his rear right side. Harry and Ramona had been hiding in the corner beyond the furnace. They rushed out at him now, tripped him up, and knocked him to the floor. They dashed in tandem up the stairs into the kitchen and locked the door behind them.

This proved conclusively that Harry had no integrity whatever. Meanwhile Keese was a prisoner in his own basement.

CHAPTER 6/

KEESE felt uneasy when below ground level. This was not the sort of place in which his strengths were at maximum efficacy. He would have been at least twenty-five percent to the good had he instead been locked in an attic. But it was no doubt a truth that we can seldom choose our place to stand against misfortune!

One thing was certain: sentimentalizing would not help. He narrowed his eyes as an aid to scheming. The windows, of course! They were set high in the wall, but a little stepladder was available. A more troublesome fact was that they were of constricted aperture, and Keese was not a slender man. He went to the nearest window and measured it crudely with spread hands, which he then applied to his body. It was hard to say whether the fit was right. What if he got stuck when halfway through?

The car! Of course! He still hadn't got around to calling the wrecker. He might do that now, from the game-room phone, and while he was at it, tell the garageman to stop by the basement first and let him out.

A copy of the directory accompanied the telephone, a wall-mounted instrument: the phone book hung beneath it on a twisted string. He found the number of Greavy's Garage. The wrecker was supposed to be available around-the-clock: therefore no offense could properly be taken by the man who owned and operated it. But in practice he was reputed to be a curmudgeon if summoned outside the frame of the normal working day. Keese could not understand the morality of offering an emergency service and then deploring its use in an emergency, but then the world was full of such discrepancies.

When Greavy answered his ring now, Keese (who could not bear being treated rudely) made a prefatory statement in which he endeavored to justify his late call and so forestall any abuse, but Greavy soon interrupted.

"It's already on its way." His voice was genial. "Harry done called for the wrecker, and it went five minutes ago, the boy at the wheel."

So he knew Harry already?

"Then sorry to have bothered you," said Keese, "if you're sure we're speaking of the same car."

"Harry called," Greavy repeated. "He said you ran his car down the swamp and locked him and his missus in the basement." He sounded as if he had difficulty in breathing, but eventually Keese understood that the man was laughing.

"Yes, it was a practical joke," said Keese.

"You just watch yourself now," said Greavy, "because if I know Harry he'll have something up his sleeve to pay you back with."

"Actually, he has already tricked *me* into going to the basement, and I'm locked here now, whereas they got out."

"There you are!" Greavy said enthusiastically. "Harry don't take it laying down."

"Known him long, have you?"

Greavy suddenly became suspicious. "What business is that of yours?"

"Now don't act like that," said Keese. "You just spoke as if you knew him fairly well. You called him Harry and you said, 'If I know him he'll want revenge.' "

"Now, I never said *that,*" Greavy replied, "and you better watch what you're saying to me, brother: I won't put up with no sarcasm: I'll take away your teeth with a wrench."

Again there was that charge of "sarcasm." Keese doubted that this was Greavy's own style. It was pretty obvious that he had been programmed by Harry.

"All right, all right. Maybe you didn't use those exact words, but you did give me the idea. I guess it was mainly that you called him Harry."

"How would I know his last name?" Greavy asked. "What is it, if you're so damned smart?"

"I don't know."

"Then what are you doing talking about him?" Greavy asked furiously. "You got no right at all. Are you trying to make a fool out of me, you mummysucker?"

Keese went cold. He could not believe that he was being spoken to so vilely. "Call yourself a businessman?" was the best rejoinder he could find at the moment, playing for time while he put down wild impulses to go the station and throw a match into one of Greavy's gasoline tanks. The more he sought aid, the more scores he had to settle. He was somehow antagonizing the entire world merely by trying to defend himself.

"Listen," said Greavy, "I'm as good as you, any old day. Just because you bring your car in here and pay me to fix it, don't mean I'm dirt under your feet."

This too was reminiscent of Harry's style in its use of bogus resentment. Keese had never been disrespectful of Greavy. Far from it: like everybody else, he was the obsequious, helpless victim of any mechanic. But he realized that it would only be playing into Greavy's, and presumably Harry's, hands to confess this.

"No, you're not as good as I," he said. "I stand there in a

good suit, shirt, tie, watching you cover yourself with grease in my interest. Furthermore, you must do what I tell you to. No matter how nicely I put it, it's an order, and you must obey because I'm a customer. You are actually my servant, my flunky. No wonder at your vicious envy."

Greavy accepted this in silence. When he finally came back on the wire his venom was gone. Indeed, he was such a sycophant that Keese regretted having brought him so low—unless, of course, this was another hoax.

"I'm a ignorant man, sir," said Greavy. "I don't know how to act with decent people. That's why I keep to myself mostly. I let the boy deal with the public."

Now he was making a bid for Keese's sympathy. That could not be suffered. First, because it was needless; and for another, Keese needed all his strength to use against Harry & Ramona.

"You're a fraud, Greavy! I'm glad to have had the opportunity to tell you that." Keese hung up. This had been no impassioned outburst. He was cool and serene. Greavy had been vile to him for no reason at all. But he had nothing against his son. In future, when he needed service he would either apply directly to Perry Greavy or take his car to one of the garages in Allenby.

Meanwhile he was still locked in his own basement. Apparently he would not get out without destroying something. He must break the lock on one of the doors, and if so, that to the kitchen was preferable to the one leading to the yard. For strategy, however, it would be more cunning to get out without the knowledge of one's captors. He had a marked advantage over Harry & Ramona if they believed him still safely incarcerated, completely harmless to them. He could then range freely about the property, swooping in for a guerilla attack when such was least expected. In this light the door to the yard could be seen as the better one to breach.

Nor would it be necessary to break anything at all! Simply

removing the hinges, or rather the pins which secured them, would do the job. Keese chuckled to himself as he searched for a tool with which to accomplish the task. He could find nothing better than an archaic hooked beer-can opener of yesteryear, now rusted.

The hinges were painted over and would not have been quick to respond to the proper tools; to Keese's application the door was impervious, and more than once he stabbed his other hand when the can opener slipped. He was getting nowhere.

He stopped laboring, to entertain this rueful thought, and now for the first time he looked up the stairs which rose to his right, and he saw that the door to the kitchen was ajar. He had no way of knowing how long this had been the case. He threw down his makeshift tool and plodded deliberately up the steps, preparing to be sheepish when he faced his neighbors. In fact, he was ready to shake hands with Harry and call an end to this whole futile business.

But when he emerged into the kitchen his neighbors were gone. Cold clanking noises from outside attracted him to the window. Perry Greavy had arrived with the wrecker. In the light from the two lamps on its rear superstructure he was attaching the chains to the front bumper of the car in the driveway. Perry wore a billed hunting cap made of lustrous orange-hued synthetic. Keese had once poked the crown of such a cap in a hardware store: it looked as if it might be hard to the touch, but actually it was resilient, even spongy.

Keese continued to stand passively at the window, the victim of a loss of will. He unprotestingly watched Perry Greavy climb into the cab of the wrecker and drive away, pulling his car along on its hind wheels.

When the red taillights were finally extinguished by intervening trees, Keese left the window and reconnoitered the entire ground floor of his house. No Harry was to be found, and no Ramona! God be praised. Obviously Harry believed that his final trick had evened the score, and they had gone home at last. The loss of Keese's own car, plus thirty-two dollars in cash, was a small price to pay for their absence, and anyway Perry would hardly destroy the automobile. No doubt he would park it at the station overnight and get to it in the morning. Keese might have to pay him for the useless round-trip haul, as well as for the subsequent retrieving of Harry's car and the repair thereof, but this did not worry him. He intended to study his insurance policies.

In the living room Keese settled in the large overstuffed chair that he regarded as his personal property, though when guests were present he always sincerely urged other persons to sit there, even children. As a small boy himself he had always adored the grown man who invited him to use the regal chair, in which a child sat so far back that his shoes hung far above the floor.

This neighborly contest had ended just in time. There had been no damage that could not be mended—and the assessment applied to the emotions as well as to material considerations. Keese intended to limit his subsequent association with Harry & Ramona, but he did not hate them. He would wave across yards, he might even shout a greeting now and again. Sending an Xmas card was a must. Packages might be accepted in their absence. Small items might be lent: an egg, a cup of confectioners' sugar, a fifteen-amp fuse. But even such transactions were nearing the yellow-colored or warning zone. A man like Harry might try to parlay a rake, say, into something much more ambitious. And Keese could not picture Ramona in the kitchen, baking a pie. Lewdness emanated from her. Obviously she was the sort who would sunbathe in her back yard while dressed in little or nothing: from May to October her navel would never be covered.

Elaine was due to graduate on one day in June and on the next to go to France for postgraduate study, paid for by some foundation and not her father, though of course Keese had always bought her anything she wanted. Though happy for her, until this moment he had found the prospect of a daughterless summer to be without recommendation. Yet now he found himself almost happy, in a negative sense, to think that she would not be here to witness the decline of the neighborhood.

But the answer at the moment was to return to the routine. To see where he should be at this hour under normal circumstances Keese consulted the little clock on the bookshelf. Past 11:00 P.M.! One way to kill an evening was to entertain your neighbors. He decided he could not do better than to retire at this point.

He locked the doors and turned out all the lights but that which illuminated the staircase. He ascended to the second floor. The door to the master bedroom was closed and no thin line of light could be seen along the threshold. Why Enid had retired so early he could not say: she had hardly exhausted herself in the matter of Harry & Ramona. He would not soon forgive her for that performance.

Keese entered the bathroom. His pajamas were habitually kept all day on a hook that was fastened to the inner door, that which opened on the bedroom. But the pair that he had hung up in the morning was not to be found in place. If Enid had declared them ready for laundering, she was wrong. In fact, they were new, fresh from the plastic bag! To support this argument to himself, he went to the waste can to find that bag —and discovered the pajama coat. It was balled and befouled, soaked in some oily fluid as if it had been used to clean a piece of machinery.

He was too shocked to be angry. Obviously someone had spilled something, probably bath oil, and used half of his new pair of pajamas to clean it off the floor. For a long moment he could not imagine who might be responsible for this crime. Certainly Enid was incapable of it; he might sooner suppose he had done it himself in some overwrought transport. But then he remembered Ramona's incursion into the second floor. The little bitch! Now his anger came, and it was intensified almost to fury by his discovery of the pajama trousers, which though quite clean, still unused in fact, were rolled into a kind of limp sausage and inserted through the gooseneck beneath the washstand. If some excuse might be found for ruining the coat—fallen bottle, flood of oil, panic—there could be none at all for the degradation of the pants.

It was all Keese could do, as he used the toothbrush, not to bite off the bristles. One of his disadvantages in dealing with Harry & Ramona was that he had no one to assist him. Enid had obviously disqualified herself: she was definitely not in sympathy with him. Certainly he had received no encouragement for his position from anybody on the telephone. Even the Greavys seemed in league with his neighbors. If only Elaine were there! Nobody could stand long against Elaine, with her devastating combination of brilliance and beauty: where one failed the other could always be brought into play.

Keese rinsed his mouth and spat with great vehemence. He inspected his face in the mirror, avoiding a close study of his jowls. His teeth were in first-rate shape, and he had kept most of his hair. It was his body that could not pass muster, and furthermore he intended to do nothing whatever about it. He had given up smoking and confined his drinking to white wine. To lessen the intakes of fats and starches was too much to ask of him.

He now stripped to the buff, placing his washable clothing in the laundry hamper and his sneakers in the corner. He extinguished the bathroom light and opened the door to the bedroom. Instantly he felt a draft from the open window: the night air was chillier than he expected, but then he was naked. In the dark he found his chest of drawers and the appropriate compartment, and by touch he selected a pair of pajamas. It was unkind to put on a light in a room where Enid lay sleeping; noise disturbed her little, but any illumination however modest was ruinous to her repose.

Keese slept on the far side of the bed, near the windows. He went there now, peeled away the layered sheet and blanket, sat down on the edge of the bed, and swung himself in. With his left hand at an awkward angle, he reached for the edge of the bedclothes he had flung back, but it eluded him as such things are wont to do, and it was necessary to bring his right hand into service. He reached across himself and felt—Enid's back. She was much closer to his side than usual. The bed was king-sized, and she was now in possession of a good two-thirds of it. Ordinarily he would not have minded that so much, but after her really shameful failure to support him against Harry & Ramona, and then her early voiding of the field altogether, to come to this bed, he was not inclined towards generosity.

Impatiently he drew the blanket over him while turning his body away. He jackknifed himself then, and steering his rump into her small of back, he pushed her slowly, inexorably, towards the opposite edge. But this movement had hardly got under way when it was arrested. No further progress was possible without applying more pressure than could be justified. Such difficulties are always mysterious in the dark, but light soon solves them. Keese was in no mood to be senselessly merciful. After a day like the foregoing, he must at least be permitted to possess his half of bed. If the light awakened Enid, then so much the worse for her.

He thumbed the switch of his bedside lamp and turned back to determine why she was wedged immovably.

He lay beside Ramona, who was sleeping next to Harry. Harry however was not sleeping. He had lifted his head to stare across at Keese, and he was grinning. No, just a moment: his large teeth were in evidence, but not in the interests of a grin. A savage grimace was more like it. But Keese himself was hardly in a genteel attitude. He glared back for an instant and then leapt from bed. He marched around to Harry's side of the bed.

At his belligerent approach Harry changed his own style. He lost his snarl. He fell back and raised his hands: "Wait a minute, Earl," he said vulnerably, "don't do something you'll be sorry for. I wanted to tell you, I swear I did. It was Enid who's to blame."

"Coward," cried Keese, "hiding behind a woman!"

At this Ramona awakened, unless she had been playing possum all the while. She proved much more effective at this juncture than her husband.

"It's very simple, Earl," said she. "Our bed is still dismantled over there. When Enid heard this she insisted we stay the night. Naturally we assumed she would tell you."

Keese sucked his lips judiciously. "All right, I'll go along with you—for the moment. Where *is* Enid?"

"In your girl's room," said Ramona.

Keese pointed his finger at her. "Do you realize there's only a single bed in Elaine's room?"

"No, I didn't," Ramona said civilly, and turned to her husband. "Harry, did you know that?"

"How would I?" said Harry, his eyebrows assuming the worried look of a hound's. "Gee, Earl . . ."

He seemed genuinely sympathetic, but Keese wouldn't be taken in again. "Am I supposed to sleep on the floor?"

"Well, I wouldn't say that," said Harry.

"What would you say then?"

"The thing I'm wondering," said Ramona, "is why you pretend you don't have anyplace to sleep when the guest room is there all the while."

"For the simple reason that the guest room is presently being used for storage and is jammed full of extra furniture."

"I'm sure you can find some place to burrow in it," said

Ramona, starting to roll over on her side as she spoke. "After all, it's only for a few days." She closed her eyes.

"Days?" cried Keese. "You've got another think coming!" But she was asleep or pretending to be.

Harry shrugged, nodded at her, and smirked for Keese's benefit, as if she were an amusing eccentric who must be humored.

"Oh, yes," Keese shouted, "it's quite a joke, isn't it? So laugh at this!" He seized handfuls of sheet and blanket at the foot of the bed and walked backwards with them, exposing his new neighbors, in more ways than one: they were both naked. He sputtered incoherently for a moment, and then he dropped his end of the bedclothes. Ramona pretended to sleep through all of this. Her body was decorous: one polished hip in the air, and her near breast was beneath her elbow. But Harry, flat supine, was blatant and obscene: "A feast for the eyes," he crooned while spreading his legs.

"You dirty dog," said Keese, "I'll get you for this." He picked up the end of the bedclothes and flung them over the terrible couple.

"So we didn't have our nighties with us," said Harry. "Can't you take a little joke?"

Ramona groaned as if in her sleep. "Gawd, how long are you gonna keep this up? Either get in or get out."

Keese couldn't believe he heard her accurately, and therefore he ignored this speech, but Harry smiled at him and said: "There you are, Earl, what could be more generous?"

"Oh, thank you very much," Keese said with acid irony. "Are you inviting me to share my own bed?"

Harry stared for a moment and then nodded violently. "Come on," he said to Ramona, "it seems we ain't welcome."

This was to call Keese's bluff in another way: now he was supposed to feel guilty about routing them from bed. Where would they go? But his experience with them thus far had cured him of a tendency to assume responsibility for the difficulties people got themselves into of their own volition. If a man has willfully discarded his supply of food, by what obligation am I expected to feed him?

"That's right," he said boldly now. "Get out and be damned."

Ramona peeped at him over her shoulder. She spoke in a piping, little-girl's voice. "Why be such a mean old man? We're your neighbors. You should be nicer."

"All right," said Keese, "don't start that stuff. I began by being hospitable, if you will remember, but your technique is guaranteed to turn any normal person against you in short order, I'd say. I can't explain the Abernathys."

"Who?" Harry asked, leaving the bed deliberately and regardless of modesty.

"Enough of that," said Keese. "I've talked with them, you see."

"So?"

"So they insist they're your dearest friends."

"That's a laugh." Harry began idly to scratch his groin. Keese had seen nothing like that since his army service, many years before.

He was embarrassed by it now. He turned and asked Ramona: "I suppose you maintain you don't even know them?"

But she asked defiantly: "Are you going to stand there and play with yourself while I get dressed?"

He was onto this tactic by now, the diversionary attack. "It's my bedroom, isn't it?"

"O.K.," she said, extending one arm from the bedclothes, pointing to the chair nearby. "Please?"

He saw her clothing there, and went to fetch it. It consisted of no more than the shiny blouse, the high-waisted slacks, and the shoes. No stockings. And no underwear? He surveyed the room: no, not a stitch. Harry, across the bed, was getting into his, though. His bulging Jockey shorts looked a size too small. He stretched insouciantly. He seemed vain about his body.

Keese took the clothes to Ramona. She had retracted her hand and was staring at him in an intense fashion. But he refused to play more games, and dropped his burdens onto the bed.

Wearing T-shirt and drawers, Harry rubbed his blond head, the curls springing up as his fingers went by. "Listen," he said, "how's about *paying* you for the use of the room for a night or two?"

"For God's sake," said Keese, "I don't run a hotel."

"Neither does anyone else around here," Harry said. "The long and short of it is that the house is not habitable at the moment. It needs some work before we can actually live there. But we want to be nearby while the work is done, because you can't trust 'em unless you keep an eye on 'em."

"Just a minute," Keese said. "The Walkers lived there up to the moment he died. I've seen that house: it's perfectly O.K."

"Full of vermin," Harry said. "Roaches behind the wallpaper. I hate that. Mouse turds on the kitchen shelves. But the structural weaknesses are serious. You can put your finger through the beams down cellar: dry rot. I wouldn't be surprised to look out your window and see the whole place collapse at any moment."

"Don't turn around," Ramona warned Keese. "Your heart's not strong enough." A sequence of rustling sounds indicated that she had risen.

Keese was stung by this. He squeezed his fingers into fists and, glaring murderously at Harry, he said to Ramona: "Go to hell, you bitch."

He was not as amazed as he might once have been to see

Harry throw back his head, laugh, and congratulate him: "That's telling her!"

"Look here," Keese said when he had cooled slightly, "I don't believe what you're saying. The house couldn't have degenerated that much since I last saw it. It wasn't three years ago that Walker showed me his basement: it was just fine then."

"Just a minute," said Harry, who had not made a move to don more clothing than his underwear. Keese noticed suddenly that he was slightly bowlegged. "Why did he show you his basement? You're lying, Earl."

Keese shook his head over the futility of trying to talk with either of them about the simplest matters. Anyone who is determined to frustrate an inquiry has an easy time of it: a ridiculous question can be made of every particular of life.

"Take it on faith, Harry," said Keese. "Meanwhile, put on the rest of your clothes."

"I wish there were some way I could convince you we need shelter," Harry said.

"Get going," said Keese.

Harry found his trousers on the floor: he had apparently undressed as he walked towards bed. "You wouldn't consider it—?"

"No," said Keese. "I don't want to be hateful about this, but I'm afraid I really can't stand either one of you, alone or together. It's as simple as that. I'm not making a moral judgment, calling you wicked or anything. I'm even willing to entertain the idea that you mean well. I'm not consigning you to perdition, but I wish you would henceforth make your way through life without involving me. . . . Now, that's as nice as I can put it."

Harry received this speech expressionlessly, while putting on his trousers. When Keese was finished he said, quietly zipping up his fly: "That's pretty devastating, Earl. Nobody would say something like that and not mean it. Personally, I feel as though you kicked me in the nuts."

"I assure you—" Keese began.

"No, no," said Harry. "I understand your position: you have stated it only too well. I don't need to hear it again."

"It's nothing personal," said Keese.

"Bullshit!" cried Ramona from behind him.

He turned. She was dressed now, and for the first time he realized that she had worn the turban even to bed. She was bald, was that it?

"What is it if it's not personal?" she asked.

Keese smirked. "Well, you know what I . . . it's a matter of fundamental differences of principle. What you might see as a friendly approach repels me. I take it as an attack. We're all different, you know."

"I wish you'd quit dwelling on it," said Harry. "Step on our faces if you will, but don't grind your heel. You hate our guts, pure and simple. What more's to be said?"

He wasn't exactly right, but Keese decided not to insist on an agreement that must respect the precise nuances. It was true in a general way that he detested them.

"O.K.," he said, "fair enough."

"Fair my ass," snarled Ramona. "It's your house, your bedroom, and your bed. What's fair? Do we get any kind of vote?"

Harry snorted. Keese decided to get out of their crossfire and stepped away so that he did not have to turn so far to see one after addressing or listening to the other. This movement brought his rump against Enid's dresser top.

"What *is* fair," he said, "is that you have a perfectly good house sitting empty over there while you're both over here, pestering me. There's no great vermin problem, and the beams are not rotted. In fact, it's a good sound building in all respects. If you are too tired, or too lazy, to put your bed together, then sleep on the mattress, on the floor. I've done that more than once. It can even be fun, like camping out."

Ramona continued to sneer at him: she had been nursing a grudge against him since the first, he had no idea why. Harry on the other hand was not exactly inimical even now: he seemed basically a hopeful sort. And in return one could hope he would eventually straighten out.

Keese stepped up to him now and said: "I'm sorry it worked out this way. I apologize if I hurt your feelings, but in life interests often conflict. Maybe as neighbors we can at least be neutrals, if not active enemies. I certainly hope so and will do what I can to make it so." He put out his hand. Harry took it and applied such crushing force with his own large and muscular fist that the agony was too much for Keese, who began to sag.

"Pull that sentimental stuff on me," said Harry, grinning brutally down upon him, "and you'll be punished." He gave Keese's helpless hand a final vicious squeeze and released it. Keese plunged to his knees, and his hand fell limply to the floor.

All the fight had gone out of him. He wonderingly sat back on his heels and asked himself for the nth time, as a man will, how he had got into this predicament. He dully watched Harry & Ramona exit. He heard them go downstairs, open the front door, and leave.

With the use of his left, unmaimed hand he helped himself to his feet. His strength was slow to return. Perhaps he was finished. But no, he refused to accept that. He hurled himself into the bathroom, found his old clothes in the laundry hamper, and got into them. Then he returned to the bedroom closet and searched its dim recesses for the cane he had used, many years before, while recovering from a broken leg. He intended to flog Harry within an inch of his life. Aha! There it was, but unfortunately much lighter than he remembered, not so formidable a weapon as he required. He threw it back and, unarmed, dashed into the hall. The lights were on. He ran down the stairs and threw open the door. Perhaps by hurling himself against the back of Harry's legs he could hamstring him.

Elaine stood just outside, upon the mat. She held the key in her hand but had not had time to use it.

"Dad!" she said. "I decided to come home on the spur of the moment."

"Thank God," said Keese, pulling her inside and slamming the door.

CHAPTER 7/

"ELAINE," said Keese, "did you see anybody out there?"

"Daddy, I refuse to say a word until you greet me decently."

"Sorry, dear," said Keese. He embraced her quickly and kissed her brow, then pushed himself away. "To what do we owe this honor? Certainly didn't look for you this weekend. Spur of the moment, eh? How'd you come, then? Get a ride?"

"Hitchhiked," said Elaine, watching him closely.

Keese gasped. "You don't mean it! Tell me it isn't so, Elaine. Admit that you are joking."

"I admit," said Elaine, seizing him in the elbow crook. "I just wanted to be cruel to you for a moment."

"I wonder why?"

"Just because," Elaine said. "Just because you're my very own dad. You're mine, you belong to me, you're my property." She swung around and punched him in the belly, none too lightly, as it happened. He always brought that sort of thing out in her. He was beginning to feel normal again—in fact, much better than. Harry's image was fast fading, and it was as if Ramona had never existed.

"Are you hungry, dear?" He struck himself. "If anything's there to eat! Eggs maybe." Elaine shook her head. "Who gave you the ride? You probably didn't invite them in because the lights were out. We are retiring earlier than usual, you will note. We had an unusual evening, and it seemed the wisest course to wait for tomorrow, in the idea that a new day might shed new light."

"I'm exhausted, myself," Elaine said, stepping out to demonstrate, with sagging shoulders and drooping tongue, her fatigue. "I'm going right to bed." She would have started for the stairs then, but remembering where Enid had bunked, Keese drew his daughter into the living room.

"Now, you just sit here for a moment," said he, leading her to the sofa. "You've embarrassed us by coming back without warning. We rented your room to a family of migratory workers, and I have to run them out now."

"Ah," said Elaine, and she tried to smile at this jest, but failed to sustain her effort.

"Seriously," he said, "your mother stripped the bed today to launder the mattress cover, and it hasn't been remade."

Elaine finally managed to smile. "I could insist on making the bed myself," said she, "but I'm not going to. I come home to be spoiled. I can't get away with that anywhere else in the world."

Hearing this, Keese felt as if lifted on a massive wave. He knew he should guard against inordinate pride, but he could not resist gloating: he had the better part of a weekend in which to serve Elaine as lackey. This was the one kind of abasement that did not degrade. Keese had always been like this with his daughter. As he so often thought, it was a wonder that she had turned out well after leaving home, i.e., going into the "real" world from an artificial atmosphere. In point of fact Elaine had been immediately successful at college. Apparently she was that sort of person. In his own university years Keese had been a moody type in private and socially supernumerary: genial, anonymous, crewcut, and chunky.

He now mounted to the second floor and, going past the master bedroom and bath, arrived outside the similar suite that had been Elaine's quarters since the Keeses had moved into the house. She came home about once a month during the academic year, from a university that was a hundred miles away. In between, her rooms were considered sacrosanct. That Enid would quarter herself in Elaine's room was remarkable, but then Enid's behavior had been strange throughout the evening. Also, it was true that the proper guest room had been made uninhabitable by the extra furniture stored there, former living-room pieces that were a bit too good as yet to be surrendered to charity.

Keese burst in now without knocking. He took pleasure in the assumption that he would startle Enid from sleep, but in point of fact she was sitting up, reading. An intense blue was the predominant color in Elaine's room, but its effect was subdued after dark, with only the bedlamp as a source of illumination.

"Elaine's just come home."

Enid closed her book and lowered it. She stared severely at him over the half-glasses. "I hope this is not one of your ruses."

"She's downstairs," Keese said brusquely. "Go see for yourself. Meanwhile I'll put this room in order."

Enid left the bed. She wore beige pajamas in some slippery synthetic. She opened a closet and found a pale-blue robe.

Keese's question was surly: "Isn't that Elaine's?"

"I lent mine to Ramona," Enid replied in a matter-of-fact tone which Keese found greatly exasperating in this case.

"You'll be interested to know that I threw them out," he said bitterly. "Just before Elaine got home, luckily. I sent them packing, those God-damned trash." He glared fiercely at her.

She smiled at him. "Just as well."

"What?"

"I say, it's a relief, isn't it? It just gets to the point where you have to take some sort of decisive action with people like that."

"Just a minute," said Keese. "I don't quite get this, Enid. When did you turn against them?"

"I was never *with* them," said she, solemnly shaking her head. "I was simply playing for time. Frankly, they frightened me."

Keese scowled, trying to figure this out. "Is that why you invited them to stay the night? Did they threaten you? I wish I had known this. We have a police force in this town."

"Oh, no! Imagine how it would seem if we had the *police* eject our neighbors. Could we ever live it down? Then there is that thing about their car. If provoked they could make some ugly trouble, Earl."

"Well, they've evened the score on cars," Keese said. "Perry Greavy came a while ago with his wrecker and hauled away *our* automobile. That was Harry's revenge! . . . But enough of this wretchedness! Elaine's waiting downstairs, dog-tired by the look of it. Go on down, and I'll straighten up here."

But Enid insisted it would go faster if they worked together. And as it turned out Keese was happy that she had stayed. During this common effort their seeming differences were expunged: whether or not she had truthfully explained the reasons for her seeming sycophancy to the new neighbors, Keese decided to disregard what had happened—even though he was wounded by her lack of confidence in his ability to defend their home. No doubt she had learned her lesson. He had thrown them out! He would not soon forget that victory, though his hand still ached from Harry's mauling.

When they had completed their task Keese and Enid went together to fetch Elaine, like a pair of footmen in some palace. They tended to fall into a ceremonial mood with their daughter. Now they halted in the doorway, as if awaiting permission to approach her, but she leaped from the sofa and went to embrace Enid. She also kissed her father, which she had not done on her entrance.

"Elaine," Keese said, "I seem to be getting absentminded. Did I or did I not take your case upstairs?"

Elaine dropped her lip. "I forgot it outside! Yes. I put it down while I looked for my key."

"You should get it then, Earl," said Enid, with the self-important air of one who provides necessary direction.

Keese was stung by this, but determined to rise above it. To complain would be merely to call the insult to Elaine's attention. He turned and moved briskly to the door.

But just as he was reaching for the knob, the bell sounded. This noise was very startling, because it seemed as though the bell had been touched off by his gesture.

He opened the door, and there stood Greavy—the old man, not the son. He too wore a billed cap made of padded orange plastic. He had a swarthy chicken-corded neck, a thrusting pointed pale jaw, and a thin and mean figure. Had his eyes shown a spark he might have looked like a fanatic, but they were lackluster.

"Say," he said, looking past Keese and into the hallway and seeing Elaine and Enid, "I never knew you would of have had your women up and around at this hour."

Keese believed he could identify an implication to the effect that he was being accused of tyrannical practices—unless that was due merely to Greavy's peculiar grammar. "It's only midnight," he answered, and then, annoyed with himself for accepting it as an accusation, added: "Should I have asked your permission?"

Greavy jerked his head as though he had been slapped in the face. He mouthed some silent speech, perhaps a bitter one, but aloud he addressed Keese almost obsequiously. "I give your auto a inspection, but I couldn't find nothing wrong with it, so I brung it back. Now if you was to have trouble with it tomorrow, you just bring it in." He began to nod his head in what looked like the onset of an obsession-compulsion. "Yes, sir, you just bring it in, bring it *right* in, you hear? If you have *any* trouble—"

"I'll bring it in," said Keese. "Don't worry about that." He saw Greavy continue to nod. He couldn't endure much of this. Therefore he stepped forward and down, compelling Greavy to give way and breaking the spell of which the garageman was captive.

He looked towards the driveway. "Car around back? Keys in it?"

Greavy leaned towards him and spoke discreetly. "I guess you had a good laugh out of it?"

"Pardon?"

"Made a fool of me?"

Keese studied the man's face in the light that came from inside the open door: his expression revealed nothing. "Fool? No, sir! *I* didn't ask to have my car hauled away. Someone has been playing a joke on us both."

Greavy's worn face heaved in something that was perhaps a smile, though the same gesture of mouth and set of eye would have served as his reaction to stepping in excrement. "Say, would you mind shutting that door of yours? The womenfolk, you know."

Greavy was never less than surprising. Why should he care whether Elaine and Enid were in a draft? Not to mention that Keese had suspected from his last speech that he was taking a hostile turn.

"Certainly." Keese pulled the door to.

"Now, mister," said Greavy, "I say you're a dirty shitsack. How about that?"

Keese found this cryptic. "I don't get your drift," he said equitably. "You can't be getting nasty. You were just so nice!" But he remembered how Greavy had been on the phone, turning ugly without warning.

"What are you gonna do about it?" Greavy asked.

Bored with this exchange, Keese looked again into the darkness towards the driveway that went through his side yard. "Car's round back, I guess. I'll go get the keys." He stepped down onto the path.

His trailing foot had not left the step when Greavy struck him in the stomach with wondrous force for such an emaciated-looking creature. His fist went into Keese's soft belly as far as the wrist.

Keese curled in upon himself and fell to the ground. Pain obscured such other feelings as he might have had. When he was able to breathe again and his stomach-ache had become less acute and more profound, he was alone on the walk. He raised himself onto his knees and looked blearily down the street: once again he saw the taillights of the wrecker turn the corner and go out of sight beyond the trees.

He struggled to his feet, but he stayed bent at the waist. Elaine was waiting for him to bring in her overnight case. Where was it? He shuffled, bent, to look in the shrubs on either side of the door. He followed the footpath to the public sidewalk, should she have left it anywhere along the route. He explored the curb: there was light enough to find a valise, had one been there. But none was.

He turned back and plodded up the path to the house. He didn't know how to tell Elaine that her case had been stolen. How terrible! One's own neighborhood should be a safe harbor. Suddenly the Keeses lived in a criminal slum.

Elaine and Enid were gone from the front hall. Keese dragged himself upstairs. The bed in the master bedroom remained in the tangle left behind by Harry & Ramona. It was Enid's duty to change that linen. He looked for her in his daughter's room, but she was not there. No one was anywhere on the second floor. Perhaps Elaine had opted for a snack after all and Enid had had a few delicacies put away for just such an emergency. He descended to the ground floor and went to the kitchen.

There was Elaine, and there was Enid, and Harry stood just inside the back door. He flinched when he saw Keese, and he moved his feet into a position that suggested readiness for a quick exit.

"Dad!" Elaine said with enthusiasm. "Harry found my case outside and brought it in."

Keese did not want to start any trouble in front of his child, but he could not refrain from asking: "At the back door?"

"Yes," said Harry. "It seemed the safer course." His face remained bland.

"Wasn't that nice of him?" asked Elaine, who was standing at the edge of the table in a funny twisted posture which gave prominence to her right hip. "I think he deserves a drink at least."

"Gee, Elaine," Keese said, refusing to look at Harry, "we don't have a drop of anything in the house."

Elaine swung her case from the floor to the table. She undid the clasps, opened the little valise, and reaching amongst the wadded stuffs within, found and brought forth a flat pint of colorless liquid.

"Could that be vod?" Harry asked, being emboldened to leave the door and advance on the table. He obviously could sense that Keese was stymied by the presence of Elaine.

Elaine waved the bottle at her parents, one by one. "Join us?" she asked, as if she and Harry already made a team.

Keese had gone off the hard stuff eighteen months before. He felt no better physically, but refraining from spirits and cigarettes gave him a taste of the sort of stern discipline required by certain faiths, religious and political.

"What do you want for a mix?" he now asked dolefully. "I doubt we've got any quinine water."

"I *know* we have none," said Enid, making a triumph of it.

"I take my poison plain," Elaine said, brandishing the bottle.

Harry was near the overnight case now. He leered into it and said: "Nifty undies."

Keese might have struck him then, had he been close enough, but Elaine simpered and said: "Thank you, sir!"

Keese had no explanation for that: in his presence Elaine had always been rather brittle with men. The old Elaine would have deflated Harry in short order.

At least Enid now seemed less eager to please than on the occasion of Harry's previous visit. Perhaps she had finally got his number. She stood nowhere near him. Her only weakness was her costume: her nightclothes were if anything less revealing than daytime attire, but they seemed wrong in the presence of a stranger, and of course the robe wasn't even her own.

"I'll get some ice," Keese said hastily. He could still feel the stomach-ache, and by no means had he forgotten Greavy and the need to square accounts with the old man. But first he would have to deal with Harry again. The only things that could be said for his new situation were that Ramona was absent, thank God!, and that Elaine was home, giving him even more incentive to defend his honor.

As he took the ice-cube tray from the refrigerator, Enid went into the dining room, and by the time he had levered the cubes loose and lifted away the grid she was back with two squat tumblers. She brought these to him at the sink. Harry meanwhile had pulled out a chair and offered it to Elaine. Keese looked over his shoulder to watch her sink dreamily upon it. Harry quickly chose a chair for himself and pulled it near hers. He bent towards her and began to speak in an animated undertone.

Enid came with the glasses at this point. Keese said to her, *sotto voce:* "We'll have to do something."

Enid moued and shrugged. This seemed appallingly cynical. Keese put two cubes in each glass as she extended it to him, then called each one back and added a third piece of ice. With one glass in each hand Enid went symmetrically to serve Elaine & Harry. Keese realized that he was already thinking of them as a pair.

Elaine's bottle stood on the tabletop. Enid seized it and poured one glassful of vodka and gave it to Harry, who made a parody clown-smile and said, with some attempt at a comic impediment of speech: "Thank you, ma'am, God damn."

Enid filled the other glass and began to drink it herself.

"*Muth-*er!" Elaine complained.

"Your father," Enid said, "doesn't want you to have any."

"Not true!" Keese cried. And he had thought that Enid was back in sympathy with him! He was really losing ground. He moved to take the initiative, and asked Harry, in the harshest voice he could produce: "You have a father?"

Harry had already drained the first glassful of vodka. He lifted the bottle from where Enid had placed it and poured himself a refill. "As a matter of fact, I don't," he said at last, with a sly grin. "I was conceived by artificial insemination: an anonymous semen-donor."

Keese cursed himself for giving the man that opening.

Elaine said: "Harry, please pour me some vodka."

Harry's answer was surprising. "No," said he. "If your dad says you can't have any, then that's good enough for me."

"It's my bottle," Elaine said indignantly, "and I'm almost twenty-two."

Keese now insisted on being heard. He did this by speaking unusually softly, not by turning up the volume. "Elaine, please don't believe that I didn't want you to have a drink. Why your mother told that vicious lie—I'm sorry, that's what it was—I have no idea."

Outrageously, Harry responded to this with a prolonged Bronx cheer.

Keese kept control of himself. "Why'd you do that?" he asked quietly.

"Stick to your guns, Dad!" cried Harry. Apparently he felt that Keese was in danger of abandoning some cherished principle. Wasn't it typical of a rogue like him to be concerned with the integrity of others?

Keese put his hand at Enid. "You don't need that." He remembered his suspicion, at one point earlier, that she had smelled of whiskey. He had no idea of what she did all day. She handed over her glass docilely enough now. He accepted it and gave it to Elaine.

"Don't you *ever* do anything like that again," his daughter told him, and never had he been so wounded, by her or anyone else, for never had she so admonished him: the fact was that he had never opposed a wish of hers in all her life. It was of course impossible to gratify every wish of a small child, but when the necessity had come for that, he had vanished, letting Enid do the dirty work. He could never bear to say no to Elaine, and he had no apology whatever for that weakness. But was it a kind of justice now that he should be falsely blamed for this current deprivation?

Whatever, he believed it more graceful not to insist on his guiltlessness, especially before a stranger, perhaps even an enemy, like Harry.

"All right, I won't," he said to Elaine. But he couldn't bear it long, and he asked fearfully: "You don't hate me?"

"Well," Elaine said petulantly, "I might forgive you, but you must apologize to Harry."

For *what?* Was this unspeakable swine alienating the affections of his darling daughter? Elaine was staring fiercely at him.

"Elaine . . ." he began.

"Daddy!"

"All right, I-beg-your-pardon-Harry," Keese said quickly. But acting on Elaine's command he found the apology easier to make than he had expected. It was, after all, really for Elaine's benefit and not Harry's. Despite all he did for her, Keese felt apologetic towards Elaine at all times, having been half of the conspiracy which had brought her into clamorous life from the serenity of the void.

"If you're man enough to apologize," said Harry, "I hope I'm big enough to accept it." He shoved his large hand up at Keese. On their last transaction Harry had all but broken the bones in Keese's fingers, bringing him to the floor in pain.

Therefore Keese ignored the gesture and addressed Elaine: "How's your drink? Vodka, eh? Is that a new taste?"

"Daddy, I want you to shake hands with Harry."

Keese was desperate enough to resist her: unless he evaded this demand he would be squirming in agony on the kitchen floor, for he had no doubt that Harry would not restrain himself if given the advantage.

"Oh," said he, "I don't really think that's necessary, Elaine. I'm sure that Harry understands." He smirked in hatred at Harry and walked to the sink, so that he would be nowhere near the man.

"I'm sorry, Earl," Harry said, as if in patient explanation, "but no apology can do without the shake. Oh, it's worthless without the shake!" Obviously he would not let this opportunity escape him.

Elaine said nothing more, and Keese could not bear to look at her. Nevertheless, the force of her demand weighed ever more heavily on his conscience. He could not avoid shaking with Harry, that was clear. He turned and stared into the sink —and saw the tray of loose ice cubes.

He scooped one up, walked briskly back to Harry, and grasped his hand. He enjoyed Harry's look of consternation as his neighbor closed upon the ice cube. Harry's hand lost the initiative. Keese was able to get a powerful purchase with his own fingers (the ice was as nothing to him), and he gave Harry a taste of the pain he had writhed under not long before. He sensed that Harry was struggling to maintain composure. Keese himself was immune to the cube.

The most priceless element was provided, appropriately enough, by Elaine. "Now," she asked her father, "don't you really feel better?"

"I certainly do," said Keese, smiling honestly and thus weakening himself sufficiently for Harry to make his escape. But the man had been decisively punished. To cap his victory, Keese dropped the ice cube (somewhat shrunken) into Harry's glass. "Freshen it up," he said with a jovial distention of nostril. "By the way," he added, reluctant to lose the floor, "Greavy returned my car. There was nothing wrong with it, you see."

Harry looked doleful. "I thought he was supposed to pull mine from the swamp."

"This is probably fascinating for you two," Elaine said jealously, "but it's pretty deadly to me. Next thing, you guys'll be talking about weight lifting or prostate trouble."

Harry was massaging his fingers in his lap, probably unnoticed by anyone but Keese. He winced at Elaine. "Who cares about what you think?"

Keese's breath was taken away.

But Elaine was chastened by the rebuke. She even seemed grateful to Harry. "I sometimes tend to babble pointlessly," she said, "because of a basic feeling of unimportance, I suppose. Isn't it ridiculous to try to counter this by making an even bigger fool of oneself? It would be helpful to me if you continued to point out any flaws of mine that you notice."

As if this were not enough, Enid, who had been aloof thus far, now was reconquered and came to the table, drawing up a chair. Harry was now bracketed by both of Keese's worshipful women.

"Glad to," Harry told Elaine. "First of all, your hair could use a restyling—a cut, a new shaping, and I would leave this up to you, but frankly I think a change of color might do wonders. You'll never be a beauty—who is?—but you could more than get by with a few improvements."

Keese was finally able to speak. "You degenerate!" he cried. "This girl before you has always been celebrated for her beauty. How dare you take that superior tone, you punk?"

The women were frozen by this outburst, but Harry good-naturedly threw up his hands. "So tastes are different from here to there," said he, "not to mention that love is blind. I certainly didn't mean to hurt your feelings."

"Please go on," Elaine said eagerly, "I can profit by this."

Hearing this, Keese could not keep his balance. He sank upon a chair, and now the kitchen table was fully occupied once more.

"You seem reasonably bright," Harry said to Elaine. "You have some difficulty in expressing yourself, but that's generally true of young girls, and it's not necessarily due to a feeble intelligence. At least sometimes it's merely shyness."

Keese was shaking his head involuntarily. This was too bizarre to be happening. This abominable lout, talking to Elaine in an insufferably patronizing tone—how could it be real?

Elaine chuckled gaily. "Well, I know where that leaves me! I've never been shy."

Enid chimed in, chuckling: "That's certainly true, hahaha."

"Of course, you understand this is all impromptu," said Harry. "I could do a much better job if I had a few days. I could write it up if you like, with numbered points."

"Number One," Keese shouted at Harry, "you're a moron. Two, you're a crook. Three, you're a liar. Four, you're a pervert. Five—"

While he continued to count and assign another abusive epithet to each digit, Elaine said, ignoring her father: "I'd value that, Harry. I'm very happy to have you as next-door neighbor. I know your friendship will do me all the good in the world, and I think it's wonderful that an important person like you would help a little nobody like me."

Keese finally stopped his count and went into a kind of coma. When he came to, he heard Enid addressing Harry: "I don't suppose you could spare any time for me?"

"Why, sure I could," Harry said, visibly puffing up with vanity.

"Enid!" Keese shouted, but it was as if he had kept silent. Neither of the three persons present acknowledged him in any way.

"To begin with," said Harry, looking sympathetically at Enid, "you are a nervous wreck."

"Haha!" jeered Keese. "There you are! How wrong can he be?"

"Harry," said Enid, reaching for his hand, "you're a genius."

"Oh, yeah," said Keese, *"sure* he is."

Elaine looked at her father in—well, if it wasn't supreme disgust, then it was a heartbreakingly good imitation. "Daddy," she said quietly, "what's happened to you?"

"If I could only talk to you alone," he half-whispered.

"I think if any explanation's to be made, any excuses, they should be made before the whole group," Elaine responded, in a voice louder than normal. "I don't want to form a little cabal with you."

Enid and Harry were not distracted from their colloquy. Keese listened for a moment. Harry was saying: ". . . definitely, moreover." To which Enid replied: "If, and then depending."

He returned to the appeal to Elaine. "Please be on my side. They are intentionally talking nonsense so as to drive me mad."

"Daddy, will you stop? That's ridiculous. You're simply not listening."

Keese lost patience. He turned and shouted: "He is talking nonsense, vicious nonsense, at the kitchen table in *my* house!"

Harry sighed, pushed himself away from the table, and stood up. "Sorry, Enid. I tried."

Elaine cried in dismay: "Harry, you're not leaving?"

"Yes, he is," said Keese. "Good-bye, Harry."

Harry smiled bitterly. "Are you throwing me out again?" He looked at Elaine as if for support.

And it was forthcoming. "Daddy, can't you see that Harry just wants to be friendly?"

How could he refuse his daughter's plea? Harry's well-being was neither here nor there. It was Elaine's that concerned Keese. He realized that he could not sustain a hostile role in her presence.

"All right, darling," he said. "Harry, I'm willing to bury the hatchet."

Harry looked skeptical. "Not in my back, I trust?"

"No, no," Keese murmured. "I'll even drink on it." He went to the table and took Elaine's glass. "Do you mind, dear?"

"I'll pour," said Elaine, and did so.

Harry came to get a refill. He bent over her as Keese stepped back with lifted glass. Keese could smell the fiery liquid, which was far from being odorless: it smelled like liniment.

Harry said to Elaine: "You're some little peacemaker." He put his hand in the middle of her back and slid it down onto her behind.

Keese transferred the glass to his left hand, and with his right fist he hit Harry in the eye with all his strength.

Harry did not fall, and he did not retaliate. His eye already closed and beginning to discolor, he deliberately drank the vodka, put his glass down, walked in a dignified stride to the door, opened it, and left.

CHAPTER 8/

KEESE had no regrets, but he dreaded the denunciations he would hear from Elaine and Enid.

"What else could I have done?" he asked of them both (or perhaps of neither). "How could I stand by and . . ."

Elaine broke in, relieving him of the search for the *mot juste* (if one existed when speaking of Harry): "Daddy, you're a hero!"

Keese heard this warily. He had never known Elaine to use irony on him, but there was always a first time. "Seriously, Elaine," he asked, "do you think I did the right thing?"

But Elaine gave him no spoken answer. She merely smiled at him.

Keese sank onto his chair. "You both approve, do you?" Oddly enough, only now did his respiratory rate increase and his heart grow thunderous. He felt as though he could easily faint, but he resisted this lure. A discrete victory, of course, was nothing: true success was a sequence. He must not question the merit of his actions. If he punched Harry in the eye, then that punch must be seen as deserved by the recipient, necessary in the situation, and a triumph of the thrower thereof. After that it should be forgotten, for there was new ground to gain.

"Well," he said, "then that's that."

"Of course," said Elaine, "with that type you can expect revenge."

"What's that?"

"Harry will retaliate," Elaine said. "I'm certain of that."

"To hell with him," said Keese. "Let him do his worst." He remembered Greavy, and he thought that he might be in the right rhythm now to pay off that old skunk, who would just have got home and climbed into bed again. A man is most susceptible to terror when he is in the earlier phases of his night's sleep. Let's see, he could go to Greavy's house (the phone book would tell him where), pound on the door, and when the man came stumbling, half-asleep and confused, to open the door, hurl a paper bag of excrement into his house.

The plan in this simple form was not immune to objection: perhaps Greavy wouldn't open the door but would call the police to investigate the disturbance; or would open, but be armed with a gun; or perhaps his wife would answer or some other relative. An alternative procedure was needed. . . .

"Dad," said Elaine, "I think you'd rather I hadn't come home this weekend."

He was called back to the current moment. "Don't say that, Elaine! It's just that it's new for me to be under these attacks, and I am trying to adjust to a life in which chance encounters can be brutal."

"You're blaming me, I know," Elaine said. "But what could I do? I was trying to placate him. He looks dangerous. He's the kind who would murder you without a second thought."

Enid had listened with the thinnest of smiles. She seemed to be deliberating. At last she spoke.

"There isn't an English muffin in the house."

How irrelevant could you get? But in point of fact Keese was grateful that she had made this seemingly absurd statement. He didn't want to discuss Harry with Elaine.

"I'll get up early," he said, replying to Enid but speaking for Elaine's benefit, "and go down and get some breakfast stuff in the village."

"But there's no car," Enid pointed out. "Didn't you tell me it was hauled off?"

"It was returned," said Keese. He still felt Greavy's gut-punch: perhaps his entrails had been ruptured. He hated that old swine, who for no reason at all had intruded into the private thing between himself and Harry. With Harry his primary purpose had been to correct the man's behavior. Had there been a more effective and less violent method than punching him in the eye, he would have used it. "That is," he added, "I *think* it was brought back. I suppose I should check. The way things have gone around here this evening, I must get out of the habit of making easy assumptions: that's the way I've got in trouble." He turned to Elaine. "If the car's not there, I'll walk to the store. You might join me if it would amuse you. Remember how we used to do that when you were a small girl, walk to the village?"

Elaine blandly shook her head and said: "No."

Suddenly Keese was not certain himself. "Well, maybe we didn't do it, then. Maybe I just thought we did." But Elaine was in no mood to help with the reminiscence. She continued to shake her head.

Enid said: "Why don't you go to bed? You look very exhausted."

"Yes," Keese chimed in enthusiastically, "that's good thinking. Go to bed, Elaine, and you'll find that all these things are a distant memory in the morning."

"But I meant you, Earl," said Enid.

"You're not condemning me, are you?" Keese asked sharply.

"Certainly not! How could you think such a thing!" Enid's voice was absolutely false, and even Elaine's attention was drawn away from her brooding.

"Mother," she said, "if you're thinking something, out with it!"

"Well, it just occurred to me that Harry would probably have a different interpretation."

Keese snorted. "He is a monster of self-righteousness. The crimes he commits against others are nothing as opposed to the minor inconveniences suffered by himself. He thinks he's some kind of royalty. Notice that he doesn't mention having a last name. And for that matter, what profession does he practice? You can't talk long with the average man before he refers in some way to his work, but not Harry."

Enid put her chin into her hand. "Have you told him yours?"

"That has nothing to do with it!" Keese insisted. "We've been in *my* house, not in his. I don't have to define myself: I'm here. You see what I mean? Who's he? He's never been seen before, has he? I've lived right here for more than twenty years. I can be *found,* you see. I've got a history, a local habitation and a name. Nobody can question me on the basics. But if I were to move someplace else, I'd feel an obligation to establish myself before arrogantly trying to take over."

"I'll tell you what I think he is," said Elaine. "I think he's a state trooper. Can't you imagine him in that wide-brimmed felt hat and those leather boots?"

Keese saw no reason to suppose she was right (in fact, he had reluctantly to admit that Elaine's judgments had consistently disappointed him on this visit, for the first time in her life!), and Harry seemed nothing like a cop to him, but he nevertheless commended her for a striking idea.

"The thing that worries me is that he might have gone to get his service revolver," she said next. "I don't want to get too alarmist, but it seemed to me that he showed all the earmarks of the unstable personality."

"It's easy to excuse everything in some way," said Keese.

"For example, murder can be seen in one light as merely getting rid of someone—as a mere removal."

"For that matter," asked Elaine, "what did he really do?"

"I think we should forget about Harry," said Keese. "He is really of no consequence."

Elaine nodded solemnly. "Still, he weighs on my conscience."

Keese could not help feeling exasperated with her. Until a few moments ago he should have called that impossible. Where was her old ebullience?

"We haven't heard your news," he said. "Any funny incidents take place at college?"

From his right side Enid chided him. "Is this the appropriate time for that sort of thing?"

"O.K." Keese slapped the tabletop and stood up. "I say it's bedtime for all." He looked at the clock on the wall near the refrigerator. "Your room is ready for occupancy, Elaine."

His daughter remained in place. "I think I'll stay here," said she. "In case I'm needed."

"Needed for what?"

"I have a sense of impending doom," she said.

He was very near a total loss of patience. After what he had been through this evening! "Elaine," he said severely, "please let me handle this thing. There's no reason why you should be concerned. Harry won't try any more of his tricks on you, I promise. He's a bully, you see, and a coward. Call his bluff and you have neutralized him. Now, I don't say that he won't try some new way to get back at me, but it'll undoubtedly be underhanded from now on. I anticipate finding enormous holes in my yard, or garbage dumped there in the middle of the night. The car—he may very well do little jobs of sabotage on it, let the air out of the tires or wedge a potato in the exhaust pipe." It occurred to Keese that if Greavy had brought his car back, Harry might well have disabled it already.

Elaine reluctantly got to her feet. She had unusually dark shadows under her eyes. Were they from cosmetics or illness? Keese gave her a once-over of the kind that is a preface to empty flattery, i.e., seeing nothing.

"I like your boots," said he.

"A campus policeman went berserk last week," said Elaine.

"Good God!"

"Lucky he was armed only with flashlight and club, else he might have pumped someone full of lead."

Enid came between Keese and Elaine and embraced her daughter briefly. "Who would think of something like that!" she said. "In my day at college nothing happened but youthful hijinks."

"Some people can't stand being defied," said Elaine. "Like Harry. He could make your life a living hell, Dad. He'll stop at nothing to pay you back."

Keese shivered within. Such talk was unhealthy, and enough of it could bring on a disaster. If you continued to overestimate your enemy, he would eventually realize the prediction: some law worked in such cases, perhaps the reverse of Diminishing Returns.

"Then you don't know me," he told his daughter, almost threatening her in return. "I'll give him more than he bargained for." His face was fiery; he was getting a sunburn from within.

"Now, now, Earl," Enid said, "this is not the time to blow on the coals. I thought you were about to retire."

He suddenly noticed that the vodka bottle had been emptied. By whom? Elaine? It would explain her melancholy state of mind. Why, anyway, had she carried a pint of vodka in her luggage? Elaine had always been beyond reproach: was she going bad now all at once?

"Go on," Keese said to both, "I'll get the light." He went to the wall switch and put his finger in place. He had earlier looked at the clock without seeing the time. When he looked now he could not believe it. "Is that two A.M.?"

"All these things take time, Earl," said Enid. That was a strange comment if he had ever heard one. As if something had been accomplished!

"Well," he said, "I'm wasting no more of it on the likes of Harry and Ramona. Or Greavy, for that matter. I'll deal with him tomorrow."

Elaine stopped just inside the kitchen door. "Ramona? Greavy? Who are they? Two more of your newly acquired enemies?"

"That was a slip of the tongue," Keese hastened to say. "They are of no matter at this time of the night."

"I never expected to come home and find you embattled," Elaine said, accusingly. "I always have counted on this place to be a tranquil refuge."

"Yeah, yeah," said Keese, motioning for the women to go ahead while he switched off the light.

"Are you shooing us out?" asked his daughter.

"Sorry," he said curtly. He pointed: "Don't forget your case."

Enid stopped in the doorway and asked Elaine: "You don't mind, do you, dear?" She held the lapel of the powder-blue robe that belonged to her daughter.

"Oh, that's mine," said Elaine. "Gee."

They finally left the kitchen and Keese extinguished the ceiling light. On an afterthought in the darkness he found the back door and turned the key in it. The women had gone ahead through the dining room, which was dimly illuminated by the light from the front hallway. They were on the stairs when he emerged.

Keese himself was about to ascend when he remembered the front door. He had probably not locked it after admitting Elaine. He tried the knob. Yes, the door swung open. Ramona was sitting on the step outside. He quickly slammed the door and locked it with the key and then with the twist-knob above, a device never used since the Keeses had moved in. Indeed it was almost sealed with verdigris, and a less desperate man of normal strength could probably not have sent the bolt home.

He stole upstairs, going almost on tiptoe. It never failed: every time he believed he had got things in hand at last, another threat appeared. His confidence was shattered. He may have settled with Harry, but Ramona had consistently trounced him at every encounter. She could not be disposed of by a punch in the eye, and even at the times he had expelled her from his house (he could remember two occasions) Harry had been included and, being larger, bore the loss. In a very real sense Ramona was undefeated.

And there she sat, on his front step, at two o'clock in the morning.

He climbed the stairs and wandered to the end of the second-floor hallway, at the extremest remove from the master bedroom and around the corner from Elaine's, in the toe of a short-footed L, as it were. Some former owner had added a room there, poking out a dormer from the roof, perhaps to accommodate some new addition to his family. This room had been where the Keeses put their guests before it became a repository for the surplus furniture. Keese thought now of going into the room and burrowing deep amidst the stored furniture, sandwiching himself in thick upholstery.

Goddamnit, he couldn't let Ramona sit out there in the middle of the night! What if someone drove a car to the end of the road to turn around? He came back along the hall, passing the closed doors of both bathrooms, behind which in each case was the sound of falling water. There are people who must shower before retiring, however late.

He came downstairs. He crept to the front door, bent to apply his ear to the keyhole, and listened. Did he hear sobbing?

It could be the wind. Why would Ramona be weeping out there? Her dog had run away or been killed? Harry had brutalized her? It occurred to Keese that she might be grieving because of some misfortune that had happened to Harry, but in that case she would hardly be sitting there almost silently.

Could she be expressing her unhappiness with the debacle that had resulted from her efforts to make friends in the new neighborhood? Well, whose fault was that?

He grew angry, and he put his mouth to the keyhole and said: "You can't blame me! I tried to do the right thing. I'm not in the habit of attacking guests, but you and Harry went too far."

He spoke softly, so as not to be heard upstairs if his women had finished their baths: perhaps too softly, for there was no response from outside. Was she still there? He listened again at the keyhole and heard nothing. It was of course too dark to see through the aperture.

He stood up and deliberated on the wisdom of opening the door, discreetly, to see whether she still sat there. He decided against the measure; he had after all made a decent overture. If she rejected it, well, so be it. If she had gone altogether, that was the best that could be hoped for.

But even as he turned to leave and go upstairs and (finally) retire, he heard an aspirate sound at the keyhole, and he returned to it, bending.

It was Ramona's voice. "Earl?" she whispered.

"Yes," he whispered back.

"Earl, let me in," said she.

"Now, we've had enough of that for one night."

"What?"

He whispered at a higher volume: "It's too late for that."

"I'll give you a kiss."

"Don't be absurd." He had been thrilled, on her first entrance, when she had raked him with her breasts, but he now found repulsive the thought of removing the door that kept them separate.

"You're hurting my feelings!" Ramona wailed through her whisper.

"What do I care?"

"Don't joke in that callous way, Earl," said Ramona. "It makes a bad impression."

"Ramona," asked Keese through the keyhole, "what do you want of me?"

"Let me in and you'll see," she said seductively.

"Forget about that—drop the idea completely," Keese answered. "I am thoroughly aware that you can have no amorous interest in me, so don't insult me with these preposterous insinuations. If you'd stop once and for all trying to make a fool of me, then perhaps I could help you. You do seem to have a problem if you sit sobbing on my doorstep at two o'clock in the morning. If you'd act right for once, then maybe I could perform as a decent neighbor. My intent is good—in fact it has been since the first—but you and Harry have always succeeded in alienating me, I don't know why."

"Have you got gonorrhea or something?" Ramona asked.

"Now, there's an example of what I have been talking about: for no reason that I can fathom you refuse to speak constructively here and instead ask me an irrelevant question that could also be taken as highly offensive." But Keese found himself giving her the benefit of the doubt: how much of this colloquy was getting from one side to the other could not be said. Sibilants especially were likely to be corrupted in trying to penetrate the door, while other sounds might be taken for them.

"But maybe I didn't hear you correctly," he said, "so skip my criticism. I really would like to begin with a clean slate. Please tell me why you were crying out there."

"I wasn't," Ramona whispered. "I've got an allergy to some

weeds around here, I guess. My eyes and nose are running."

"Well," said Keese with a certain strain, "I'm sorry to hear that. There are various antihistamines that can be bought without a prescription in the village drugstore, but it won't be open till eight A.M. tomorrow. In the longer view it might be worth your while to look into the matter of taking allergy shots."

"Come on, Earl," Ramona whispered back, "stop resisting me. Let me in, you horny bastard." She began to breathe loudly through the keyhole. After a moment he realized that she was taking in and letting out air in a rhythm that suggested the breather was engaged in a sexual act, indeed approaching a climax. How obnoxious! He hastily straightened up: his spine had gone stiff, and pain, as if on a spring, leaped into the small of his back.

"Earl?" It was Enid, at the top of the stairs. "Why are you down there?" She was still wearing Elaine's robe.

"Just checking to see whether the door is locked." Which actually was the truth.

"I thought you were going to bed now and intended not to think of that subject again until you had had a good night's sleep."

He walked to the foot of the stair. "I couldn't have slept without knowing whether this house was secure."

"You have checked the door?"

"Yes."

"Then come to bed." Enid shrugged. "It's as simple as that."

"I suppose so. You go on. I'll be there in a minute."

"Earl?" Enid asked.

"Yes?"

"I want you to promise you won't provoke the neighbors again tonight."

Keese stared up at her for a long moment. Then he said

deliberately: "How dare you make a statement like that to me?"

"I'll tell you how," said Enid. "I think you are planning to slip out when the rest of the house have retired."

"For what purpose?"

"Probably to harass Harry and Ramona in some fashion."

He marched up three steps. "It apparently never occurs to you that I might be the one who is harassed."

But Enid would not give him the satisfaction of arguing. She moued, then said, "Have it your own way," and returned to their bedroom.

He muttered truculently to himself, returning to the ground floor: "*My* own way. That's a laugh."

He went to the door, bent, and listened at the keyhole. It was silent out there, but when he whispered, "Ramona," she answered immediately.

"Hi."

He refrained from comment on the episode of heavy breathing. "You'd better go home now. We'll all feel better in the morning."

"I want you to know that I really like you, Earl," she said in a very clear whisper. "I don't care about your age and weight. And don't worry about your false teeth: I tell you, I don't care!"

"False teeth!" cried Keese, forgetting to whisper. "I don't have false teeth!"

Now it was Elaine who had come to the head of the stair. "Daddy," she said, "are you all right?"

He straightened up again too quickly and was stabbed in the small of the back. With that pain added to Ramona's latest comment, he was not genial.

He roared: "Why can't you let me alone?"

After a delay for disbelief, Elaine burst into tears, buried her face in her hands, and ran back down the hall.

What had he done? He had turned into a monster before his own eyes.

Emboldened by his shout, Ramona put aside her whisper and spoke in a full voice behind the door. "All right, I don't need a building to fall on me."

"No, no," said Keese, unlocking the door. She was already going down the path. "Wait, I didn't mean that." Too late he realized that he had got the girls confused: his intention had been to go after Elaine and apologize to her. She and Ramona were hardly interchangeable! He owed no apology to this one. But to slam the door in her face now that he had called her back was impossible.

Ramona was grinning slyly. "Well, I don't know, Earl, whether I should forgive you or not."

"O.K.," Keese said impatiently. "I've done what I can, anyway. I'll wish you a good night, Ramona."

"When we're just getting to know each other?"

"Look, I don't want to be rude—"

"But you're going to be anyway, right?" Ramona shrugged. "I can always tell what's coming when someone says he doesn't want to do a certain thing."

"All right, I'll come right out with it. What do you want of me?" He winced. "I mean, not only just now, but starting back at the beginning of the evening. I'll include Harry in that question. What? Why?"

Obviously she had no clear sense of what he was asking. Why was he asking her anyway? She was probably demented.

"But we're friends?" She smiled so broadly as to reveal that one of her teeth was missing on the far right. She might not be to some tastes, but Keese found her strangely attractive. Elaine however was beautiful by definition, and he had made her cry.

"Friends!" Keese cried triumphantly. Now he could close the door, and he did, on a wondering Ramona.

He went upstairs and along the hall to Elaine's room. The door was open, but the light was out.

"Elaine?" he said softly.

She turned on the bedside lamp. She was weeping no longer, and indeed her eyes were not red.

"What can I say?" asked Keese. "It wasn't you I was raging at. I hope you know that."

Elaine raised her chin. "Dad, I want you to go to bed right now. Promise me! Don't even go down to turn out the lights, lock up, or anything else. Don't even take a shower."

"You're thinking of the neighbors, aren't you?"

"I'm thinking of *you*," said Elaine. "What do they matter to me?"

"It's only that you are defending them by implication," Keese said. "As if I am responsible for this conflict, I who was peacefully finishing my glass of wine while your mother prepared dinner."

"The chronology doesn't matter," Elaine said in exasperation. "Oh, Daddy!"

"Please try to understand, Elaine," he sadly entreated her. "Your mother is out of sympathy with me, because of envy, but I expected better of you."

"Envy?"

"Harry and Ramona haven't badgered her, you see. The three of them are in total harmony."

"Then," said Elaine, "aren't *you* the one who's envious?"

"Certainly not. I don't want to get along with people like that! I abhor the type. It's really bad news for the neighborhood to have people of that sort move in."

"You're not giving them the benefit of the doubt, I see," said Elaine. "That's not the dad I know."

Keese sat down at the foot of the bed. He felt protected there, amidst all the blue: walls, bedclothes, rug. Elaine's pajamas were blue, of course.

"I really shouldn't be bothering you with these things," he said. "Suffice it to say that I have my reasons for acting as I did. Unless you resist early on when someone tries to push you, you might find yourself in a momentum that can't be halted."

Elaine smiled gently. "If Harry's car could talk, that's about what it would say."

"You know about that, do you? Mother tell you?"

"Harry told me. He introduced himself with that news, then he produced my overnight case."

"He was just trying to be cute," Keese said in disgust. "Anybody could do the same."

"Anybody whose car had been pushed into a swamp," said Elaine.

Keese felt that Elaine's belief that he had grown unfair must be corrected. "Harry isn't all bad," he said now. "I think he really wants to be friendly, but somehow can't put his ideas into practice successfully. Actually there was something fetching about the way he fixed the spaghetti himself when we found the restaurant was closed." He gave her an account of that incident.

Elaine's eyes sparkled. "Gee, I wish I'd have got here earlier. I'd have loved that."

Keese said jealously: "It wasn't really good. It wasn't anywhere near as good as the kind you used to love as a kid."

She wrinkled her nose. "You mean that awful canned stuff?"

"You didn't like it? We always thought—"

"Please don't be hurt," said Elaine.

Keese threw up his left hand. "Sure. But my point about Harry is that if he could be content just to be friendly in a modest way, but he can't let it go at that. He has to boast, he has to gloat—"

Elaine broke in: "You have to get right back to your obsession, don't you? It's as if you feel secure there and there alone."

Keese bit his lip. "I'm trying to defend myself. You have a low opinion of me, and I'm trying to explain my position. I don't want to be an object of contempt to my own daughter."

She had an adequate opportunity here to relieve his concern, but she neglected it. "O.K.," she said, "then what's the justification for throwing them out in the cold after Mother invited them to stay overnight?"

"Mother tell you that?" He was not surprised to hear her attribute it to Harry once more. "Ha, he's a great one for listing his injuries. I'm sure, though, that he failed to mention tricking me into giving him thirty-two dollars, pushing me face down into the swamp, locking me in the basement, and calling Greavy to haul away *my* car."

"Really?" asked Elaine, beginning to chuckle. "He did all that?" Her face broke apart and she laughed heartily. Elaine lost her beauty at such a time: her mouth was distorted and her eyes were pinched, which in turn caused a crookedness of nose. "Ha-a-a-ry did tha-a—" But she could not reach the end of the sentence. She was virtually weeping with laughter.

Keese hurled himself erect. He was too angry and hurt to protest. He left the room, her laughter pursuing him. In twenty-two years he had never seen this stupid side to Elaine, and he was devastated by witnessing it now. That canned spaghetti *was* abominable went without saying: what galled him was that as a child she had demanded that he eat spoonful after spoonful along with her. He had half a mind to return and confront her with that memory. He was dissuaded by a projection of her argument: if *she* had to eat it, then misery loved company!

He entered the master bedroom. Enid was propped up in bed, reading a magazine with large pages.

"Were you aware," he asked, "that Elaine detested that canned spaghetti?"

"Which canned spaghetti?"

"The kind we always went out of our way to get her when she was a little girl."

"No."

"*No?*" Keese happened to catch sight of the little clock on the table next to her. "Oh, that can't be right: *three thirty?*" He went to the dresser, opened the lowest drawer, and found a pair of pajamas. "I trust you changed the sheets after the neighbors left? I don't want to contract a disease." He walked to the door of the bathroom. "You could do me a favor, you know. Get a paper and pencil and list in chronological order the events of the evening, as you remember them. Then I'll fill in the blanks from my experience. It'll be pretty formidable, I promise you."

Enid nodded and returned to her magazine. Keese entered the bathroom and examined himself in the mirror. It was the same familiar face, inappropriate for melodrama. Still in his day clothes, he went back into the bedroom.

"I'm sorry to say that Elaine has let me down."

"Because of the canned spaghetti?" asked Enid.

"Her whole manner is strange. Why was she humble with Harry? That's not like Elaine. Come to think of it, why did she creep in at midnight without warning? I have never known her not to phone from school."

"Are you ready to talk seriously?" asked Enid, lowering her magazine.

"What does that mean? Another slur?"

Enid raised her magazine. "Obviously you're not."

"Goddammit, Enid!"

Her face came into view once more. "Elaine," said she, "has been expelled."

"No," said Keese.

"But at least they've dropped the charges."

"No."

"It could have been uglier. Actually it was grand theft."

"Lies," said Keese. "It's extraordinary the lengths certain people will go to discredit their betters. No one is immune."

"The ring belonged to the dean's wife. It was to everybody's advantage that no stink was raised."

"Someone like Ramona steals something," said Keese, "and an exemplary person like Elaine is blamed. Is that not the way of the world, to befoul the superior person?"

"Earl, if you want to cope with this, you'll just have to accept the truth."

Keese became very haughty. "No, I don't," he said. "I don't have to accept anything that doesn't suit me."

He left the room. He considered going to see Elaine, but what did he have to say to a thief? He went downstairs. He decided to take Ramona's offer, whatever it was.

He was not astonished to find her gone from his front step. That's the way it always worked. He crossed his lawn and half of that of his neighbors, climbed to their porch, and, not being able to locate a bell-button in the dark, knocked upon their door.

At length an indistinguishable voice shouted down from an upstairs window on what seemed to be the side of the house that faced Keese's property. Keese left the porch and went around there.

"Hello!" he shouted at the window. "It's Earl Keese."

The answer was a blaze of red and yellow and a deafening report. Someone had fired a gun at him.

CHAPTER **9/**

IT was a new experience
for Keese; his military service had been put in between wars.
He fell down and embraced the earth. He had not been struck,
nor had he heard the passage of a projectile. But the explosion
continued for a time to resound throughout his head, as though
his skull were a hall of marble.

After the worst of the shock had passed he began to approach the problem of interpretation. There were several pos-
sibilities. That the shooter had tried to kill him was foremost,
but perhaps the attempt had been but to wound. In either case
his enemy had failed. But was not this very failure a promise
that the effort would be renewed?

He was on ground that made self-preservation difficult indeed: where he lay was altogether flat and naked of vegetation.
Only the darkness protected him at the moment. But when a
lantern came on, a hose of glow which soaked him in a torrent
of light, he assumed the chance of his survival was so feeble
that any measure he could take, however degrading, was justified; and he rose upon his knees, clasping his wrists, and
piteously entreated the gunman to show him mercy.

"Why, Earl!" said Harry's voice, and it was quite near. He
had had time to come down from upstairs. "Good God," said

he, "it's lucky I didn't take aim the first time. I took you for a prowler."

Keese clawed at the beam of light, which was still fastened to his face.

"Oh, 'scuse me," Harry said finally, directing his lantern towards the ground.

For a moment Keese heard only his own labored breathing. *"Whff,"* he gasped, "that's quite an experience." The effect of the bright light lingered: he couldn't see Harry as yet, but he had the feeling that he must provide his end of a polite conversation: "Keep a gun, do you?"

"Yes I do," Harry said almost smugly. "It is my practice to have at hand the means with which to defend my own home."

Keese felt very ill. "Yes," he said, "you are well within your rights. . . ." He staggered away a few paces, bent over with his hands on his thighs, and vomited.

"Wow," he said when he could, "the aftereffect just arrived!"

Harry spoke with a marked lack of sympathy: "Maybe you'll get around to telling me what you're doing here?"

Keese wiped his face. "Yeah."

"You haven't come to apologize, have you, Earl?" Harry asked impatiently. "Because if you have, it'll take some thought on my part, I promise you."

Keese had forgotten until this moment about punching Harry in the eye! "God," he said, "I do apologize for that, Harry. It was a stupid mistake."

"Making stupid mistakes seems to be a profession with you, Earl. Who needs any more? I can't afford being on close terms with you."

"Excuse me," Keese said weakly. He turned and vomited again.

"And you might do your puking at home."

"Sorry."

But Harry wasn't going to pass up an opportunity like this. "Is that why you woke me up and got me to come downstairs: to watch you heave?"

Keese's eyes had now adjusted to the darkness, and he could see a shadowy area around Harry's right eye. As it turned out, punishing him for pawing Elaine had been foolish. She was a common thief. She had disgraced him. Why should he protect her from molestation?

Harry kept it up: "You were making a symbolic comment on my spaghetti, is that it? Still another act of vengeance?"

Keese waved his hands above his head; he was still standing in the position of an upended L. "No, no, nothing like that, Harry. I'm sick."

"I can see that, Earl. You're also disgusting."

"I know," Keese confessed. "And I'm going to make it up to you, Harry."

"I get scared when I hear your good intentions," said Harry. "Just keep your distance, and I'll keep mine."

Keese breathed deeply to discourage his viscera from rising in protest again. "Look," he said, "I can really use your friendship."

"At an earlier date," said Harry, "I might have been taken in by that statement. But that's before I served as your dupe —and more than once. Jesus, how often must a guy get bitten before he shies away at the approach of a dog?"

Keese cleared his throat, which was like sandpapering an open wound: the stomach acids had made it raw. "Well," he said, "we're on *your* property now. Now *you're* the boss. You can make short work of me if I get out of line."

Harry struck an attitude. "Vengeance doesn't appeal to me, Earl," he said loftily. "That's your game, not mine."

"I didn't mean that. I meant that you have the moral advantage and that I'm in a subordinate position. I'm coming to you, not vice versa, and that gives you a tremendous edge."

Harry laughed bitterly. "The way you look at life! All I bargained for was a bit of neighborliness, for God's sake."

This was hypocrisy, but Keese was in no position to identify it aloud. "That's what I'm asking now," he said. "There's an awful crisis in my personal life, and I need some help."

Harry suddenly noticed that his lantern was still alight, spilling its illumination uselessly on the ground. He snapped it off and said curtly: "Sorry, it's against my principles."

"Oh, I don't mean money," Keese said in haste.

"Then don't call your problem serious!" cried Harry. "I have no respect for people who have none for money."

"I wonder," Keese said mostly to himself but aloud, "if Elaine can be explained that simply. Did she steal the ring only to sell it? But I thought I always provided her with sufficient funds. I only know this: she never asked for any extra."

Without warning Harry became compassionate. "It does sound as if you're perplexed, Earl my boy," he said. "Come on, we'll talk about it." He led Keese around to the back of the house, and they entered the kitchen, which looked more or less as it had when the Walkers lived there. The boxes that Keese had seen through the window when watching Harry prepare spaghetti were stacked to one side.

Keese became aware that Harry had been unobtrusively carrying the gun he had fired from the upstairs window. While they spoke in the darkness outside he had kept it close against his side.

"So that's your shotgun?"

Harry peered quickly at him and then carried the weapon across the kitchen and propped it in a corner alongside a cupboard. "Don't worry about it, Earl," he said when he was done, "a gun never goes off by itself."

"And no one," Keese said, sagely shaking his chin, "has ever been shot by an unloaded gun."

"That's a strange thing to say," Harry replied. He sat down

at the table. "Take a pew. Has it occurred to you that we are inevitably drawn back to a kitchen table whenever we have tried to talk all evening? Maybe that does suggest we're in some basic sympathy, like members of the same family?"

"I'm sure it does," said Keese. His need for Harry's friendship seemed to increase by the moment.

"But this time it's *my* kitchen—is that your point?"

"Well," said Keese, "yours, mine, what difference does it make after all?" He saw Harry for the first time since entering the kitchen (he had not looked at him since coming into the light; instead he had peered at the room, the boxes, and the gun). Harry's right eye was extravagantly discolored. Identified in haste, the hue could probably be labeled blue-black, but on brief examination almost any color could have been found somewhere in the bruised eye-socket. The lid was half closed.

"Know what that statement represents?" asked Harry. "The kind of falsity of a politician or entertainer who wishes the *whole world* good luck. How can *everybody* be fortunate simultaneously? How can the bank robber be successful without the loss of the banker?"

Keese couldn't get over the damage he had done to Harry's eye. Actually he had no memory of hitting anyone in the eye before, not even as a kid. It was probably the most savage kind of blow to administer, given its visible effect. It was certainly worse than the punch Greavy had buried in his stomach.

"Look," he said, "will you accept my apology? I shouldn't have swung. I probably misinterpreted your gesture. I've been completely disoriented since that girl came home." He genuinely believed now that he had punched Harry because of his confusion and horror regarding Elaine's disgrace—whereas he had learned of the latter only afterwards. But he was desperate to find any answer for his predicament. "I've never been a violent man," he said. "All these things are without precedent, believe me."

Harry peered speculatively at him. "Maybe you're right," he said finally. "I guess it *does* matter that you're in my house now. Whatever happens, you eventually have to go home. Isn't that what it comes down to? Whereas this is where I belong?"

Without warning he threw a punch at Keese's eye, but by chance Keese turned his head at just that instant, as a man will, and he was instead hit on the ear, and not a direct blow there, either, but rather a glancing strike which stung the lobe, scarcely the most sensitive of organs.

Keese retained his composure, though his ear burned slightly. But Harry was apparently embarrassed by his failure to connect. He turned away in probable chagrin. When he turned back after a moment, however, his manner was bland.

"A cuppa coffee, Earl? Sleep seems out of the question this night."

Keese assented to the offer, and as Harry rose from the table he said: "I also apologize for keeping you up at this hour."

"It couldn't be helped," Harry said in a happy-go-lucky fashion, with matching grin.

Keese shrank back as Harry passed him, but the larger man made no attempt to throw another punch. A tea kettle sat on the stove: someone had long since found it amongst the kitchen boxes. Harry swished the contents, decided that it held sufficient water for his needs, and turned on the gas. He went to the sink, where two cups, upside down, rested on the drain-board. Their situation suggested they had been washed and put to dry. But when Harry brought them to the table and put one, right side up, before him, Keese saw it was dirty; vilely so, in fact, with a dried swarthy sediment in the bowl and a scalloping of lipstick under the brim.

He didn't know quite what to say, given the tenuous peace between them; therefore he silently lifted the cup and displayed its condition to his host.

Harry nodded, but did nothing about it. He put another cup at his own place and went to a counter and found a jar of instant coffee. While his back was turned Keese deftly switched cups: obviously that was the least offensive way to deal with the matter.

A recognizable stench reached his nostrils at that point. Gas! "Harry," he said urgently, "I don't think that burner's lighted."

Harry turned with the bottle of powdered coffee. "Put it on for me, willya?" he asked, thrusting his hip towards Keese. "Pilot's not operating yet." He did a sidewards bump at Keese. "Matches in my pocket," he said, "and don't roam around when you put your hand in there: being groped is not my game."

Keese ignored this bit of gratuitous offensiveness. He went to the stove and turned off the burner, then headed for the back door. "Too much gas in here now to light up."

But Harry was at the stove before Keese could open the door. He turned on the burner and then searched himself for some deliberate moments before he found a match and lighted it. Nothing happened, except that the gas came bluely visible. He moved the kettle over it. "What an alarmist you are, Earl," he said. He returned to the counter and came subsequently to the table with the coffee jar and brown-stained spoon. He looked at Keese, his eyebrows rising above both eyes, normal and blackened, and asked: "Strong?"

"So-so."

Harry put a rounded teaspoonful of brown powder in the cup before his own place and exchanged it for the cleaner cup at Keese's.

Keese really thought he should say something at this point. "This cup's not clean." To show his good intentions he rose. "I'll just rinse it out."

"And waste that coffee?" Harry asked belligerently.

"Maybe I can just put it someplace temporarily," said Keese, "until I have washed the cup." He looked desperately about and could find nothing. Therefore he emptied the cup's contents into his left palm. He was enroute to the sink when arrested by Harry's command.

"Sit down, Earl."

"Just let me—"

"Sit *down*," Harry roared. When Keese had complied with this order Harry said: "Now just pour the coffee powder back into the cup."

Keese did so. Owing to the natural moisture of his palm, some of the powder adhered to it. He displayed this to Harry.

"May I wash my hand?"

"No," said Harry.

Keese smirked and got up anyway. Harry hurled himself upon his guest. He maneuvered himself around in back of Keese and got him with a forearm across the throat. Keese's left arm was twisted behind him by Harry's viselike left fist. Not only did this put him absolutely into Harry's power, but it was extremely painful. He would have been loud to announce his surrender had he been able to speak, but the mugger's grip across his windpipe rendered him mute.

Harry steered him back to the chair and forced him to sit down. The first few moments of Keese's liberation were consumed by swallowing and breathing, which seemed new exercises. He coughed for a while, once to the point of choking briefly. Then, after determining that his handkerchief had been left behind in the clothes he had removed hours before, he dried his streaming eyes on the cuff of his old shirt.

Nevertheless, as soon as Harry turned his back again Keese switched cups. Then ensued one of those seemingly endless phases of time in which emotions are left hanging, when all the world waits upon the rising of water to the boil.

At last Harry brought the kettle to the table and transformed into muddy coffee the powder in the cups. Then he went to the corner where he had left his shotgun, lifted the weapon, and pointed it at Keese, and said: "Take the cup you tried to trick me into using."

Of course Keese obeyed. "Well," he said bluffly, "it's neither here nor there to me." What a childish kind of revenge! While Harry put the shotgun down, Keese with one quick thumb-rub lifted off some of the lipstick. This material might be attractive on a woman but it always looked filthy, even diseased, when adhering to an inanimate surface. He discreetly cleansed his thumb on the inseam of his trousers. His left palm was still gritty-sticky from the powdered coffee: he rubbed it in the same place.

Harry came to the table and sat down. "Just a minute, Earl. What are you doing, playing with yourself?"

Keese's hands were still beneath the table, being rubbed clean in his pants. He brought them into sight now. "Please, Harry, I'm trying to tell you something. My daughter—"

Harry shook a large forefinger at him. "Now, there is a problem, if I ever saw one."

Keese was taken aback. " 'Problem'? Why do you say that?" He began to breathe rapidly. "What do you mean?"

"Sticks out all over her," said Harry. He took an exceptionally loud, slurping drink of coffee. "I suppose, though, you couldn't see it. Fathers are that way, aren't they?"

"Listen, Harry," Keese said, and he laughed in keen chagrin. "This is a crazy situation. I don't quite know where to begin." He shouted: "Elaine is a superior person, for God's sake! She's beautiful and brilliant and was always at the head of her class. Don't act as if she is some neurotic warped soul, some mediocrity. Elaine is fluent in several European languages. Elaine belongs to several honor societies, and she will graduate *cum laude.*"

"Or so she tells you," Harry said cynically.

Keese repeated his bitter laugh. "Why won't you believe me? How would *you* know better?"

"I don't pretend to, Earl. I'm just asking the question. If everything is so perfect about her, then why are you here now?"

Keese hung his head. "O.K.," he said, "you've got a point. . . . Now, what has happened—this isn't easy to say . . ."

"But I'm a stranger, really," said Harry. "Remember that. It should make it easier." He said this with what certainly sounded like genuine sympathy. He was an unpredictable devil, that Harry.

"Elaine stole a ring!" Keese cried.

"Oh, is that all?" Harry smiled, fluttering his hands at the wrists. "I thought there was some major catastrophe."

"If this isn't major, then there is none such," said Keese. "She's been expelled, two months before graduation."

"What's that to me?" asked Harry. "I have only the slightest acquaintance with her." He stared back at Keese's wild look, and then he said, leaning forward: "Devil's advocate, Earl. Prove it to me!"

"Prove what?"

"Why," said Harry, "relate this to the human condition. Aren't we all victims of fate? Why should your daughter be exempt? How are you going to make her predicament important to some poor devil dying of illness?"

Keese frowned for a while, and then he said quietly: "Harry, you really are a shit."

Harry took no apparent offense. He shook his head. "You're still not getting it, are you, Earl? I don't mean that your troubles, your daughter's, are to be dismissed. I just mean that I want to have them proved as serious."

"I don't know how they could *not* be serious!" cried Keese. "This is the culmination of twenty-two years."

"There's something that's a good deal more important," said Harry, "and you are ignoring it entirely."

"Yes?"

"What's Elaine do about sex?" asked Harry. "Where's she getting it?"

Keese had not touched his coffee. He looked into it now, then lifted the cup deliberately and dashed it at Harry. But in anticipation of this move, Harry had slid his chair away as Keese slowly lifted the cup, and by the time the fluid-laden missile was flung, Harry had dived behind the piled cartons.

He came out when the splattering was done. "That was foolish, Earl, and it could have got you killed." He nodded towards the shotgun. "Don't think I'll allow you to abuse me in my own home."

Keese gritted his teeth and said: "And don't think *just because* it's your house you can say anything you want about my daughter!"

Harry came forward, avoiding the brown pool and the crockery fragments on the floor. The cup had landed four or five feet beyond the table; therefore the immediate area was clear.

"If you'll reflect," said Harry, "I said nothing insulting."

Keese got up, raving. "How do I get sucked into these degrading conversations? Why do I keep assuming that you and Ramona will straighten out?"

"Ramona?" asked Harry. "What have you been doing with her?"

"Nothing whatever," said Keese, "and you know it very well. In fact, that's why you make your loathsome insinuations about my daughter: you've got your wife to worry about, haven't you?"

"Your daughter is sacrosanct, is that it?" asked Harry. "Yet it would be quite O.K. by you if you had some dirt on my wife."

His tone was not indignant, but resigned, and Keese saw that his neighbor had an argument. "No," he answered reasonably, "it wouldn't be O.K. at all. I'm not looking for dirt on anybody, believe me. This has been a crazy night. Many of the things I've done are completely alien to my normal character. I'm not nursing a grudge against you, and I don't have a thing on Ramona."

"Then," asked Harry, "where is she? What have you done with her?"

"She's not here?"

"I wouldn't be asking if she were," Harry said sternly. "I assumed she was with you. She has some sort of weird fascination with you, old and fat as you are."

Keese sighed. "Now there you are, Harry. Every time I make a peaceful overture you never fail to insult me in return."

Harry scowled in puzzlement. "Insult? I should think you'd find it flattering."

"I meant your characterization of me as old and fat."

"Well, aren't you? Should I lie? Are you underweight? Ramona is twenty-seven. You're at least in your late fifties, no?"

"I am forty-nine years of age," Keese said frostily.

Harry groaned. "The hell you are."

"You're arguing with me about *my own* age?" Keese pounded the table. What a humiliating dispute! He had every motive to turn vicious. "If she's wandering around at this hour of the night, what does it say about your capacity?"

"What's that supposed to mean?"

Keese had turned the tide! He pressed his advantage. "Am I right in gathering that you are inadequate, old boy?"

Harry winced, quite a dramatic show on such a large face with a bruised eye. "You're a disgusting man, Earl. You'll stoop to any measure."

"You started it with your vile insinuations about Elaine!"

"The thief," said Harry. He pointed at Keese. "Don't deny it. It's your own story."

Keese sagged, and then took some air. "Hadn't we better look for Ramona?" he asked finally. "Where can she be at this hour?"

Harry made a nasty face. "I assume she's at your house, Earl."

"No, she left."

"Then you admit she was there?"

"Now, please don't try to make anything of that," Keese said. "She was on my threshold briefly. We exchanged a few words and she left. That was, oh, say an hour ago."

"Well, she never came back," Harry said. "What 'words' did you exchange?"

"Commonplaces," said Keese.

"If I know you," said Harry, "it was actually a bitter argument. One word led to another. You finally rose to a pitch of rage and slapped her face savagely. She slipped and fell. Her head struck the concrete with the sound of a smashed cantaloupe. You knelt to examine her. She was dead, her skull crushed." Harry gave this extravagant narrative in an emotionless monotone.

"You must be mad," Keese said, echoing a cliché from the sort of movie he had seen as a child, because the event that Harry had sketched came from the same source in popular entertainment, in which people were always being killed so easily.

"You saw your chance to get back at me through her," said Harry.

Keese believed that the only way he could arrest this train of thought before Harry reached the point of no return (which, given the shotgun, might be dangerous) was to leap to the attack. "You're actually projecting onto me your own crime, aren't you, Harry? *You* had the argument with her, *you* slapped her face and watched her fall and break her neck, and then you carried her body down to the swamp!" Keese was proud of his embellishment. He then thought of how to better it. "You put her behind the wheel of the car! You count on the police to assume her neck was broken when the automobile plunged down the embankment."

The whole thing had been a joke in questionable taste at the outset. Now Keese began to get a horrible sense of disaster, as if by chance he had hit upon the truth: that Harry had murdered Ramona and was trying to pin the crime on *him:* ineptly trying, because of course Keese had been home all the while, with two witnesses.

But as it happened neither Enid nor Elaine had seen Ramona during his conversation with her through the door. They had seen only that he was lurking in the front hall. Actually he had no evidence whatever to support his statement, were the police to call it into question. Was there a possibility that he could be railroaded for a crime he did not commit? But if he had no alibi, could Harry have a better one? Also, Keese had no motive. That was the most telling point on his side.

As if Harry had been privy to Keese's internal dialogues, he spoke up now. "You cornered her somewhere, made the same indecent advances that you have been making all evening"— he ignored Keese's strangulated protest—"and when she resisted, you brutally knocked her down. You would have raped her at that point, but she was dead."

"On my front step," Keese said sardonically.

"Is that where it happened?" Harry asked. "Ah, you're beginning to confess, are you? Then I'll have to give you the usual cautions: You have the right to remain silent, you have—"

Had Elaine been right? Was the man a *cop?* Keese felt an inchoate agitation at the base of his spine. But then he heard Harry falter in his recitation and finish with: "And so on."

"No," said Keese, "the law says you've got to repeat them all."

"Don't think a picayune incidental like that is going to get you off," said Harry. "You're guilty, all right."

"I want some proof you're a policeman!"

"I don't have to show you anything," Harry said softly. "You're on my property now. If I feel like it, I can shoot you as an intruder. If you're killed, then it's only my version that would be heard: you broke in here, threatened my life with a shotgun, we grappled, and you were killed when the weapon was discharged in the struggle."

Keese began to worry that Harry wanted this very sort of encounter and intended to bait him until one began, so as to murder him and be done with it. He decided to be on guard against any attempt of Harry's to lure him into an act of violence. "Look," he said, raising both hands, "I'm not resisting. You're the boss. It would be foolish to deny that."

"Where's Ramona?" Harry asked. He licked his lips in a desperate way. He hurled himself up, leaned over, and grasped the front of Keese's old shirt. "By God, I'll beat it out of you." He balled his right fist and drew it back, as if stretching a slingshot, to a position opposite his ear.

Keese suddenly couldn't bear the idea of passively allowing Harry to batter his face—that it might be considered as deserved retaliation for his earlier blackening of Harry's eye was an argument without eloquence for him. He found that the large hand on his shirt did not impede him from rising and moving sideways, away from the table. To pursue him Harry had to alter his own situation and let the shirt go.

Keese then kicked him powerfully in the groin. Harry grunted in pain, doubled up, moved backwards, and fell into the pool of coffee. Keese left the kitchen by the back door. He was astounded to see that the dawn was well under way. Appealing to Harry had been useless. The man simply did not work out as a friend.

He was now faced with going back to the same problem

from which he had come away. His car was in the drive, around back. Then Greavy had at least returned it before assaulting him. Keese had by no means forgotten that incident.

But now he had still another score to settle. Someone, presumably Greavy himself, had written in large white-paint letters, along the left side of the blue car, with two painted arrows, from as many directions, to indicate the driver's window:

PIMP

CHAPTER 10/

BUT for the infamous inscription Keese would have jumped into his car and driven away to the end of the earth. Of course that was unthinkable now.

What had he done to Greavy to call for such savage retaliation? It was strange how a man whom he had not aggressed against would punish him so severely, while Harry, for all the damage received at Keese's hand, had been able to do so little against him.

Keese had been a young man when he was last outdoors at dawn, and he had forgotten its peculiar aroma, at least in spring: green, it went without saying, but also with a touch of mustiness. There was now light by which to see Harry's car, and he went to the end of the road and looked over the smashed guardrail. The vehicle had vanished without a trace: sunk, probably, in quicksand. No, there it was, to the left. He had been looking in the wrong spot. Perhaps the wheels had struck an object which caused them to turn leftwards. The car looked undamaged from the rear, and the water in which it sat rose not even so far as the hubcaps. One had the illusion that it could be driven away, none the worse for the experience.

If the past could not be changed, sometimes measures could

be taken to cause it to be forgotten. Even at this late date he was sure he could expunge the foregoing night from memory insofar as were concerned the friends he had consulted by telephone. A confession of drunkenness and an abject apology would surely suffice. If Ramona could be taken as an individual, separate from Harry, then she had no great claim against him. Twice he had ordered her from his premises, true enough, but between those moments had been extended intervals in which he had been very genial, even hospitable. On their latest meeting he had not been unpleasant for so much as an instant.

Harry was another case. Keese had definitely damaged him in several ways, and it could not be said that his few and usually unsuccessful bids for retaliation had brought things anywhere near even. Were his car retrieved, however, and not only restored in appearance but improved—e.g., a completely new coat of paint!—he would not come away empty-handed. Which left only the matter of bodily harm. This was somewhat more serious. Harry had after all been repeatedly bested in hand-to-hand encounters with a shorter, older, fat man. His physical hurts were probably inconsequential, but the damage to his pride should not be underestimated. Keese could appreciate that. He was no monster. That Harry had brought it on himself was true, but that was no excuse for gloating.

Then there were the Greavys. The boy (in his thirties) was hardly involved, but he was unlikely to stand by when his father was under fire (unlike Keese's daughter). The attack must therefore be stealthy or, if open, include Perry though he had no quarrel with him. Keese frankly would have jumped at the chance to forgive the old man. The surprise blow to his gut had been barbarous, but he had himself sucker-punched Harry for what he believed a good cause.

But the painted epithet on the car cried out for vengeance.

As Keese reached his front door he remembered that Ramona was supposed to be missing. This was where he had seen her last: just here he had closed the door in her face. If, locked out of his house, she had been carried off by a bear or band of gypsies, he supposed *he* would be blamed. Neighbors!

"Earl!"

He looked up and saw Enid in the window of the master bedroom. He expected her to be disapproving; therefore his response was a silent glower.

"Earl," said she, "have you been up all night?"

"Enid," he said, "I'll thank you for showing me a certain tolerance. If you reflect you will realize that it takes all kinds."

"I wanted to tell you something."

"Please," he moaned, "no moralizing at this point. I'm worn thin."

"There's a new version now." Only her head could be seen, as if she were standing erect and looking from a window that was five feet above the floor. This annoyed Keese. Even at his angle he should get some sense of where her body was.

He shouted angrily: "Are you kneeling?"

"Now it seems that the ring was taken, but no one confessed to the theft, and there would seem to be no evidence against the thief—or so, anyway, it is supposed."

Keese lowered his head, only to raise it and say: "Do you realize what this means? Nothing is lost. All is O.K., as it was before. *Everything can be put back where it belongs.*" He had to restrain himself, else he might have wept in relief.

He twisted the knob. The door was locked! He pressed the button. When this summons was not responded to within a reasonable period of time, he stepped down onto the path and shouted at the window from which Enid had spoken.

But it was Ramona who appeared there. Notwithstanding his great joy at what he believed Elaine's deliverance, this latest event reacquainted him with very negative feelings.

"What are you doing there?" he cried.

She grinned triumphantly down at him in silence. He saw

that her turban was off for the first time since he had greeted her from the other side of this very door. Funny, he had assumed that her hair would be woolly, wiry, springy; instead it looked lank and lifeless. By contrast, her features were stronger than ever.

While he stared at her the door opened. It was Enid.

As he entered the house he asked indignantly: "What's that woman doing here?"

"Huh?"

"The person from next door!"

"I know where she's from," said Enid, "but doesn't she have a name?"

"What's she doing in our bedroom?"

Enid was still wearing Elaine's robe. She shook her head and said: "What difference does it make? You had gone."

"And she was lurking around outside, trying to get in again, wasn't she?" Keese sneered. "And you fell for it. There's nothing wrong over at their house. There's no reason why she had to come over here and apply for entrance like some waif from the storm. In fact, Harry's over there wondering where she is. He accused me of doing away with her."

"Ah," said Enid.

"You know how they love to whip me up, but I'm learning how to deal with them."

"Good."

Keese showed his teeth. "What's she doing here?"

"I thought the simplest way to handle the situation was to let her in and be done with it."

"Yes," he said sardonically, "your old strategy of the early evening, as I remember, and it was certainly successful then!"

They stood in the entrance hall. He was about to go upstairs, but Enid drew him into the living room. "Be decent, Earl. As long as she's here, why not let her rest for a while. She's been up all night."

"What do you think *I've* been doing?" Keese asked with great feeling. "Not only have I not had any sleep at all, but I didn't really have any dinner. But the deprivations are not the least of it: I've been fighting a good deal of the night. I'm almost half a century old, and I've been taking and giving punches like a kid. I wouldn't have believed this possible twelve short hours ago."

Enid drew him to the couch, sat him down, took a place near him, and looking soberly into his eyes, said: "You're bearing up under it amazingly well."

"I'll say this," said Keese. "I've given more than I've got. I don't mind admitting I'm proud of myself."

"You certainly should be."

He considered the possibility that she was mocking him. "I'm amazed that you don't mention my blood pressure."

"Well," said Enid, "it is *yours,* after all. It would be arrogant for me to say much about it."

Keese still wasn't clear about her motives. "Now," he said, "I don't really want to probe too deeply into the matter, but I gather that the ring which was proved so troublesome to Elaine is in her possession."

"I don't know," said Enid. "I know only the latest version of the story, which I passed on to you."

Keese rose from the couch. "That's a good deal more important than your friend Ramona," said he. "I'm going up to talk to Elaine—and I don't care whether she is asleep. This problem must be resolved and concluded immediately."

He went upstairs and knocked at Elaine's door and, a moment later, without an invitation, entered the darkened room. "Excuse me, Elaine," he said, going to the window. He raised the shade. But he had never liked the niggard look of early morning light in a bedroom unless it came from the east.

Elaine was pretending to be asleep: her imposture could be detected from the stress lines at her eyes.

"Come on, dear," Keese said jollily, "you're squinting."

Elaine began to speak reproachfully even before opening her eyelids. "I'm just trying to get to sleep after that awful night."

"Elaine," Keese said, taking a generous seat on the bed where it was available, down near the foot, "I want to settle this matter about the ring."

"Well," Elaine said, her two hands appearing at the top of the bedclothes, as if they were independent of her head, "it *is* a difficult problem. My friend doesn't know what to do."

"Your friend?"

Elaine stared. "The one who took the ring. She was invited to tea at the dean's house, you see, and at one point she used the bathroom, which has a second door, like ours, which leads into a bedroom. She opened this door and she went into that bedroom and she saw a dressing table there and she went to it and she saw a sapphire ring there and she took it."

Keese nodded judiciously. "Your friend—an impulse suddenly came over her? An ungovernable impulse?"

Elaine blinked in impatience. "How should I know? Perhaps she's simply a crook at heart."

Keese gasped. "No, no."

Elaine grimaced. "How'd you know? Are you acquainted with this person?"

He drew back. "No, certainly not. But what would a crook be doing as a friend of yours?"

She peered at him. "You think it's me, don't you?"

"No," said Keese. "What a thing to say!"

"But you're not really sure, are you?" Elaine asked sternly. "You were sure about Harry, so certain you punched him in the eye, but you're not sure you can believe or disbelieve in me at this moment."

"Please don't bring Harry into this. We've had enough of him! Look, let's forget about *who* took the ring. That matters not at all. A student could be expelled for such an act. I'm sure your friend is aware of that. My advice to her would be to return the ring. I don't think, frankly, that she should trust the dean to be forgiving. Maybe he'd be and maybe not. Therefore the most effective procedure would be to return the ring by mail, anonymously. Restitution having been made, I think we could count on all concerned to forget the incident."

Elaine's expression brightened. "Say, that's an excellent idea! Give me the phone, will you?"

The instrument was on a lower level of the bedside table. Keese lifted it out and gave it to his daughter.

Elaine vigorously worked the dial. The other party must have answered on the first ring, for she spoke before her finger had quite been removed from the last aperture.

"Say, here's an idea!" she said brightly into the mouthpiece. "Mail it back." She hung up.

Keese was amazed. But was it not too blatant to be a pose? If she really intended to fool him, wouldn't she have been a bit more painstaking?

"Elaine," he said, hand on chin, "will your friend understand that message?"

"Oh, sure," was her breezy answer.

"One moment," said he. "I am an easygoing sort, as you should be the first to know, but—"

"Daddy!"

"Here's my point," said Keese. "You share an apartment with three others. How can you be sure who would answer? Two: even if the right person answered, how would she know what you meant when you said as little as you did?"

"She'd know," said Elaine, sliding down in bed and pulling the covers over her head.

"I'm sorry, Elaine," Keese said, pulling the covers down to expose her face, "I may be doing you an injustice, but that answer's not enough for me."

Elaine's face suddenly seemed to have become a decade

younger. It looked as though she might stick out her tongue. But instead she wailed: "Why are you doing this to me?"

"Oh, it's to *you*, is it?" asked Keese, in a rush of self-pity.

Elaine reared up, seized the telephone from the bedside table, and gave it to her father. "Dial this number," she demanded. He did so.

Hardly had the last digit been signified when a young woman's voice came through the instrument: "Scotty Muldoon."

"Is that Scotty Muldoon?" asked Elaine.

"Yes."

"Ask her: 'Did Elaine Keese call just now with a message?' "

Keese put this question, and Scotty Muldoon said: "Yes."

"Ask her," said Elaine, "whether she understood it."

"Did you understand it?"

Keese asked, and Scotty Muldoon said: "No," and hung up.

"Well, there you are," said Elaine, as though her bluff had been successful.

"There I'm nowhere," said Keese. "Scotty Muldoon just said no."

Elaine laughed heartily. "That's Scotty all right. That's her way. You know the type."

"But I don't know Scotty Muldoon," Keese cried.

Elaine raised her hands in exasperation. "Gawd! O.K., call this number—"

"Who's this?"

"Rags Rafferty. He knows Scotty Muldoon better than anyone in the world. He can tell you whether it is her custom to say no when she means yes and so on."

"Elaine!" Keese cried. "I don't want to have to call half the world!"

"You have impugned my veracity," said Elaine. "At least be decent enough to hear the evidence on my side."

Keese nodded stoically and dialed the number. This time the

answer was not immediate. Indeed, the bell having rung a dozen times, Keese felt he had met his obligation, and he was on the point of hanging up when a young male voice came on to say, flatly: "Yeah?"

"Rags Rafferty?" Keese asked.

"Who says so?"

"Elaine Keese."

"Oh, *that* bitch," said the voice, and the line went dead.

Keese furiously redialed the number, and when the young man came on Keese said: "I'm her father. I'm sure you didn't know that."

"*Whose* father?" asked the voice, in such an innocent intonation that Keese was almost convinced the boy had forgotten the call of six seconds before.

"Elaine's."

"Sorry, sir, I don't know any Elaine except my mother, and you're obviously not my grandfather, who is not among the living."

"You're not the same fellow I spoke to earlier?"

"No, sir, not on this telephone."

"Are you Rags Rafferty?"

"No, sir."

"Do you know him?"

"No, sir."

"Sure?" asked Keese, shrugging for Elaine's benefit.

"I'm sure of only one thing," said the young man.

"And that is—?"

"That you can kiss my ass." He hung up.

"Well," Keese said accusingly to Elaine, "that only earned me more vicious abuse." He hung up and lifted the phone from his lap and banged it down on the bedside table. "This hoax was without purpose. Whoever stole the ring is not my concern. Whoever did will not suffer for what was obviously the crazy impulse of the moment, if she mails it back to the owner." He stood up. "That's my statement on the matter."

Elaine narrowed her eyes at him. Her forefinger came out of the blankets to crook and summon him to close quarters. When he had reached her she gave him a kiss on the cheek and she said: "Thanks, Daddy."

Keese was almost overwhelmed. He suppressed a sob and gained the hallway. One of his problems was apparently solved. He looked down the hall at the closed door of the master bedroom and his heart was warm. Let Ramona get a morning's sleep if she wanted it.

He descended to the ground floor and looked for Enid. He found her in the kitchen, writing on a notepad.

"I gave Elaine an idea that will work," he said, "if she'll use it. I think she will, though there was some preliminary dodging and feinting, with a cast of bogus characters. It was simply this: the ring can be mailed back anonymously. Of course she denies taking it."

"And you believe her?"

"I think we should give our daughter the benefit of the doubt," Keese said pompously. "As to the motive for the act, call it some temporary aberration. The best of us will have a few of those before we're dead!" He was attempting to be jolly, to put the best face on it.

"You're speaking of yourself?"

"Not really," said Keese.

"Oh." Enid flung her hands up and closed her eyes. It was really the most effective gesture of noncommittal he had ever seen.

"Look," said Keese, "there are people who kill and maim and torture and enslave. There are people who stink and make loathsome noises and scratch themselves and writhe and cavort and are ugly and awkward and rude. All of these are worse than someone who acts badly once in a very great while owing to an ungovernable impulse."

Enid shrugged and began to leave the kitchen.

"Stop!" Keese commanded. "Why are you leaving?"

"If you have reached a consideration of universal principles I feel redundant," said she.

"Don't be ridiculous."

"Well, what do you want of me?"

Keese squinted. "I decided to let Ramona have her forty winks, you'll be happy to know. Not that there is any reason why she deserves them. With an entire empty house just across the yard—not to mention her husband. And the dog—you never answered the question about that animal." He decided to make a stand there, and he maintained his defiant, quizzical stare until Enid responded.

"The dog is all right."

"Oh. Well, I feel I owe Ramona precisely nothing. But the relief I felt when I had solved Elaine's problem—" He realized he was thinking out loud, a poor procedure for anyone who has enemies. "Wait here a minute, will you?" He went down the stairs and explored the lowest level of his house. He returned to the kitchen and said to Enid: "The dog is not in the basement."

"No."

"Then how can you say he's all right?"

"It was just a figure of speech."

"I doubt it," said Keese. "You don't speak loosely, Enid. I've always admired you for your succinctness."

She smiled faintly.

"I do," said Keese, "and that's far from being all the story. I admire you in many ways."

Enid smiled more broadly. "Your purpose is to flatter me into finding the dog for you?"

Keese winked and asked slyly: "Is that so bad?" In the early years of marriage he had been wont to jolly her in this fashion. Somehow the technique had been put aside: perhaps because it was the sort of thing that did not age to advantage.

But Enid seemed touched by it now. "What a nice thing to say," said she. "You're an interesting man, Earl. Your principles are quite as good as most, and your methods may be eccentric but they are always founded in rectitude."

"That's not the preface to an obituary, is it?" Keese asked, not altogether lightheartedly. He began to regret his praise for her way of speaking. It sounded as though she might go too far. "I'll explain my concern: those people have a three-phased tactic, like an army, really. First the dog is sent in to scout the territory. Then Ramona launches the first assault. While the adversary is reeling from this attack, Harry arrives with the lethal strike. Then all join together for the *coup de grâce.*"

"Oh, you're back to that subject."

"I can't get far from it," said Keese. "These neighbors have brought out certain traits I didn't know I had. That may be all to the good, mind you. I am merely trying to understand it."

"They didn't succeed with you!" Enid said, moving closer towards the door with every syllable.

"Ramona managed to get my very bed away from me!" Keese vehemently admitted. "I may have immobilized Harry, but while my back was turned she made her successful move." He grinned. "Well, hell, let her rest—on her laurels. She deserves them! I failed to protect my rear: it's as simple as that."

"O.K.," said Enid. "Then we've got that settled." She escaped.

Keese made no attempt to stop her again. He was satisfied that his version of the outcome was fair. He was not, at the moment, thinking of the dog, but without warning a sense of where it could be found came to him: it was with Ramona. Not only had his bedroom been taken from him, but it had also been transformed into a kennel.

He left the kitchen at a brisk pace and soon arrived before

the door of the master bedroom. His knock was a little drum-roll, followed by two separate explosions.

He was answered by a rumbling growl.

"Go away, Earl," said Enid's voice behind the door. "You can't do any good here."

"Good?" he asked. "You fill my room with enemies and lock the door against me, and you talk of good?"

"You've got the wrong slant on things," said Enid.

Then Ramona's voice was heard. "You had your chance, Earl. Now go away."

He threw himself, spread-eagle, against the door, cursing. In an instant he felt a massive vibration as the dog, Baby, assaulted the wood panel from the other side. The beast would be a formidable foe, especially if it considered itself to be at bay. Unlike Harry he kept no weapons. Fool that he was, he had assumed he would never need one. He despised his harmless self of old. Were he to do it all over again he would go everywhere armed to the teeth: you could never know when you might be jumped, and taking revenge at some later time was never really satisfactory. Timing was all. A minute passes and the world is changed in every respect. The landscape out the window looks the same, but every atom of it is different.

If he found Greavy now and punched him in the stomach, the man would have no memory of having done him dirty. Greavy would believe himself the accidental victim of a lunatic. God, how unfair it all was!

But he was not to be counted out yet. He spoke to the door.

"Enid, are you aware of the impression you are creating?"

"Leave us in peace," said Ramona.

"Enid!"

At last a sleepy voice answered: "What do you want now?"

"Enid, the inevitable impression one gets here is that you are behaving like a deviate."

"Well."

"Behind a locked bedroom door with a person of your own sex—"

"Then," Enid murmured, "there's the dog."

"The fact is, Earl," said Ramona, "you've been outmaneuvered. It's as simple as that."

Strangely enough he was, momentarily at least, pacified by the ineluctable truth of this statement. He turned away and shuffled towards the stairway.

Down the hall Elaine was peeking timorously from the door of her room. She whispered so softly he could not hear her. He went close.

Elaine asked: "What's happened?"

"Your mother is entertaining a friend."

"Do you have to be disagreeable about that?" she asked, raising her voice to its normal level.

"Don't push me, Elaine, I warn you. You've been getting a free ride for many years. Don't start acting like a paying passenger."

"Daddy," said Elaine, "please don't start telling me the truth about anything. I hate showdowns. There's always something false about them, anyway."

He was touched by her plaintiveness. "All right, I'm sorry. I didn't mean that."

"I think you meant it." Elaine's expression was smug. "What you regret is having said it."

"Why am I always being suckered?" Keese asked of himself as he turned and went downstairs. It now had happened: women were in utter control of his house.

He went outside, through the kitchen, and looked at his car. The painted legend was the cruelest of ironies, though Greavy, a near-moron, had no doubt chosen it for its mere ugliness of sound. *Pimp.* He supposed he was one, in a way—like everybody else.

He examined the letters closely, and suddenly he was, of all things, grateful to Greavy, of all people, and for an odd reason: the paint was not enamel, but whitewash! Good old Greavy. Keese wet a finger and swiped it through the first *P*. Then he went back to the garage and found a pail and a sponge, and at the corner of the house he got water from a hose attached to an outdoor faucet. In a trice his car had one clean and shiny door. But this too looked out of the way, and therefore he began to wash the entire vehicle.

He had reached the trunk when from behind he was hit by a gush of water, and he turned and took it, blindingly, in his face for a while before he could dodge and identify Harry as his tormentor.

Harry however was not discouraged by the recognition and continued to advance with the pouring hose. This was not the ultimate in punishment: the weather was temperate and in washing the car Keese had already got himself damp enough, but as Harry got closer the stream of water, having less far to travel, increased in pressure. It was still not precisely painful, but the inexorable approach began to suggest to Keese that Harry might just be desperate enough, at this point, to plunge the nozzle into one of his neighbor's orifices.

He therefore flung the contents of the bucket at Harry. This was no deterrent, the pail being by now but half full, and anyway the blob of flung water was split and pretty well dissipated by the gush from the hose, which Harry quickly brought to his own defense. After an instant it was back on target, on Keese, and advancing once more.

Moving swiftly and deftly for a man of his bulk, Keese got to close quarters with Harry, reached up and slammed a bucket over his head, and while Harry was groping to claw it away, Keese ran to the faucet and shut off the water.

Harry got the pail free and hurled it at Keese. Being of weightless plastic, it flew not far. Harry picked up the hose he had dropped and tried, with a great whipping movement, to snake it at Keese. But it was rather too long and sluggish to permit this.

Harry's eye looked worse than it had in his kitchen at dawn. For all practical purposes he was a Cyclops now. Keese did not want to hurt him again.

"Harry!" he cried. "You really got me then. Look, I'm soaked!" Harry looked dubious. Keese would have to convince him, else the stupidity would start up all over again. "Harry, I think we're even now!"

Harry dropped the hose and stood deliberating. He wore a pouty expression. "I don't know, Earl. I don't know at all. Do you really think so?"

"Who would know better than I?" Keese tried to say it wryly: "I'm soaked to the buff."

"But they're your old clothes," said Harry. "And you were anyway washing the car. I don't see that's much damage. I won't mention again the major dirty deals I got from you last night. I'll just point out the final kick in the nuts. I writhed on the floor for a quarter hour! I thought I was permanently ruptured. You're not a nice guy, Earl! You're a malignant little bastard. You're a dirty fighter. You're a hood, for Christ sake!" He was working himself up, that was clear. "You pretend to be a normal kind of neighborhood guy, respectable, stuffy, overweight, and so on, but that's a mask."

This portrait of himself was not altogether repugnant to Keese. He was not displeased to be considered dangerous. Distracted by vanity, he had failed to register that Harry was moving closer. Now his neighbor leaped upon him, bore him to the ground, and began to throttle him with a loop of the plastic hose.

Keese resisted Harry's effort to strangle him, but he was weakening. Could Harry be seriously trying to murder him? His arms were pinned by Harry's powerful elbows, while the huge hands twisted the hose ever more tightly. Keese's eyeballs were ready to pop from their sockets, and his tongue was oozing from his pursed lips like toothpaste from a tube. His face was maroon; his white-of-eye, bloody. . . . These symptoms were the work of his imagination, as he understood when Harry relaxed the pressure for a moment.

"Are you trying to kill me?" he croaked dramatically.

"Don't exaggerate your damage," Harry said with disgust, wincing down at him with one good eye. "That's the trouble: I don't know what to do. Anything effective as revenge *would* be lethal."

"Then may I get up?"

Harry sighed and began to lift one of the thighs with which he was straddling his victim. But then he lowered it and seized Keese by the shirt front and slapped his face a half-dozen times, backhand-and-forehand, movie-style. "I always wanted to do that to someone!" he said exultantly. But he frowned and added: "I guess the *whap-whap-whap* sound must be made by artificial means."

Keese struggled away from him and got up. He reclaimed his bucket and filled it from the hose, which he made no attempt to turn on Harry. He found the sponge that had been hurled away, and he returned to the washing of the car.

"Ah," said Harry, stretching, "turned out to be nice weather for our first day in the country. Say, Earl, you know a sponging isn't enough: might as well chamois it if you're going to all that trouble."

Obviously he didn't know about the abusive sign, though it had faced his house (where he had been writhing from the groin-kick), and it wasn't the sort of thing that Keese wanted him to know.

"You're right," Keese said now, and he went to the garage and brought back a chamois.

"Give that here," said Harry, amazingly, and he was as good as his word. He took the hard leather, wet it till it wilted, and began to stroke it across the body of the car, absorbing the beads of dirty water.

"Oh, you were looking for your wife last night," said Keese.

"Correction," said Harry. "I noted that she was gone. I was not actively seeking her out."

"She's in my house," said Keese, sponging the right-hand door.

"Figured she was," Harry said, chamoising the fender just behind.

"I had nothing to do with it."

"I didn't think you did," said Harry.

"She and my wife seem to hit it off."

"Yes," said Harry, "that's because they're both women."

"That's true," Keese said. He moved onto the front fender. The job went swiftly on the buddy-system.

"Damn right," said Harry. He reached into his pocket—he was wearing what appeared to be a brand-new pair of blue jeans, on which the rivets sparkled—and brought out an opened package of chewing gum. He offered this to Keese, who hadn't chewed a stick of gum in at least twenty years.

"O.K.," Keese said, "I will." He took a piece and he thanked Harry. Fortunately his teeth were in good condition, for the gum was stale and tough going at the outset.

Harry stopped chamoising and leaned against the car. "Kind of nice to chew gum with a pal."

Keese would never have expected such an ingenuous statement from Harry. "Real man-stuff, to clean a car on the weekend," he said. "I haven't done this myself in years. I usually run it through the automatic car-wash in Allenby, when the impulse occurs."

"Well, I—" Harry began, and then he and Keese stared at each other for a moment and then they laughed uproariously.

"Man," said Harry, "last night was really something, wasn't it?" He continued to laugh. His black eye looked better when it was squinting in mirth. "I can't remember how it started. But you know, talking of man-stuff, that was it, all right: paying one another back."

Keese was chewing vigorously. "You know, this gum isn't bad," he said. "I used to smoke cigarettes."

"That's how I got started on the gum," said Harry. "I gave up the smokes. Only thing that won't make you fat is gum,"

Keese said hastily: "I've got no worries about that."

Harry sucked air and said: "No offense intended."

"It never would occur to me," said Keese. "I've been heavy all my life."

"You're all right, Earl," said Harry, smiling. "Damn if you aren't." He winked with his good eye. "Nice to have a friend."

"And neighbor," Keese added robustly. Harry joined him in the chuckle.

And Harry added: "It certainly beats having an enemy as a neighbor!"

"Doesn't it, though?" said Keese.

"A lot of countries are like that," Harry said. "Pillboxes at the border, barbed wire, minefields. And who's on the other side? Human beings, just other men."

Keese had earlier observed Harry's tendency to philosophize in a banal fashion, and it made him vaguely uneasy to hear these political commonplaces: he felt he might be asked to join in the affirmation of some truism which would embarrass him intellectually.

He cocked an eye towards the heavens and cried: "Oh, no, that's not a rain cloud!"

Harry did not bother to glance upwards. He simply said: "No, certainly not." He appeared slightly miffed to have been diverted from his train of thought. He resumed: "The good old human condition . . ." But the initiative was gone now, and his voice petered out.

Keese had not wished to offend him. At whatever cost the

old strife must not be permitted to have a renascence. "Your remarks are well taken," he told Harry. He at first regretted having come up with nothing better than that, but in point of fact Harry gave every evidence of being flattered.

"The only thing I ever claim for myself is that I strive for moderation," Harry said. "I try to rise above, to get the general picture, to find the perspective which would allow . . ." He continued, and Keese, wearing a glazed smile, pretended to listen but heard nothing.

Finally it seemed fair enough to move on. "Well," Keese said, emptying the pail on the ground, "I'd better get clean water." He went to the nozzle end of the hose, seized it, and proceeded to the faucet. Harry continued to speak all this while. When Keese turned off the water Harry was just finishing a sentence with "on it."

Keese walked past him with the bucket, saying: "That's very interesting."

"Well," said Harry, "you're an easy man to talk with, Earl." He followed along and when Keese put the pail on the ground, Harry rinsed his chamois in it. Side by side they bent and cleaned the grille.

"I did the other side," said Keese, pointing with his sponge-laden hand, "but it wasn't chamoised, and it's probably dried by now."

He went there and looked. The whitewash had apparently disappeared with a few swipes of the sponge, but some of it, concealed by the damp, had secretly remained, and now that the metal was completely dry the outlines of the word PIMP were once again clearly discernible.

After making the last few touches of his chamois to the grille, Harry came around to join Keese, who was frantically scrubbing with his sponge.

"Hold on, Earl," said Harry, reaching for Keese's elbow. "Something's been painted there."

Keese yanked his arm beyond Harry's range, and continued to scour.

"What's it say?" asked Harry. "Can you read it?"

"Little punks," Keese said. "They come from across the creek."

"Jesus," Harry said fervently, "if you get graffiti here, how's it better than the city?"

"Well, it doesn't happen very often," Keese said.

Harry moved in and put his head at an angle. "What's it say? 'Chump'?" He firmly, gently forced Keese to move left. "Oh, I see. Yeah. Well." He seemed to be chewing on something the size of a caraway seed.

Keese suspected that Harry was, underneath it all, enjoying himself immensely. Well, why not? If one stepped away, so to speak, and looked back, it *was* funny.

He began to laugh. After all, he was chewing gum with his best friend. "Yeah, 'Pimp,' " he said. "Whoever wrote that was trying to summon up the ultimate in abusive terms."

"He found a pretty good one," said Harry.

But then the light came on! "*You* wrote that, didn't you, Harry?"

Too bad. They really had begun to build a friendship.

CHAPTER **11/**

BUT Harry surprised him. "No, Earl, I didn't—and you know I'd be the first to admit it if I did."

Keese did not "know" that, but he chose to believe Harry for another reason: at this point he would accept almost any excuse so as not to begin the strife again.

"I'm glad to hear that, Harry. I'm sick of tangling with you. But I'm afraid that I cannot help striking back when I'm attacked: it's my nature. And I don't mean to suggest that I am exceptionally courageous or anything. It's just a kind of reflex. If I were convinced that you wrote this on my car, I couldn't rest till I had retaliated in some way."

Harry flipped his chamois back and forth between his hands. "I can understand that, Earl, though I don't think I am as sensitive as you in that area. And by the way, I didn't mean a moment ago that the term was deserved: I meant by 'pretty good one' only that it is the kind of thing that would get under your skin."

Keese drew back slightly, thrusting his jaw forward. "Wouldn't it get under yours?"

"It might," said Harry.

"I'll take you into my confidence," Keese said. "This was done by Greavy, I'm pretty sure."

"The garage guy?" Harry shook his head. "This gets worse and worse! This guy you hire to come with his wrecker—he writes insulting terms on your car? That wouldn't even happen in the city."

Keese sighed. "I'm afraid you have a pretty bad impression of our area."

Harry continued to weigh his chamois, as if it represented the issue at hand. "What are your plans for getting revenge on Greavy?"

Keese worked his sponge on the minuscule white fragments that remained of the insulting epithet. "I haven't decided yet."

"If you're on the outs with him," said Harry, "how will my car ever get out of the swamp?"

Keese stopped working and straightened up. "My quarrel's not with Greavy's son Perry, who usually drives the wrecker. It was he who came last night and hauled my car away—no doubt as the result of, well, I guess it was your call, wasn't it?"

"My call?" asked Harry.

Keese said: "I assumed when he hauled my car away it was on your orders, it was your act of vengeance."

But Harry shook his head decisively. "Would that be likely, Earl? Think about it. Wouldn't I first want my own car pulled out of the muck down there?"

"Golly," said Keese, "wouldn't you though?" He slapped the car with his sponge. "Do you know something, Harry?" He gestured at the house with his thumb. "It must have been one of *them.*" He nodded as if in the possession of wisdom.

"I don't suppose it makes much difference by now whose fault or purpose it was," Harry said. "But I really would like to get my car up and out as soon as possible today. I have an idea it might run, and I've got a lot of things to do."

"Harry," said Keese, "I want you to regard my car, this car, as your own until your own is back in service, and I don't mean *as is*, but rather until it is restored to exactly the same condition it was in before it took the plunge. In fact—" Keese opened the driver's door and took the keys from the ignition. "Here." He gave them to Harry. "When we've got it cleaned, take it over to your driveway. I'll assume full responsibility for the recovery of your car. Nothing is more important than that."

"All right, Earl," said Harry. "I'll accept the offer, and in return I'll run down to the village, get the ingredients, and make a big breakfast for us."

"You and me?"

"Who else?" asked Harry. "Who needs those women?" He energetically chamoised a patch of car that Keese had sponged. "I don't think we'd have had any trouble last night if it had been just between you and me."

"I wonder." This was Keese's only response, and it was literal. Thus far he had preferred dealing with Harry to confronting Ramona, but he couldn't go so far as to make some absolute judgment that would apply to all possible conditions. And there was the basic truth that whatever he thought of her personality, he did find her sexually attractive—which is more than he could say of Harry.

For some reason it seemed a good idea now to finish the job as soon as possible, and they did so in unison. Harry insisted on shaking hands when he put down the chamois.

"We're quite a team, Earl," said he, pumping Keese's wrist. "I hope you like blueberry pancakes and little pig sausages." He opened the door and climbed into the driver's seat. He slammed the door, rolled down the window, poked his large fair head out, and added: "Because that's what you're getting."

"With slatherings of pure creamery butter and real maple syrup?" asked Keese, quoting from the TV commercial of a fast-food chain.

Harry frowned, as if he had been disparaged, closed the window (though the air was warm), and backed out the driveway at a much slower speed than he had shown the night before.

Keese watched his car disappear and then he went into the kitchen and consulted the clock. The time was 7:30! He was still not inured to this new losing of time. On the other hand, there *had* been a thrill a minute, by a certain interpretation.

Once again he looked up Greavy's number and dialed it. There was no problem now: it was Perry who answered. Keese told him about the car in the swamp. He decided not to mention Perry's useless errand of the night before—whoever had called the man.

Perry for his own part said nothing to suggest that he remembered the address. Indeed he said nothing whatever; he grunted and hung up. But he must have left the garage immediately thereafter, for no sooner had Keese passed his water in the ground-floor lavatory off the front hallway than through the little washroom window came the clanking sounds, and Keese went out the front door and saw Perry Greavy already unreeling a cable from a large spool on the cranelike structure of the wrecker.

By the time Keese had reached the outdoors Perry had taken the large iron hook on the business end of the cable and gone through the broken guardrail and descended into the swamp.

Keese became aware that the engine of the wrecker was running: to be sure, that was where the power would come from to work the winch and haul out the car. He looked into the cab and saw old Greavy. He would have stolen away had Greavy not seen him at the same instant.

"How do?" respectfully said the old man, and even touched his cap-brim with a dirty finger.

"Hi," said Keese.

"Be O.K. if the sonbitch's long enough."

"How's that?"

"Cable," said Greavy, with a smile that displayed the gaps in his dingy teeth. "And that mutterfrick can snep off and whop back, and it wool take your head clean off, or even come up between your legs and lash your whacker off, I tell you, I seen it heppen, so you look out and go behind the truck when Perry's hooked her." He was certainly genial this morning; obviously he had no memory of the night before. Keese was happy he had not sought to retaliate against Greavy—though if he tensed his abdominal muscles he could still feel the old man's sucker punch.

"I seen one take a greaser's foot off at the angle," Greavy went on chummily. "That was down in the warm country."

"Is that right?"

"Oh, I been all over," said Greavy, "and done everything, too. Everything but one. Know what that is?"

"No," said Keese.

"I never went down on a midget," Greavy cried, almost choking on his mirth.

Keese joined him in laughter. Funny how once the night was over he was getting along very well with his recent enemies.

Greavy looked at him with momentary interest, as if to repay him for enjoying the witticism. "Say," he asked, "you putting in another cesspool?"

"No." Keese wondered whether this too was a joke.

"Aren't you the gemman I saw last week over on Roose Road, putting in a new cesspool?" Greavy seemed serious enough.

"No," said Keese. So that was why Greavy had been so friendly: he hadn't recognized him in the daylight.

Greavy ignored the negation. "I want to talk about a seepage problem I got over to my place. I think there's shit in my water.

You come around there Monday morning." At this point Perry's voice could be heard, shouting up from the hollow.

Keese watched Harry's car leave the swamp. This was a slow process, and the cable was frighteningly taut. He moved farther off when the car gained the summit, which it did somewhat on the bias before correcting itself—or rather, as Keese saw now, was straightened by Perry, who had ridden up inside, at the steering wheel, giving some guidance during the backwards climb.

When the vehicle bumped down over the curb and at long last was again in its proper habitat, a paved road, Perry looked out of the window and asked Keese for the ignition key.

"Oh," said Keese, "it isn't my car."

Perry climbed out, went to the wrecker, and brought back a toolbox. He lifted the hood, did something underneath, and the engine started up without hesitation. He stopped it and closed the hood. He inspected the front of the car.

He asked Keese: "Where's the man owns this?"

"He'll be back." Keese walked to the nose of the car and looked at the grille: it was unmarked. "This looks O.K.," he said with relief. "The bumper must have taken all the punishment." He squatted and looked at the latter, seeing only some inconsequential scratches and blurs, which might well have been there before.

"That there rail was all rotten," said Perry. He boldly scratched his crotch, taking great handfuls of coverall. He bore no resemblance whatever to the elder Greavy, being a burly fellow, with a bulging paunch. He lifted off the cap of orange plastic and wiped his brow with the wrist of his other arm. This put a slash of oily dirt across his forehead. Then he worked up some saliva into a foamy blob and spat it upon the asphalt.

Keese interpreted this series of gestures as being Perry's nonverbal announcement to the effect that he did not now know what to do with the automobile.

"It doesn't seem to need much work," he said to Perry. "Why not move it over to the curb and leave it? Then when Harry comes back, if he wants to have something done to it, he can bring it down to your place. But he probably won't, because it looks in good shape."

Perry frowned. "We don't do body work. If you need that, you go to Sanford in Allenby. Now we'll tow you there, and you won't have to pay the basic charge again, just the mileage. But if we leave now, and then have to come back with the wrecker and tow it to Sanford's, why, that's another different trip altogether, and it's the basic charge again plus the mileage, so you lose quite a bit right there." He spat again. "I always tell that to people so they won't call me a fucking crook later on."

This would be all Keese's money, in accordance with his promise, and therefore he listened soberly. "Well," he said, "I don't see the need, and I don't think Harry will."

Perry nodded, but continued to stand there. Keese said: "So if you'll move it over to the curb . . ."

Perry nodded and spat again, but stayed in place. He seemed to have some difficulty in focusing his eyes. Finally he asked Keese: "Am I right? Are you the bastard who mouthed off to my dad last night?"

So there it was. Keese thought for a moment, and then he said: "No."

Perry chewed on his tongue. He brought a finger up slowly and rubbed it beneath his nostrils. At last he said, narrowing his intensely blue eyes: "You telling me the truth?"

"No," said Keese.

Perry looked down and scratched his foot on the road. "You going to apologize?"

"No."

"You're not?"

"No."

Perry leaned towards him and spoke in a confidential tone: "I'm going to kick your belly through your back."

"No," said Keese.

Perry winced and backed away. He began to lower his head, as though he were about to charge.

At that moment old Greavy looked out of the cab of the wrecker and said: "Come on, Perry, if you got the job done. I got to take a dump."

Perry nodded and hitched up his trousers. "You're a lucky man," he said to Keese.

"No," Keese said.

Perry went to the rear bumper of Harry's car and bent to disengage the hook-and-cable. Keese considered jumping him from behind, zapping Perry before he was aware, hurting him so badly that he would not think of revenge—because that was possible, but only to a real technician of mayhem, he suspected. Anything less and he would insure for himself a nightmarish future; anything more and he would kill the garageman.

Chagrining though it might be, he would probably have to wipe the slate clean of the Greavys' crimes against him. He had never even figured out a way to avenge the old man's punch. With the son's threat the whole affair became too complicated to endure.

Perry had the hook loose. He seemed to have forgotten Keese entirely. He cried to his father to switch on the power for the reeling up of the cable, but literally the shout was only a single sound, like a hoot. When this business was finished Perry got into the wrecker and drove it away.

Keese walked up the path to his house and took a seat on the front step, where Ramona had perched at one point last night. The trees seemed to have doubled their greenery overnight, which is April's way. But spring was not Keese's favorite season. While he thought about this peculiarity of taste, his car swung into the road. Harry had returned.

When he had parked the car in the driveway and got out, Keese hailed him.

"Yes," said Harry, "I see it. Does it run?" He and Keese joined forces at the edge of the driveway and went down to Harry's car.

Keese said: "It started right away when he tried it."

Harry found an ignition key in some hideaway under the seat, put it in place, and started the car. "Well," he said out the window, "that's it." He got out and walked quickly around the front, saying: "Uh-huh, uh-huh."

"Looks O.K., doesn't it?" Keese asked.

Harry reached the right rear fender. "Oh-oh," said he.

Keese went there and saw a rust-filled dent of two or three inches in length.

Harry bent and touched it. "This is the major damage, right here. Of course, there's a good deal of grass-burn on the painted areas in front and some chrome-torture on the bumper and grille."

Keese was sure that Harry had invented these terms, though he must admit they were professional-sounding, and if that had been all, he might have bantered with him on the subject. But he could not let the man get away with pinning responsibility on him for a dent that had obviously been on the car some time before its plunge into the swamp.

"Come on," said he, "look at that rust. That dent was there long since."

Harry stared earnestly (or with that air) into his eyes. "Earl," he said reproachfully, "you're not reneging?"

"Of course I'm not," said Keese, "but I really think my obligation, in all fairness, would be to rectify anything that had been damaged by what I did last night. Now, I have looked the car over pretty carefully, and I don't think it needs much work —except maybe a good wash and waxing. Put a nice shine on her and she'll be good as new, eh, Harry? If you'd like I'll run her over to the car wash in Allenby soon as we have eaten breakfast."

Harry grinned and shook his head. "Oh, you're something, Earl. Aren't you a prize! Sky's the limit, so long as you don't have to pick up the tab."

Keese shook his own head. "Harry," he said.

"Earl," said Harry. "I thought you were really trying to turn over a new leaf."

"Why," Keese asked plaintively, "is it always *me* who's to blame?"

"I might ask the same," said Harry. "You've been prejudiced against me since the first."

"Because you're usually in the wrong!" cried Keese. "It's as simple as that."

"Who wrecked the car?"

Keese said: "*Usually* in the wrong. I didn't say 'always.' " He shook his head. " 'Grass-burn' and 'chrome-torture.' "

Harry raised both fists to the level of his chest and struck them together. "Earl, that car needs a paint job. There's no two ways about it. Now, if you want to renege, O.K., I won't sue you. I'll make it a matter of honor. I'm saying what's right."

Keese's eyes were burning, and there was an odd sensation in the back of his neck. He recognized these as the results of his night of no sleep. Nor was he in possession of his old fighting spirit. Suddenly he submitted. "All right," he said, "I'll buy you a paint job. I'm not agreeing to your argument, but I'll pay for a complete repainting. Will that do it? Are we square?"

"Absolutely," said Harry. "Earl, you're one hell of a guy!" He clapped Keese on the shoulder, and then he seized his hand and pumped it. "I'm proud to call you friend."

"And neighbor," said Keese, vastly relieved. It was a small price to pay, to achieve this rapprochement. "Listen, after breakfast we'll go over and get an estimate from the body shop in Allenby. I'll follow you in my car. We'll leave yours there right now. Heck, you'll probably have it back in a couple of days."

Harry put his head on the side and grimaced as if thinking this over. And then he said: "Why should you bother? Naw, I know of a cut-rate place in the city that's good enough." Keese must have frowned involuntarily, for Harry stared at him and added: "I'll get a receipt."

Keese was embarrassed now. He said: "Oh, I . . ."

"Of course," Harry said, "it's cash on delivery, so maybe you'd give me a check right now."

Keese began to grin bitterly. He said only: "Uh-huh."

Harry got the point. He put his hands in the air as if he were being held up, backed away, and said: "O.K., O.K., it was just a suggestion, Earl. Don't give me that look. I'm no confidence man. Forget about it. I'll pay it out of my own pocket and bring you the receipt."

"This place you know, what do they get for a paint job?"

Harry brought his bushy eyebrows together: there was something canine in his frown, especially with the black eye. "Depends on the make and model."

He was lying, of course. Keese was exhausted now, but he had enough energy left to make Harry squirm a little. "What's the name of this place?"

"Excuse me?"

"The name of the auto-painting company?"

"Oh," said Harry, "it's, uh, let me, uh . . ."

Liar. Keese said maliciously: "You probably haven't noticed the name, just the location."

"Yeah," said Harry, "that's it. You know how it goes."

"Then where can it be located?"

"Huh?"

Keese asked harshly: "Where is it?"

Harry ignored this question to give an answer that had been

sought earlier. "I think I remember the name," said he. "It's just 'Auto Painters.'"

"Oh, it is, is it?" said Keese. "Well, Harry, I'm getting pretty—"

"I'm fairly certain the phone number is— Wait a minute, I'd better write it down." He ran to his car, opened the door on the passenger's side, and rummaged in the glove compartment. He found a pencil therein, and a yellow receipt or bill, which he turned over and on the reverse he scribbled something.

When Keese was handed this slip of paper he said to Harry: "What would you do if I actually called this number?"

"I'd ask them for an estimate on a paint job for the car."

Keese had to admit that Harry's ingenuousness of voice and eye was impeccable, but he didn't trust him for a moment.

"Would you be willing to come in with me while I call them now?"

Harry shrugged. "Sure."

Keese feinted at the front door, but decided to go around to the kitchen. He went to the wall phone. Harry sat himself down in his old place at the table, now familiar terrain.

Keese dialed the number from the back of the receipt. The phone rang for several sequences at the other end of the wire. At last the drowsy voice of a woman was heard: "Hullo."

"Is this Auto Painters?"

"I'll get him."

"Wait—" cried Keese, but she had already put the phone down.

A harsh-voiced man came on the line. "Yes?"

"What is this place?" Keese demanded.

"Don't get fresh with me," said the man. "*You're* calling *me,* and I should tell you who I am? Who are you, General of the World?"

"I'm sorry," said Keese, who was not in the market for more

enemies, "I apologize to you, sir. It's just that I suspect I am the victim of a hoax. I was given your number as that of a company that paints cars, you see." He waited, but there was only silence at the other end. "Sir? Are you there?"

"I'm here," said the heavy voice.

"I don't suppose you're the Auto Painters, then, are you?" Keese wanted to give Harry every chance, so that he could not later be accused of having been unjust.

"My name's not Otto Painters," said the man.

"O.K., then please forget it. Thank you. Once again I apologize."

But the man spoke before Keese could hang up. "You want your car painted, is that it? I can do it for you, but not today, I'm busy. Tomorrow's O.K., though. I'm off tomorrow, and I can paint your car for you. What color you want? The hardware store's still open when I get off work, and I'll pick up the paint and brush. Tell me what color."

Keese asked: "You're not a professional painter of cars, are you?"

"Don't knock the job before you see it," whined the man. "That ain't fair. What's it, a hot car? What do you care how good it's painted, or why would you have called me?"

"Good question," said Keese. The voice sounded vaguely familiar to him by now. "Tell me this, you don't work at Caesar's Garlic Wars, do you?"

"Not me," said the man.

Keese sighed and hung up. He turned, flopping his hands; in one of them the yellow paper fluttered. "I don't know why I even bothered to check this out."

"Weren't they open on Saturday?" asked Harry.

"Harry, I dialed this number and talked to the persons who answered: they do not have such a business as you say."

"He won't paint your car?"

Keese twitched his nose. "With a brush?"

"What do you have to complain about?" said Harry. "*You're* paying, right? I'm doing you a favor. We could go to the body shop in Allenby if you prefer, and pay the standard price, which would be plenty, I assure you. Is that what you want?"

Keese was thinking.

"It's *my* car, isn't it?" said Harry.

Keese grimaced. "I have the feeling that you have just shown me up," he said.

"Well, if I have it wasn't intentional," Harry replied. "I've had enough, Earl. I'm leaving."

"Now, wait a minute, Harry," Keese cried. "Don't go off half-cocked. I admit that once again I failed to act well. It may be that we speak a different language. Some of your ways apparently have another significance for me than what you intend. That may be due to a difference in milieu or age or even size—"

"Well, whatever," said Harry, "I'm clearing out."

Keese smiled. "I think I can understand your chagrin. But you'll see, mark my words, things will improve after you've lived here for a while. I can still remember—"

Harry interrupted. "But I'm not going to live here any more, Earl. I said I'm leaving. I'm moving away."

Keese smiled sympathetically. "But not today, at any rate, Harry. So let's talk about it, think it over. Besides, you couldn't get a mover that quickly! Say, let's have that breakfast you promised. Where's the stuff, in the car?"

"Can't you get it through your head, Earl? I just got back from hiring a truck and some guys down at the service station. They should be on their way by now. I'm moving out immediately."

"You're not joking, are you, Harry?" Keese asked after a moment. "I can see that now. I don't know what to say. Do you mean you're moving away after less than twenty-four hours? Where are you moving to, Harry? How can you have found another home so quickly?"

"I don't have time to go into all those details," Harry shouted, opening the door. "Can't you see that, Earl?"

Keese caught the door and followed him. "Harry," he cried, "do you blame me for this? Did I ruin this place for you?"

Harry was striding rapidly towards his house, but he stopped here, turned, and said: "Don't blame yourself, Earl. You had little to do with my decision, though it is true enough that you could scarcely be called hospitable—until perhaps this morning, when it's too late. Frankly, this place began to sour on me as soon as I set foot in it."

"Well, Harry," said Keese, a bit breathlessly, owing to the haste with which he pursued him, "if I'm not to be blamed, then what's the matter?"

"Everything," said Harry. "But nothing that can really be explained: noises and drafts, where the sun sets and how the horizon looks at different times of the day, where the electric switches are, and why the toilet drips all the time."

"Old Walker put in some alterations himself, as I recall," said Keese. "Some Rube Goldberg plumbing, I think."

"Well, it's not just the house," Harry said. "Actually, I could put up with the house itself. Oh, to get it right in all respects I'd have to tear it to the ground and start all over. Which I might be willing to do if I liked any part of the neighborhood. But I don't." He pointed across the road to the field, the property of the Power & Light Company. "Who wants to look at those transformers day in and day out?"

He had a clearer view of them from his property than Keese had from his own. "But after a while," said Keese, "you forget they're there. Really. I'm a veteran of these parts."

"What about that swamp where my car was? That must be a mosquito hatchery. They must rise in clouds on summer nights!" Harry shuddered dramatically.

"County sprays that every year," Keese told him. "I can testify to the fact that hardly a bug survives." This was a barefaced lie.

Harry sniffed violently. "Yeah? Well, what does anybody do about the stink?"

"Stink?"

Harry performed a kind of reverse sneeze, so forcefully did he take air into his nostrils. "What would you call it, then? God almighty, I never smelled anything like it." He pointed his nose at heaven. "It's a rotting smell. I think it comes from that garbage pile behind your garage."

He was on the attack now. Keese's job, as he saw it, was to stand his ground without turning vicious again and giving him even more reason to dislike the neighborhood.

"Oh," Keese said, "you mean Enid's compost heap. That's where she gets her mulch. She's quite a gardener."

"It's certainly an eyesore. Will you admit that, at least?"

From where they stood, actually now on Harry's property, they had an angle on a corner of the compost pile. It was essentially a heap of dead leaves, so far as Keese could see.

"Come on, Harry," said he. "It's really not so bad." When he glanced back he saw his neighbor marching away again. "Harry, hold on!" he cried and went after him.

Harry stopped and said: "Earl, I find it curious that you are acting now as though you wanted me to stay. I should think you of all people would be ecstatic at my decision to leave."

"Aw, Harry," said Keese, playing on his sentimentality (if he had any), "you can be unfair at times."

"I'll tell you this, too, Earl: I don't like to be off to the side like this."

"Pardon?"

"This dead end," said Harry, his lip rising. "You call it a neighborhood, but it's not. There's nobody else here but us. You've got to go around the turn of the road to find another house. That's not a real neighborhood, at least not to anybody from the city."

"You mean, you want a delly, a gutterful of refuse, and a couple of whores in a liquor-store doorway?" Keese was joking. "I've lived in the city in my day."

Harry stared at him. "What I mean is, I'd feel safer if there was somebody here other than *you*. Or at least in addition to."

"Now I know where I stand."

"I don't much like the looks of your house, either, Earl, so long as we're being frank."

"Are we?"

"That fake colonial, and with an extra dormer? And a window greenhouse?" Harry was really pouring in one salvo after another. "Mock-orange bush? Jesus."

"I see you can't be dissuaded, then," said Keese, to whom it occurred to the threat to move might merely be a ruse by which Harry could denigrate him with impunity. "O.K., I hope it works out better with your next home, wherever you make it. I also sympathize with your new neighbors." He couldn't resist adding that.

Harry stabbed a finger towards him. "Haha, Earl! I knew you'd show your true colors sooner or later. My congratulations on concealing them so long, you dirty little hypocrite, you. You almost took me in, do you realize that? I was jus⁺ about talked into staying. This was my last trick, and it certainly paid off."

"Harry, you really are a bastard," said Keese, but he said it genially. "You're just playing hard to get, aren't you? You want to be begged. Well, I'm not going to do that, because that sort of thing has a way of backfiring. But if you want an honest statement of my feelings, I'll be glad to give it. It's your right to move, certainly, but so far as I am concerned, I'd really like you to stay." He turned away. "The truth is, I don't have any friends around here."

"Earl, you're breaking my heart," said Harry.

"No, Harry," Keese said, "don't ridicule me at this moment, when my response to you is altogether positive, in spite of certain provocations. I'm saying I realize now that while hating your guts most of the night I was really having a good time."

"You could have fooled me," said Harry.

"Come on, Harry, stay."

Harry started walking towards his house again. He spoke as if to himself: "So I can get locked in the cellar again? Thrown out of his house several times, once when I had already gone to bed? So I could be punched in the other eye? So my car could be rolled back into the swamp?"

"Next time it will be your turn," Keese said. "You can abuse me in various ways, and my resistance will be ineffectual. Is it a deal?"

"No more deals," said Harry. "They have a way of souring on me around here. I'll tell you this: I never had that trouble in the city. Everything went *my* way!"

"I'll bet it did," said Keese, "and it can here, too, Harry. All you need is one good break."

"I doubt I'll get it if you're anywhere near, Earl."

"Aw, sure you will, Harry. The wind's gotta change for you."

Harry made a face. "And blow more of your stink my way?"

If someone had earlier told Keese that the time might come when he would plead with Harry to remain in the house next door! But he was desperate now to find an argument with which to detain him.

"Ramona!" he cried. "Ramona doesn't want to leave, I'll bet."

Harry sneered. "She's not leaving."

"You're going and she's—"

"You can have her," said Harry. "You've nothing to fear from me, Earl. She's yours."

"Oh, no," Keese said, walking backwards while he talked. "I've got no need, Harry. I'm a happily married man. I've got a daughter almost as old as—no, you'd better take your wife along. You might need her when you least expect. No—"

"Earl, as a return for all your hospitality to me as a new neighbor," said Harry, *I am presenting her to you with my compliments.*" He turned and hiked rapidly towards his house.

Keese realized that at the moment, at any rate, it would be useless to talk further to Harry on this theme. The only thing to do was to go at the problem from Ramona's end. He started back to his house. There wasn't a moment to lose. He heard the approach of a heavy vehicle, and he turned and watched an enormous U-Haul van lumbering into Harry's driveway.

If Harry was bluffing, he had gone pretty far.

CHAPTER 12/

KEESE entered the front door—and almost knocked his daughter down. She was fully dressed and carrying her overnight case.

"What's this?" he asked. "Elaine!"

"I hoped to get out without the rigmarole," said she.

"But you've hardly been here."

"It seems like months."

"Was it that bad?" He answered himself: "Worse." He tried to seize her case, but she swung it away. "Look, Elaine, you know this isn't the normal weekend so far, but why not give it a chance? It may pick up steam."

Elaine shuddered. "That's what scares me. Who was that shooting a gun at dawn?"

Keese had forgotten that incident! "Oh, that was an accident. No harm done."

"He's a cop, isn't he?"

"Harry? No, I don't think so. By the way, he claims he is leaving already, moving out. Can you beat that?"

"Small wonder," said Elaine. "I'm on my way, too, Dad. Oh, I forgot. I have to call a cab." She put her case down, and Keese seized it.

"I can't let you leave until I get things in order!"

She smiled and picked up the handpiece from the telephone alcove. She began to dial: she had a good memory for seldom-used numbers. Keese usually drove her to the bus station at Allenby.

"Elaine, please!" But she continued to dial. Keese apparently lapsed into stoicism, but actually he went behind her back, opened the triangular door of the understair closet, and reaching within, removed the phone plug from the jack that was concealed there. He counted on her to have forgotten, if she had ever known, that this instrument could be unplugged, its wire going through a U-slot at the base of the paneling. Some predecessor had made that arrangement. Until now Keese had been saving his knowledge of it.

"Oh, damn," Elaine said, "now the phone has gone off."

"Hmm," said Keese, coming around and hypocritically taking the instrument from her and pretending to test it.

"I've got it!" she cried. "You say Harry's leaving? I'll catch a ride with him."

This was worse. "Elaine," Keese said earnestly, "can't you stay a bit longer? Later on, at your convenience, I'll drive you to Allenby—or, if you'll permit, to Collegeville." (For indeed that was the quaint name of the town where her university was situated.)

She squinted at him. "The idea is to get away from you, Dad, while I can still walk."

"What's that supposed to mean?"

"I'm too young to die needlessly while on a weekend visit with my parents. It's as simple as that."

"Oh, come on, Elaine. What are you talking about?"

She put her hands on her hips and confronted him. "Why is Harry leaving? This has become a lethal neighborhood."

Keese said: "Oh, Harry—in case you didn't notice it last night—is a remarkable eccentric. On the spur of the moment he'll move his entire household."

"When has he done that?" Elaine asked defiantly.

"He's doing it now, Elaine. Don't ask me to explain the man. Anyway, look at what he did last night."

"I don't recall his doing much," said she. "You punched him in the eye."

"And why?" asked Keese. "Simply to be brutal? What's come over you, Elaine?"

She rolled her eyes.

"Harry has announced he is moving away," Keese said in a calmer voice, "having got here only yesterday. Now, can't you see what an unfortunate reflection that is on the neighborhood? In effect, isn't he rejecting this street? And if so, can we afford to let it happen?"

"If Harry's made up his mind to go," said Elaine, "I doubt there's much that could be done to dissuade him. He seems pretty stubborn to me."

"Not at all," said Keese. "He's a spiteful man, Elaine, and that type's never stubborn. He's moving out now, or perhaps merely feinting at it, for the purpose of shaming me. Spite, all of it. He believes he's demonstrating how badly I've treated him. And, mind you, there may be people who will believe him. The Abernathys, no doubt."

"Your best friends?"

"Deceitful people, Elaine. They're no friends of mine."

"Good," said Elaine. "Marge has very bad breath."

Keese had not been aware of this failing, but he did not betray his ignorance here, lest he lose face.

He was silent for a moment, and then he said: "Just bear with me for a few minutes. I'll run you to Allenby, but I don't dare leave at this moment. The moving van's already pulled in next door. Please!" He took Elaine's hand. "Promise you'll stay right here."

"Well, if it's really that important . . ."

"It is, believe me."

"All right, then, I'll stay."

Keese kissed her forehead, which looked cool but was actually so warm it may have been feverish, but he had no time to worry about that now. He climbed the stairs, marched to the door of the master bedroom, and was about to rap on the door when Enid emerged. She was fully dressed. She gave him a piercing look.

"I'll bet you didn't even try to sleep."

"How could I?" Keese asked accusingly.

"Yes, blame me. That makes sense."

"Have I your permission to address your girl friend?" Keese asked.

"No," said Enid, "the poor little thing needs her rest."

Keese grunted huffily, turned the knob, and pushed in. There was a strong odor of dog, but all in all it was a pleasant, homely smell. The wolfhound lay on an oval scatter rug below the foot of the bed. It had curled its large body so that it fitted the rug precisely.

Keese went to the left side of the bed, properly his own, and looked down at Ramona, who was apparently sleeping. He had been in the Army, and he had never seen a sleeping human being without being sensible of an overwhelmingly sympathetic emotion, even if the person when awake was despicable.

"What the fuck do you want now?" Ramona asked while in the act of opening her eyes. No doubt she had been playing possum. "Throwing me out again?"

"Not really," said Keese. He would never become inured to her foul mouth. Her features looked more delicate in her current attitude, but her lank hair adhered unpleasantly to her skull, as though wet. "I thought you should know," he said, "that Harry's pulling out."

"Of whom?" Ramona asked idly, yawning cavernously. She didn't seem to have a filling in her large and savage teeth.

"Harry is leaving, moving away," said Keese. "The van is there already. I thought you would want to know."

"Why?"

"Isn't it your home too?"

"I can't see it was much of anybody's home in that short a time," said Ramona. "I certainly wasn't looking forward to it as mine."

"I know," said Keese, "you miss the city. I've been through all that with Harry."

Ramona scowled. "I hate the city! What I love is the country—the real country, not this. I mean the Mountains or the Desert or the North Woods."

"Or the Lake Region?" Keese asked sardonically. He wanted to deride her, but as usual he felt she was actually winning.

"Is that the only reason you woke me up?" she asked in disgust.

"All right," said Keese, "if you really want to know: Harry told me he was leaving you here."

"That sounds like him," said Ramona, rubbing her nose.

"Actually he said I could have you."

She raised her eyebrows and let them fall.

Keese said: "Does he have the power to give you away?"

"Why not?" said Ramona, stretching under the covers. "Isn't that exciting?"

"I think it's appalling," Keese said solemnly, "if you're being serious."

"That's because you are thinking ethically." She smiled sweetly. Suddenly she slipped from view beneath the bedclothes.

Keese had been bested again. He impotently addressed the covers: "Well, I've done my duty."

"Like hell you have," said Ramona from within the bed. Her head reappeared. "I'm not going to let you get away with that!"

Keese was amazed by her passion. "You mean I am giving up too soon?" It was the only thing he could think of.

Ramona said: "Your version of neighborliness is a farce, Earl."

Keese did secretly feel a kind of contrition with respect to the figure he had cut, but he retained enough of his old indignation to serve. "Your performance as a neighbor newly arrived leaves much to be desired, too," he said, "but I don't want to relive last night. For your information, I told Harry I wanted him to stay. I pleaded with him."

"He probably recognized your hypocrisy," said Ramona. "I do."

"Then you don't understand me. I'm very sincere in this. I realize we didn't hit it off last night, but I say give it a chance! It was different with the Walkers: in all the years we scarcely knew them. I forgot what it was like to have neighbors as real friends."

Ramona's expression softened. "If you'd only give a guy a chance . . ."

"All right," said Keese, "I know I've made mistakes, but I don't think all the fault was on my side."

Ramona's face was working. Suddenly she opened the bed-clothes at the side towards him. She was naked. She said: "Get in here, Earl."

"For God's sake, Ramona."

"Don't worry," she said soberly, "we only want you to be happy."

Keese avoided looking at her ivory body in the warm stratum of bed. "I can't do that sort of thing! It isn't the kind of thing that is done. Do I have to explain it?"

"I am just extending the hand of friendship," said Ramona. "Can't you see that?"

"You're making me very nervous," said Keese. He walked around to the other side of the bed.

Ramona shook her head and dropped the covers. "Well, there you are again. You say you have turned over a new leaf, but you haven't changed one iota, Earl. You repel any offer of affection, any attempt at neighborliness."

"Neighborliness?"

Ramona sighed. "Are you a freak of some kind, Earl? Must you have dead chickens or the smell of pee? Can't you simply and honestly be with a woman in the natural way?"

What was the use? The situation had got so warped that nothing would really serve but for Keese to confirm her assessment, as the only means by which he could persuade her to let him alone.

"I guess that's my trouble, all right."

Ramona nodded sympathetically. "Yes, I knew that. I was just being cruel now, I couldn't help myself."

"You 'knew that'?" Keese said furiously. He removed his clothes in a trice, threw back the covers, and climbed in beside Ramona's nudity.

But no sooner had this happened than a pounding came at the door and a voice crying: "Earl! Earl!" It took a repetition for him to identify Harry.

Moaning to himself, he scrambled from bed. These trash had tricked him into the old badger game! He seized up his clothes from the floor and stole into the bathroom, where he dressed quickly in the old "work" pants and shirt and unlaced shoes, omitting underclothes and socks. Harry was still pounding and shouting. Why didn't he enter the bedroom?

At last Harry shouted: "Sorry, Earl!" The door could be heard to open.

Keese instantly glided from bathroom to hall and then, soundless on the runner rug, stole around the corner. In a moment he heard Harry come back into the hall and shout: "Earl, Earl!"

Keese could have concealed himself in the former guest room, amidst the extra furniture, but he was determined to face the music. He swung around the corner and came marching down the hall.

"Harry," he said, "I thought you'd be moved out by now."

"Earl," said Harry. His face was streaked black, as if from soot, and his hands were filthy, his clothes torn and apparently singed here and there. "Please, Earl," he begged, "none of your cruel humor at this point. My house is burning down."

"I assume you've called the fire department?"

"I don't have a phone and yours is out of order!"

Keese said: "All right, Harry, all right. I'll do something." He felt amazingly competent in a general way, but he had no particular idea of what to do. "You'll see," he added. He descended the stairs.

Enid and Elaine were roaming about the front hall, apparently distraught. Keese decided he'd better look at Harry's house, to see whether his neighbor might be lying or at least exaggerating. He went to the dining-room windows and looked.

He could see nothing amiss, not a wisp of smoke, let alone a flame. The moving van was gone.

He returned to the front hallway, where Harry had joined the two women. Indeed, they seemed to be supporting him, each under a shoulder.

"Let him go," said Keese. "It's another of his hoaxes."

"Earl," Harry croaked out, "have you no humanity at all? For the love of God, man, drive to the fire department. I couldn't find your ignition key."

"Aha," cried Keese, "you thereby reveal yourself, Harry old boy. Why didn't you use your own car? It has been recovered, you know."

"Because—" And here Harry went into a racking cough, for all the world as if he had inhaled too much smoke.

"Earl," said Enid, "an axle is broken on his car. It won't run."

That idiot Perry Greavy! He had tested only the engine. Damn! Now Keese was in for a nice bill. An axle! He had a feeling this day, too, was going bad.

He opened the little triangular door beneath the stairs, reached inside the space, found the telephone plug, and inserted it in the jack. He straightened up and took the phone off the cradle.

"Here," he said to Harry, "I'm calling your bluff. Get the fire department."

But Harry waved him off, coughing violently.

"I saw what you did, Daddy," said Elaine, with reference to the telephone plug, "and I'll never forgive you."

Keese bared his teeth at her and dialed the fire-department number, which he saw on a little label affixed to the base of the instrument, along with the numbers of the police and ambulance service. Then he went out the front door to await the arrival of the firemen. He eagerly looked forward to fingering Harry as the person who had entered the false alarm.

As he stood at the curb a window suddenly collapsed on the second floor of Harry's house, and a burst of red-and-orange flame billowed from it.

He ran back into the house and shouted at Harry: "You're right! It *is* on fire!"

Harry was still gasping, but he managed to shake a fist at Keese and gargle out a word of abuse.

Soon afterwards the volunteer fire department arrived in two trucks, with, except for a discreet bell, a strange lack of noise. The company consisted of local lads. They made a recreational club of the firehouse in the village, gave dances, and marched in parades. Luckily Keese regularly bought chances in their raffles. They now immediately wetted down the roof of his house. The brawny fellow manning the nozzle of the hose turned out, under the leather helmet, to be Perry Greavy.

But while this was being done, Harry's house burned ever more furiously, and when the firemen finally turned to it, their chief, a pudgy man wearing a white helmet, necktie, and red felt jacket, pronounced the case to be hopeless and therefore a foolish extravagance for the full department, and he sent the larger truck away.

Keese was all alone in the yard. Neither Harry nor the women had emerged. Keese walked over to the fire chief and recognized him as Doc, the village pharmacist. Doc looked markedly different without his glasses.

"Not going to bother with it?" Keese asked Doc.

"She's kaputt," said Doc. Even at this distance the radiated heat was uncomfortable. Doc commanded some of his men to return to the wetting down of Keese's house.

Keese fought against being hypnotized by the fire and almost lost the struggle: it was utterly fascinating to him. He could understand the emotional rewards of arson. But duty called. He must go inside and console Harry. With a last fond glance at the flames, he went inside.

He found Harry and Enid in the kitchen. They had apparently been having an animated conversation, which stopped suddenly when his step was heard.

"Harry," Keese said on entering the room, "your house is a total loss, I'm afraid. But at least you got out alive. What happened?"

Harry's face was still sooty, though he had had plenty of time to wash it. Here and there were burn-holes in his knitted shirt of royal blue, yet there was no evidence of his body's being burned. The flesh seen through these apertures (he wore no undershirt) looked hale enough.

Harry squinted at Keese through his good eye. "All right, Earl," he said, "you can drop the act."

"And what does that mean?"

"It didn't just burst into flame of its own accord," said Harry. "Come on."

"No," said Keese, "I'm sure it did not."

"Then are you admitting you set the fire?"

Keese smacked his hands together, almost in glee. "I might have known! But *you* set the fire, didn't you? You burned down your own house!"

Harry looked at Enid. They were sitting side by side at the table. "Didn't I tell you?"

Enid appealed to Keese. "I think he's got you this time, Earl."

"He's got nothing." To Harry he said: "All right, *don't* tell me how you set fire to your house. Tell me how your clothes were burned while they were on your body, without your skin being hurt!"

Harry grinned ruefully at Enid. "He's like a cornered rat!"

"You have no explanation?" asked Keese.

"He's clutching at straws," said Harry.

Keese could hear the water from the firemen's hose falling on the roof of the kitchen, which had no second story above it. "We were just lucky that they came quickly enough to protect this house," said he. "I suppose that didn't occur to you, Harry? That you would endanger us as well?"

"He doesn't miss a trick," Harry said to Enid.

"If *I* did it, then when?" asked Keese.

"While we were distracted by the moving," Harry said.

"All this aside," said Keese, "I hope you were able to get some of your furniture out. I noticed that the van was gone when I first looked over there, before the flames had burst out the window."

"Not a stick!" Harry cried bitterly. "You've wiped me out, Keese!"

"Just stop that, Harry!" Keese shouted across the table. "I

had nothing to do with the fire. If you think about it for one minute you'll realize that I had nothing to gain. And furthermore, by that time you and I had become friends."

Enid asked: "Would that be enough to restrain you, Earl?"

Keese said: "Look, to continue to accuse me is misguided, and it's also unproductive. Let's see what we can salvage from this catastrophe. Surely the house was insured. . . . Now, forgive me for saying this, but if you *did* set the fire, I hope you left behind no evidence that would affect your insurance claim—"

"God, how you can twist the knife," Harry moaned. "You're really a sort of fiend, Earl." He whimpered at Enid, who took his hand and patted it.

"All right," said Keese. "I'm sorry, Harry. Maybe it was spontaneous combustion in the straw used to pack the dishes. Or maybe the moving men carelessly threw down a cigarette butt or something."

"I didn't see either of the Greavys smoking," said Harry. "And the dishes weren't packed in straw!" He seemed to see the failure of these theories as a personal triumph.

"The Greavys! Were *they* your movers?"

"Of course," said Harry. "They rent out the U-Haul, and I couldn't do the job by myself, so I hired the two of them."

"And how did they work out?" Keese slyly asked.

"Not well. The old man agreed to one price down at the station, but he upped it once he got here."

"Did you quarrel with him?"

"We had a difference of opinion, and they left. That's why nothing was saved."

"There's your fire," said Keese triumphantly. "They set it in revenge. Guess who's a fireman? Perry Greavy." He was greatly relieved to have solved the mystery. He and Harry could be greater friends than ever.

"Well, Earl," said Harry, "nobody can fault your ingenuity."

"Think I am inventing this explanation to conceal my own guilt?"

"You said it. *I* didn't."

Enid asked with concern: "Earl, have you had any breakfast?"

"No!" Keese said passionately. "Nor no decent dinner last evening, nor no sleep at all!" He turned to Harry. "I thought *you* were going to make blueberry pancakes and little pig sausages."

Harry raised his eyebrows. "Forgive me, Earl. It's really outrageous of me to neglect breakfast, to be distracted by a fire that destroyed everything I owned." He laughed bitterly for Enid's benefit.

"Well, I've got you there as it happens." Keese too appealed to Enid: "Breakfast was supposed to have occurred long before the fire. In fact, there wouldn't have been a fire at all if he had kept his promise to make breakfast—if, instead of hiring the Greavys to move him out, he would have bought pancake mix and little pig sausages and come back here promptly and cooked them!"

Harry asked Enid: "Can you believe this? That a civilized man would be so devoid of common decency?"

"Talk about someone with a bias!" said Keese. "Listen, you quarreled with Greavy about the price, you said. What was his reaction?"

"I didn't say we quarreled. I said we disagreed. He stuck to his position, I to mine, and he shrugged and drove away."

"You mean the old man?" asked Keese. "What about the son?"

"He was in the toilet."

"Well, there you are," Keese said. "He was starting the fire. It's clear enough to me."

But Harry would not submit to reason: he stared defiantly at his neighbor. "First you hated my being in what you call your neighborhood, and then, when I try to leave, you stop me. What *do* you want, Earl?"

"I just wish you acted *right,*" said Keese. "That's the only thing I've ever had against you, Harry. It's like that breakfast thing. I didn't even want any pancakes until you brought up the subject. Why did you mention them if you weren't going to make them after all? What's the point? To ingratiate yourself *at that moment,* to hell with the next? But the next always comes, doesn't it? And it reveals you as a liar."

"Earl," said Enid, "is this the time to be moralistic with Harry? He just lost his home."

Harry said: "That's when old Earl swings the boot—when a man's down."

Keese realized that there was some justice in the complaint. "O.K.," said he, "but I am being accused of arson. I'm going to defend myself. I tell you it was the Greavys, one or the other. They are degenerates. Funny, I didn't realize that until last night, though I've dealt with them for years."

Harry put his head on the side. "You're serious about this, aren't you?"

"Yes, I am," said Keese. "The old man hit me without warning in the pit of my stomach, and the son threatened me."

"First I heard of it," said Harry, with a puzzled look at Enid, who shrugged in return.

"Earl," said she, "why not have a bit of breakfast?"

Keese looked back and forth between them, as if they were playing table tennis. "You don't believe me, do you? Either of you." To Enid he said: "Yes, I'll have half a grapefruit, a lot of bacon and eggs, toast with butter and jam, and coffee."

"Uh-huh," said she.

"You don't have any food, do you?" he asked harshly. "You've taken up Harry's style. Some nerve!"

Enid rose and silently stole away.

"All right, Earl," said Harry, "suppose I believe your theory? What should I do?"

Acting on it had not occurred to Keese. He was momentarily embarrassed by the question—a failure which could do no good for Harry's sense of his reliability. "Well," he said finally, "we can at least tell the fire inspector of our suspicions."

"Ours?"

"Mine."

A noise not loud but massive came from outside. Keese left the house by the kitchen door and looked across to Harry's property. The building burned heartily, but a good deal of it was still there. The heat cast by the fire had increased, and the firemen continued to hose down Keese's house. They had pushed his car around back, and they had wet it as well and soaked the garage.

Keese went to Doc. "I thought I heard something."

Doc held a bullhorn and gestured with it. "Second story fell onto the first."

"Who runs the drugstore when you're here?"

"The boy. I'm semiretired anyway."

"You're doing a great job keeping my house out of it," said Keese. "Thanks, Doc."

" 'Chief,' " said Doc.

"Sorry. Chief . . . say, could I get you a cup of coffee?"

The chief said nobly: "Not when my boys don't get any. And you wouldn't have that much." He had everything well worked out.

"I'll have my wife make enough," Keese said. He went inside and told Enid.

She sighed. "You won't believe it."

Keese looked at her and his eyelids drooped. "You don't even have any coffee, do you?"

"All out, I'm afraid."

Keese blinked. "No humiliation is too petty to be denied me." He then noticed an absence. "Where's Harry?"

"He's looking for Elaine."

Keese felt a rush of terror. "Oh, no, he doesn't!" he cried, and went rapidly in search of his neighbor.

He found Harry in the upstairs hallway, lingering before the closed door of the master bedroom. Keese felt vulnerable when he remembered his moment with Ramona, though in all truth nothing had happened.

"Harry," he said, "feel free to use the bathroom to wash up. Then take any clothes of mine that'll fit you. My closet's on the left side of the bedroom."

Harry put a finger to his lips and pointed to the door with another. Keese came near. Harry beckoned him even closer and bent and whispered into his ear: "They're making a pair."

Keese suddenly understood he meant Ramona and Elaine.

CHAPTER 13/

KEESE rapped smartly on the door.

"Yes?"

"Which one is it?" He couldn't tell who it was from one word.

"Who wants to know?"

Keese regarded this answer as insolent. "I am the owner of this house!" Furthermore, he still couldn't identify the person on the other side of the door. All at once he understood why. The speaker was using falsetto!

He cried: "I demand to know who this is!"

"It's Baby," said the high-pitched voice. "I can speak only behind closed doors. If you see me, I'll never say another word. I'll just go *woof, woof!*"

This mockery caused Keese to lose his patience, and he would have entered the room without further ado had he been able to, but the door was locked.

"Look at this," he said to Harry, twisting the knob.

"They certainly seem to be hitting it off," Harry said.

Keese boiled over and attacked the door with both fists. "Get out, get out, get out!" Somewhere along the line he remembered the inner door that opened into the bathroom.

Could it be that they had overlooked it? He pounded once more for good luck, then dashed at the bathroom door. He had, from his angle, assumed it was ajar, but when he reached the entrance he found the door to be not only shut, but locked! In other words, they had themselves a little self-sustaining private suite under his roof.

"Look at this!" he said again to Harry.

Harry shook his head. He seemed utterly confused, and of course he was still filthy and dressed in what could be called, loosely, tatters. Keese doubted that Harry would be of much help to him, but it was good to have him there.

"The damnable thing is," Keese said, "I wanted to get you some clean clothes, Harry."

Harry shrugged, and then he smiled feebly. "Well, what does it matter, eh, Earl?"

Keese reflected that there was something noble in the man, to be so stoical in view of all that had happened. "Your luck can't always stay bad," he said, knowing it was a useless banality and in many cases not true: losing was routine enough.

Keese went back to the bedroom door and shouted at its off-white paneling: "How dare you commandeer the bathroom too?"

He was answered by Elaine, speaking in her normal voice. "Ramona is taking a bath, Daddy. For God's sake will you stop making a racket out there!"

He was silent for a moment, and then he said: "I'm ready to drive you to the bus station now. Let's go."

"That's just a ruse, Daddy," said Elaine. "Besides, I've decided not to go back to school. Actually, I haven't even been enrolled this entire term."

Keese turned to Harry. "Don't think you're the only one who has lost everything this weekend."

Harry said wisely: "She's just trying to impress Ramona, Earl. You know how they are—"

"Who?"

"Women."

Keese supposed it made sense. "Harry," he said now, "you're really helping. I wanted you to know that. I've been on my own too much. It's good to have a pal."

Harry squinted at him. "Sure you didn't burn my house down?"

"Aw . . ."

"Well," said Harry, "who wouldn't be suspicious? If I had left, you would have been the only man at the end of this street."

"But I was that before you came," said Keese. "I did not burn your house."

"I suppose it doesn't make much difference," Harry said. "It's destroyed. Now I've got to decide what to do, where to go. Funny, now that I've got no choice but to leave, I'm not all that eager to do so. This neighborhood is not the worst I've lived in."

"Good!" said Keese. "I'm glad you're beginning to think better of it."

"I've been here less than twenty-four hours," said Harry, "but already history has been made—and isn't that what makes a place a home?"

"Of course," Keese pointed out, "unusual incidents can take place on a vacation."

"But so many?" asked Harry. "And in such a sequence? We're talking of something more than getting the shits or buying fake antiques."

"You're right, of course," Keese said quickly. "You've made your mark here already: I didn't mean to cast doubt on that."

Harry put out his hand. "I know that's sincere, Earl. It took a long time to get around to this, but it's worth waiting for."

Keese shook hands with him. They were still standing in front of the bedroom door. Keese stuck his thumb at the door.

"I'm in a quandary," he said. "I don't know what to do about *them.*"

"Want me to handle it?" Harry suddenly asked.

"Would you?" Keese asked Harry. "After all . . ."

Harry smiled in a distant way. "Remember, Earl, when I was jealous? How I warned you to stay away from Ramona?"

Keese shrugged. "Well . . ."

"No, no," Harry said, "it doesn't bother me."

"The best thing I could do now, I think," Keese said, "would be to leave you here. I believe you would prefer to be alone for this job."

Harry said: "You're right about that, Earl. I'll get everything straightened out in short order, and when I do, I think my plans for the future will follow suit."

Keese waved at him and descended the stairs.

Enid was still in the kitchen. When he entered she said brightly: "I found some bouillon cubes!"

"All right, I'll have a cup then." He drew out a chair for himself. "Listen, Enid, suddenly it has all come together. This is quite exciting, really. It took all these things to happen for a whole new vista to open up before us. God, isn't it strange, though?"

"You've done enough now to set up suspense," said Enid. "Unless you tell me right now what you are talking about, the result will be an anticlimax."

"All right," said Keese. "Here it is—"

And she turned then and began to run water loudly into the teakettle. When this was done she clattered the kettle onto the stove, and then she made crockery noises in the cupboard where the cups were stacked.

Keese said: "I've decided to murder everybody and commit suicide." Just as he supposed, she went on making a pointless kitchen din. When she put a cup and saucer before him he picked them up and hurled them against the refrigerator.

"Will you listen?"

"You haven't become more reasonable throughout the morning," said Enid. "I hope this is not the beginning of another last night."

"We're going to move to the city!" Keese cried. "And Harry and Ramona are going to live here."

Enid swept up the fragments of crockery and disposed of them. She brought him a new cup and saucer. On her next trip she dropped an adamantine cube of bouillon into the cup and rushed it with steaming water.

"I don't hear your huzzas," said Keese, "and no wonder. It sounds demented on the face of it, I grant you." He smiled wildly and took a sip at, rather than of, his bouillon. The aroma was rather more medicinal than beefy. He lowered the cup. "Here's my thinking: we're on the verge of a new phase."

Enid made some bouillon for herself and sat down at the table across from him.

Keese went on. "And we are at that time of life when contracting our holdings makes the only sense. Why do we need three bedrooms, or a dining room, or two and a half baths? Why two stories? Why a yard?"

Enid sipped her bouillon. "Why indeed?"

"Perhaps you're being ironic," said Keese, "but if you reflect you'll see I'm right."

"That may well be," Enid said gravely.

"And this may shock you, but I don't intend to reveal our new address to Elaine."

"That would be unnatural," said Enid, "but, from your point of view, effective."

"You're damned right," Keese said vehemently. "She's almost twenty-two. How long are we required to keep rocking her cradle? When I think of the sacrifices we made . . ."

Enid frowned. "I can't think of a one."

"Still, the principle is valid," Keese said with heat. "And

we're growing stale here, Enid, with so-called friends like the Abernathys. We belong in a different kind of crowd, Enid: people with more depth but at the same time a lighter touch. Suavity without unctuousness, genial but responsible—I'm sure they can be found, but not out here."

"And Harry and Ramona will take this house?"

"Rent or purchase," said Keese, "it wouldn't matter to us. But what a favor to them! Harry is not the world's worst. I may have misjudged him. His ways are a bit eccentric at times, but that can be said of us all. The important thing is that, underneath it all, he means well, unlike so many of the people who pose as friends."

"You may be right," said Enid, "but he makes my flesh crawl."

Keese shook his head to clear his ears. He could not have heard that correctly. "I thought you liked him all the while I was having trouble with him?"

"Me?" asked Enid. "He turns my stomach."

"Well," said Keese, "you certainly like Ramona."

"That disgusting little bitch?" Enid made a face.

Keese did not want to become emotionally exercised again. He had had no sleep for more than twenty-four hours and nothing to eat. This bouillon smelled like kerosene and was already cold. "Then are you saying that we shouldn't turn over the house to these people?" he asked, as calmly as he could manage.

"No," said Enid, "I'm not saying that at all."

"Good," said Keese, "because I happen to think that my idea's flawless. It combines self-interest with care-for-others."

"And perhaps if Elaine is so attached to the place she might rent her old room from Harry and Ramona."

Keese peered closely at his wife, to see whether she might show a smirk of irony, but her face was expressionless. "Elaine will survive," said he. "I hope you are thinking of the advantages of living in the city: no matter where we are, we'll be near a novelty shop. Various public-library branches have collections that are peculiarly strong in certain subjects: magic, for example, or aeronautics. Scores of educational institutions offer courses in every imaginable subject: bookbinding, the folk dancing of all nations . . ."

"I'm not saying your idea is bad," said Enid, after drinking deliberately from her cup.

"*But,*" said Keese. "I feel a *but* coming on. . . ."

"I hope you won't take this as a slight," his wife said, "but I think I'll ask Harry and Ramona whether they might be willing to rent a room to me too."

Keese flapped his elbows, bird-fashion. "Then my plan is out of the question!"

"You're not moving to the city?"

"Not alone." He pushed away his bouillon and sighed. "I guess there's nothing I can do for Harry, then."

"You might have his car repaired."

Keese scowled. "I'm not looking forward to that: replacing an axle, wow. That won't be inexpensive." He laughed bitterly. "You see—between you and me—I was hoping to do him a favor from which I too would profit. Does that seem so terrible?"

"Who am I to say?" asked Enid. "Of all people."

Keese looked narrowly at her. "You've seen my dark side this weekend. I realize that your opinion of me has probably been altered."

Enid seemed startled. "Certainly not!"

He didn't know whether he liked that answer. On the one hand it was reassuring, but on the other it might be disingenuous. Of some of his stunts of the night before it would be no more than justice to say he had made an ass of himself, and to pretend otherwise did no service to him.

"I played the fool," he announced now. "This morning I see

things in a different light. This idea about moving represented my new approach—not so ponderous, so humorless, so, uh, passive. Why defend this place any further? Who cares? I wanted to turn it over to Harry and get a little apartment in town. But if you say no, so be it."

"I shudder to think of how those two would treat this place," said Enid.

"Now, isn't that funny? Yet you would rent a room from them."

"Yes," said Enid, "but in that case I would be a tenant."

"Uh-huh," said Keese. No doubt the distinction was more significant to her than to him. "In any case I never mentioned the idea to Harry," he said. "He probably would not have been interested. He claims that he likes it better here since his house burned down, but he was probably just being polite."

"Then you intend to stay?" Enid finished her bouillon with every suggestion of satisfaction.

"I don't have a choice," said he. "I don't mind admitting to you that I'm too incompetent to live alone."

"I don't know if I should take that as a compliment or not," Enid observed.

"You should," said Keese. He was not equipped to be more effusive. Indeed, even this much embarrassed him thoroughly. He got up from the table, opened the curtains of the window that looked onto Harry's property, and saw that of the house next door only half the ground floor remained, and that was blazing lustily.

"If we're going to stay," he said, "I guess I should try to patch things up with the Abernathys and the other people I insulted last night. I'll have to eat some crow, damn!"

"Are they worth it?"

"Probably not, but the way I see it if we stay we'll have no alternative but to go back to the old ways. My new concept was predicated on moving to the city. New friends, new pursuits and amusements. Speaking for myself, I might be able to walk to work. It would be a completely different way of life."

"Earl, I can see that you were really counting on this move," Enid said sympathetically. "Gosh, why deny yourself?"

"You mean, you'll come?"

"No, unfortunately, I can't. I'm too old."

"You're four years younger than I!"

"That was just a figure of speech," said Enid. "I don't like crowds."

"All right," said Keese, "then why discuss the matter? Can't you see you're being false? We'll stay and continue as before. There'll be some difference, of course: no more Walker place, the neighborhood landmark. Only a blackened ruin will be there now." He opened the curtains and looked out again. "I doubt that Harry will rebuild. He claims he likes it here better than he did, but even if he was being serious, will he spend that kind of money? Can he? The costs of new construction are prohibitive."

"What kind of work does he do?"

"I haven't the slightest idea!" cried Keese.

"I think he's a pimp," said Enid.

This was so unexpected that Keese burst into a guffaw of embarrassment. His own car, after all, had been painted with that term. Could Greavy have mistaken it for Harry's automobile, or was it merely one of those fortuitous strokes with which life abounds?

"Elaine insists he's a cop, on the other hand," Keese said. "But what interests me most is how you've turned against the man."

"I told you all along that I was playing for time, and wasn't I right?" Enid went to the stove and lighted the gas under the kettle. "Wasn't that bouillon delicious! Do you want another cup?"

"What do you mean, weren't you right?"

"Well, hasn't he lost all his worldly goods by now?"

"Shouldn't that make you more sympathetic to the poor devil?"

"If fate has turned against him," Enid said, "I'm somewhat apprehensive of being his friend."

"How ruthless!" Keese said. "You really shock me, Enid."

"Would you habitually walk across an open field during rainstorms with a person who had often been struck by lightning? Isn't common sense to be considered?"

"But unless you're a religious fanatic of some sort, it doesn't mean that he's evil."

"What's morality have to do with it?" Enid asked. "I'm speaking of self-preservation." The kettle was already spewing steam. She turned it off and fetched the the vial of bouillon cubes. "Do you want another cup?"

"No thanks," said Keese, "tasty as it is." He wished to keep on her good side, cowed as he was by her apparent heartlessness.

Someone knocked on the kitchen door. Keese saw the fire chief through the glass. He opened up.

"We're pulling out," said the chief. "It'll burn for a time yet, but the emergency's past. Your home is out of danger."

"Safe for you to go?"

"We've got another call," said the chief. "Could leave one man here to keep an eye on it, if you'd feel better. Could leave Perry Greavy."

Keese asked himself: *Is there no one else in town?* But to Doc, the chief, he said: "We'll keep an eye on it ourselves."

"Reason to leave Perry," said Doc, "is he feels responsible."

"Oh, he does, does he?"

"He came to move Harry, you see, and he saw him smoking near an open can of paint remover, throwing matches down."

"Harry doesn't smoke," said Keese to Doc, who stood there in his white helmet and black boots, one step down.

"He was puffing on a pipe."

"That's what Perry says, does he?"

"I don't know about that," said Doc, "but that's what Harry was smoking when he came into the pharmacy this morning."

"He was in your drugstore?"

"He bought a can of tobacco," said Doc. "Well, we've got to get to this call over on Sprague." He turned and slopped away in his large boots.

Keese closed the door and brooded awhile. "Gosh," he finally said to Enid. "I hate to say this, but my old feeling about Harry might be coming back."

Enid gasped. "Not that! Please don't start that fighting again and locking people up!"

"You're right about that," he said. "I don't intend to lose control. But could you hear what the chief said?"

"Was that Doc, from the drugstore?"

"Yes, he's the fire chief. He doesn't want to be called Doc in this role."

"I heard him," said Enid.

"Could it be that Harry decided, since he was leaving the house, to burn it for the insurance? Does that make sense?"

"I wonder," said Enid.

Keese slapped himself on the leg. "This is lousy! The guy is doing me a favor at this very moment! Anyway, it's his business, isn't it? And no one got hurt. I hate to have suspicious feelings towards somebody; they prey on my mind and have a corrosive effect." No sooner had he finished this statement than a wild peal of laughter came from upstairs. "Was that Elaine or Ramona?" he asked. "I can never tell unless they say more."

"Search me," said Enid, but she frowned. "Do you like the sound of that? He burns his house to the ground and then comes over here and makes girls laugh?"

"Funny," said Keese, "but I find it reassuring. I doubt that an arsonist would be so carefree. But no one got hurt. I keep coming back to that. If Harry did it, then at least he is not the callous kind of fellow who would burn up other people for his own gain. It's important to remember that, because he's under our roof at the moment."

"Have I got it straight now?" Enid asked, moving her empty cup as if it were the counter in a game. "*Even if* Harry burned down his house, he's still O.K. with you, and you like him?"

"The only thing that hurts is that he accused *me* of setting the fire. That's pretty dishonest if he did the thing himself, and in any case it leaves something to be desired as a friend and neighbor, that he'd suspect me first of all."

Enid leaned forward and asked earnestly: "But you did do it, didn't you, Earl?"

Keese slammed his hands down and pushed himself erect. "This whole line of conversation was a trick of yours, wasn't it?" He left the kitchen and went to see how his friend was handling the situation upstairs.

On his way to the front hallway he heard the laughter again and the sound of running feet.

"What's going on up there?" he cried jovially, not expecting to be heard or, in any event, answered. But as he came up the stairs he saw Ramona.

"Playing hide-and-go-seek," she said. "If you want in, you're It."

"I haven't played this in forty years," said Keese. "Think of it." On an impulse of foolishness he agreed. "Now go and hide."

"You must turn away and put your hands in front of your eyes," said Ramona.

Keese went to face the wall. He shut his eyes and put his hands over them. "One . . . two . . . three . . ." At ten he halted: was that enough? He couldn't remember.

He had heard no sound whatever from Ramona, not footsteps nor noise of door. In fact he expected to open his eyes and find her waiting there to leap at Home—there were always children who had done that: it had never seemed right to him.

He opened his eyes and whirled. The hall was empty, and the two visible doors were open. The bedroom-bathroom complex was an especially tricky arrangement, which made this one a player's game and put It under a decided handicap. If you penetrated too much of the bedroom, the bathroom exit would be unguarded, and vice versa. The nimble hider could always keep a partition between himself and the seeker—but only if he could tell where the other was from the sound. Keese went up onto tiptoe. He remembered with pride that he had been reasonably cunning at this as a child. And though he was now larger by a hundred fifty pounds, he had that not unusual attribute of the fat man in lightness of foot. The master bedroom was the closer enclosure: by taking his post just inside its door he could guard the entire field of play.

He entered the bedroom and searched it insofar as he could without getting too far from the door. Silently he slipped into the hall and over to the bedroom threshold. But the unseen prey had apparently anticipated his move and crossed into the bedroom through the inner door. Quickly, then!

He dashed at the banister. . . . But no one raced him for it.

It occurred to him that his assessment of the situation had been utterly in error: no one had been hiding in either bedroom or bath. He headed up the hallway, towards Elaine's room . . . and behind him he heard the triumphant shrieks of the players who came from nowhere to get Home Free.

He could hardly believe the disappointment, even the bitterness, he felt. But he certainly did his best to conceal it. "Well," said he, returning, "you gave me the works, didn't you? Of course it's been years since I played this."

Slightly flushed and grinning, Harry said: "You'll do better next time." He wasn't rubbing it in: he really was staying a friend. He was, incidentally, still wearing his torn clothes from the fire, nor had he so much as wiped the soot from his face. But the costume did give him, for all his size, a kind of street-urchin air that was appropriate to the game.

But Elaine made an ugly face. "Are you kidding? He'll never get me!"

"We'll see, Elaine, we'll see," Keese said. Suddenly he realized that Ramona wasn't there. If he could beat her he would not remain It. "Shh!" he cautioned the others, with a finger to his lips. He peeped into the bedroom again, and next the bath, but these were perfunctory gestures: obviously, if she had been with Elaine and Harry she would already have run Home with them. He went up the hall again, and no sooner had he passed the bathroom than Ramona ran from it and joined the little group at the head of the banister. Elaine cheered her raucously. But Harry was almost apologetic.

"It's your first time in a while, Earl," he said. "Takes some getting onto."

"What hurts is I *thought* I looked carefully into those rooms!" Keese said, trying to show good humor. He remembered why Harry was here, and he realized that his friend had been successful in getting the girls to open the bedroom door and engage in this harmless game. All was going well, then; it was not necessary that he win at hide-and-go-seek. Yet . . .

"Who's on for another round?" he cried. "I don't want to quit while I'm the goat!"

This time he was more thorough in searching the bedroom, and Elaine and Harry escaped via the bathroom and scored. Then Keese penetrated the bath, and Ramona leaped from the bedroom to get Home Free.

"By God," said Keese, who was scant of breath now, "skunked again!" He grinned savagely at the runner rug: he had suddenly got a vengeful idea. "Have you got guts for another?" he shouted.

"You're the one who needs that," said Elaine. "*We're* winning."

But again Harry was mollifying. "Hell, Earl, it's just a game. Nobody's scoring permanently off anybody."

And even Ramona said: "Now don't get too desperate, Earl. If you want, I'll take over as It. I don't mind." The game seemed to have sweetened her.

"Oh, no," said Keese, "not until I beat at least one of you." He went against the wall, covered his eyes, and counted. He heard suppressed giggles and gasps, muffled footsteps, and what suggested a silent tussle. Having reached ten, he opened his eyes, stepped over to the bedroom threshold, reached behind the door, and removed the key. He then closed the door and locked it from the outside. His vengeful glee could not be denied. He chuckled audibly as he entered the bathroom. He searched this enclosure thoroughly, though there was nowhere, apart from the shower curtain, where anybody could hide.

"I've got you now!" he gloated as he entered the bedroom by the inner door. But no one was flushed from hiding. Indeed, as a subsequent search established, no one had hidden in that room.

He took the key from his pocket and unlocked the door from inside. He expected to see the three of them in a cluster at the top of the banister, awaiting his display of chagrin, but the hallway was empty. He felt he had been granted a magical reprieve. His trick, which had been both unfair and unsuccessful, the maximum in failure, would at least remain unknown. He went down the hall in a stride that could be called jaunty. He was in a commanding position: they were in a cul-de-sac now, and he was between them and Home.

He found Ramona immediately, merely by opening the door of Elaine's bedroom. She sat at the dressing table, face very near the mirror, applying a bluish tint over her eyes with a tiny paddle.

"Have you forgotten the game?" asked Keese, posing himself for the dash to the banister-end.

"No," said Ramona. "You've beat me, so you're off the hook. You're no longer It." She smiled flutteringly at him in the mirror.

"Come on," he said, "that's no game. I don't want to win without competing. It's not that much different from losing."

"The old game is over, Earl," said Ramona. "We'll have to start a new one. That is, of course, if you insist on playing a game of some kind."

Keese sat down on the bed behind her. "No, of course I don't. I was just going along with it to be one of the crowd. I don't need games. In fact, I haven't played any since I was a child."

"Then we'll just be quiet together," said she, turning on the stool to face him. "Did you ever do that with anybody? It's *very* nice."

Ramona was revealing unsuspected depths, but he suddenly thought about the other players. "I'd like to try that," he said. "But hadn't I better tell Harry and Elaine? They're still hiding somewhere."

"Don't worry about them," Ramona said breezily.

"Have they quit?"

"They're gone."

"Gone?"

"We won't see them again," said Ramona. "They have left in your car. Elaine had a key. Harry made a trade."

"Trade?"

"Yes," said Ramona. "For me."

CHAPTER **14**/

KEESE asked: "This isn't another game of some kind?"

"Not really," said Ramona.

He sighed deeply. "When I think of how I'd have felt if this had happened yesterday! . . . But the strange thing now is, well, I should be ashamed to say it, I suppose, but I am actually relieved."

Ramona looked at him with what might have been identified as affection. "I think we all, in our hearts, felt that you would react that way, Earl."

"You did?" In embarrassment Keese coughed into his hand.

"Everybody wishes you well." Ramona leaned across from her stool as if she might touch him, but it seemed that she couldn't decide where, and she withdrew.

"Not the Greavys!"

"They are not among my circle of acquaintances out here," said Ramona. "But then, I don't know anybody here except you and your family."

"I feel much the same way," said Keese, "even though I've lived in these parts since time out of memory. But I assumed from what they said that you were thick as thieves with the Abernathys."

"Harry maybe. He's the popular one."

"But since he just moved here, how'd he know them?"

"Harry will meet a lot of people if he stops for gas or buys a loaf of bread. He has friends everywhere. He'll stop some stranger to ask directions and they'll give him a valuable present."

"Hmm," said Keese, "I guess I didn't measure up in that respect—even if you are exaggerating."

"Listen, you should see the watches and rings and cameras—" She lost her grin. "I guess they're all burned up now."

Yes, thought Keese, *so the story can't be checked.* But the principle might well be valid, that Harry was instantly likable to most mortals. Keese was not really ashamed not to be counted amongst the herd, if so. An affection that required a bit more in effort would seem to be worth more.

"Say, Ramona, where do you think he might be going?"

"Harry? I don't know." Ramona smiled. "This is a big country, and it's wide open."

"Of course, that's easy enough to say," Keese noted, "but in point of fact most people tend to move in patterns and act in rituals. And then a lot depends on one's profession: you'll find few cotton pickers in northern Minnesota, I'd say, or snow-shovel salesmen in Key West." He cleared his throat and said: "I see you're not going to bite. You're not going to tell me what Harry does?"

"He doesn't like it," said Ramona with a straight face. "He wants to get into something more creative."

"Does he have any special qualifications?"

"Don't expect a little thing like that to stop him!" She shook her head. "If you knew Harry like I did—"

"Won't you miss him?" asked Keese. "He really is an interesting guy."

Ramona deliberated for a moment, and then she said: "It's time for a new phase."

Keese was struck by her use of the term. He slapped his hands together. "You won't believe this, but I said the same thing just a few minutes ago to Enid."

"There you are!" cried Ramona.

He had begun to find himself at ease with her—which is more than he could say of his associations with either of his own women in recent hours.

He rose from his seat on the bed. "You wouldn't be hungry, would you? I haven't eaten for a whole day."

"Sure I am!" She jumped up and linked arms with him. "That's a terrific idea, Earl."

"Oh, damn." He sagged. "Harry took my car, and his won't run. We can't go anywhere to get food. Isn't that lousy?" He shook his chin at her. "I tell you, Enid has always been a good wife, but she really has let me down starting yesterday. Imagine not having enough food on hand to make a decent dinner Friday night. I work hard all week. Now here it is, Saturday . . ." He looked at the little electric alarm clock on Elaine's bedside table. ". . . *One* P.M., for God's sake! Can that be right?"

"We had a box of stuff," said Ramona, "but I guess it's been burned up. The spaghetti came from that, and the sauce and meatballs. There was also some oxtail soup and black bean with sherry and shrimp bisque, and cocktail franks and an aerosol can of that cheese that comes out like toothpaste and Argentine corned beef and frozen sukiyaki."

"Makes me feel worse to hear that list," said Keese. "But there must be something in the fridge downstairs or the cupboards: raisins or anchovy paste or macaroni elbows, blanched almonds, bread-and-butter pickles, dry yeast, caraway seeds, or extract of vanilla."

"Of course that's not really food."

"Damn! Maple syrup, piccalilli, chili sauce, reconstituted lemon juice. . . ."

"You're just tormenting yourself, Earl."

"I was trying to find some edible combination or version of those items."

"If you've got ketchup and hot water you can make tomato soup," said Ramona. "That's a free dish at a restaurant."

"Or the old college thing of my day," said Keese. "Bread and butter, which used to be provided as soon as you sat down and picked up the menu, covered with the maple syrup that in many places was available all day long in its little metal pitcher with the hinged lid. Get it? French toast! Free."

"Oh, yeah," said Ramona, "I guess you could actually toast the bread with a match."

He was having a good time with this nonsense. Enid had been more receptive to that sort of thing when younger. Ramona was turning out to be a valuable addition to the household.

"Well," he said, "shall we go downstairs and rummage around in the cupboards?"

Ramona was all for it. Keese liked people, especially women, who were cooperative when it came to new ventures. They went down to the kitchen.

"Now where's Enid got to?" he asked rhetorically. He wanted to see her reaction when she learned of Elaine's replacement by Ramona.

Ramona said: "She went with Harry."

Keese took this as a joke: he had not even put the question to her. He opened a cupboard door and found a jar of grated Parmesan cheese. "Hey," he said, "here's another free meal. In an Italian restaurant, see: those shakers of grated cheese on every table. Put on bread, with ketchup: pizza, right?"

"Hey, yeah," said Ramona. She went to the neighboring cabinet and opened its door. "Capers? Stewed tomatoes? Cocktail onions? Sauce Diable?"

"Damn," said Keese, "cornstarch isn't food, nor cream of

tartar." He closed the doors. "We'll have to get Enid's help on this."

"At least Harry *said* he was going to invite her along. If she's gone, that must be where."

Keese thought about this for a moment, and then he said: "You should be flattered: you replaced them both."

She replied without smugness: "Harry thinks a lot of me."

"Hmm," Keese muttered. He staggered to a chair and sat down. "The full realization is just hitting me."

"Would you like a drink of water?" asked Ramona, looking at him with concern.

Keese said: "I don't mean to be rude."

"I know that, Earl," she said. "You're a gentleman. I have always admired that about you. Fond as I am of Harry, I have to admit he's kind of a thug."

"Oh, I wouldn't say that."

"Uncouth, you know?" She cleared her throat. "Want me to go on looking?"

"Huh?"

"For edible combinations, you know?"

"Oh," said Keese, "you won't find anything. I have that feeling."

"Why don't I walk to town and get some food?"

"It's three miles round trip," Keese said, "and on the return route you'd be carrying a load."

"Can't you call a cab?"

"God," he exclaimed, "you see how stupefied I am after all the surprises added to my lack of meals and sleep? Look in the phone book. There must be a taxi service, though when you live here you never use one."

Ramona went to the counter near the wall phone, where the directory lay. "That's what I hate about the country," she said. "All the shit about cars." She lifted the book and began to leaf through the yellow section. "Haha! Greavy's Garage!"

"What's that got to do with a cab?"

"It's under the heading of 'Taxi Service.'" Ramona looked owlishly at him over the opened telephone directory.

"That's in error," said Keese.

"No," said Ramona, "it's listed right here. I'll call them."

"No," cried Keese, "you must not. They are bad people. Perverts, degenerates, fiends. You don't want to ride in their cab. They will molest or maim you. They will beat you savagely."

"But why?" Ramona grimaced in puzzlement.

"Merely to exercise their love of wreaking mayhem," said Keese.

"Do such people operate businesses that deal with the public?" she asked in disbelief. "How can they get away with beating up their customers?"

"A good question," said Keese. He realized he had bitten off more than he could chew. "They can't. They don't actually have a taxi service. The listing is a hoax."

Ramona's upper lip disappeared under her nose. "*Really?* Well, why? What's the joke?"

"They used to have a legitimate cab service, but they've given it up since that edition of the directory was published."

"Why didn't you tell me that in the first place?" asked Ramona. "You have some ways that take getting used to, Earl." She smiled affectionately at him. "But you're sweet. And I suspect that it's really that you don't want me to leave even for as long as it would take to get some food. Now *that's* flattering."

Suddenly she was on his lap, her hands snaking around his neck.

Keese could feel himself blush so furiously that he pulled his face away, so as not to singe her. "I had hoped I wouldn't have to tell you this," said he, "but I have a venereal disease."

"So have I," Ramona said enthusiastically, not budging.

"You think that's another ruse," said he. Actually he could feel the bones of her rump in an odd and uncomfortable way. His first motive for wishing her off him was to remove a cause of pain.

"Come on, Earl."

"I'm a deviate."

"So am I."

"All right, I'm not really."

"Me neither."

"You don't have to echo me, Ramona. It may seem ridiculous to you, but I can't simply jump into bed with you just like that, though I know I was provoked into doing so this morning. But I am in a state of calm at this moment." He gently dislodged her from his lap. "I could if I knew you better or on the other hand hardly knew you at all. Does that make sense?"

"Sure," said Ramona, returning to her chair. "Like being madly in love *or* picking up a whore."

"I suppose that's it."

"We see eye to eye on every single detail," said Ramona.

Keese pondered on this for a while, and found an exception to the rule. "But I must confess I don't really like dogs."

"You mean certain kinds of dogs. Or certain dogs. Neither do I."

She had nailed him, all right. Of course dogs in general were very likable. Only particular examples, shitting on one's lawn, snapping at one's ankles, were obnoxious. He had no pleasure in taking the ultimate step.

"Forgive me, Ramona, but I don't like Baby."

"Then everything's perfect," she cried. "Harry took him along too!"

"Then there really isn't a living thing left at this end of the road but you and me!" Keese got up and ambled around the kitchen. "Makes you think, doesn't it?"

"It's a big relief, for my money," said she. "Now only one style is needed. You don't have to placate the whole world."

Keese stopped and looked at her. "You really can be eloquent, Ramona. I never heard it put that way before."

"Not that I won't miss Baby!" she cried. "But I thought with Harry he'd have advantages he could never get out here with me."

"I wonder how Harry will *really* get along with Enid and Elaine?" Keese asked of the air. To Ramona he said: "Strange, isn't it? It's all so *goddamned strange.*"

"Harry's one in a million," she said smiling.

"I imagine he'll dominate them," said Keese. "That was his manner when sitting in this kitchen last night. He was very masterful. And they knuckled under—or at least pretended to. Enid claimed it was just courtesy, but I don't know."

"Oh, Harry makes his wants known, but I'll say this: he doesn't hold a grudge."

"I realize that," Keese said sheepishly. "He was pretty good about my blunders last night."

A knock came at the back door. When Keese opened up he saw Perry Greavy, still in his fire helmet and carrying the special axe for fires, blade on one side, spike on the other.

"You'll see smoke for maybe a couple days, and thell be live coals for a while, but theys nothing left much to burn. So it's safe enough unless the wind should blow up."

Perry said all of this in a decent manner, and Keese saw no reason not to be civil in return. "Thanks. You fellows did one whale of a good job."

Perry's piggish face, still clean, grew pink. (Obviously, despite the axe, he had not been in the thick of things.) "You're being sarcastic again."

"Oh, come on." Keese sighed wearily.

"It burnt to the ground, didn't it? So that was the good job we done, you—"

Keese broke in before the vicious word (whatever it was) could be uttered. He shouted: "I mean, you saved my house by wetting it down, didn't you?"

"Oh, that." Perry sneered at the ground.

Keese had stopped him in his tracks. Now for the kill— But no! That was precisely the wrong way. No *coups de grâce*, not even a telling thrust. It was a new era.

He put out his open hand. "I'm really grateful to you, Perry. I'll say more: we're all in your debt around here. You and your dad practically run the town."

But Perry ignored the outthrust hand, and said surlily: "I could use a cuppa coffee after all that work."

Keese retrieved his hand and put it at his chin. "By golly," he said ruefully, "we've got bouillon, but not any coffee."

"Bullion?" Perry asked belligerently. "You mean tea?"

"No," said Keese. "Beef broth."

"You blowhole!" Perry cried with violent emotion. "Did I ask for soup?" He fingered the handle of his axe, as if he could hardly restrain himself from swinging it. "Don't have any coffee? They is nobody who don't have coffee, you skunk-dump you."

"Who is that?" cried Ramona from behind. From her angle she could not see Perry. "And what does he want?"

"Coffee," said Keese.

"We don't have any. We only have bouillon."

Keese turned back to Perry Greavy. "There you are," he said. "I'm telling the truth."

Perry squinted malevolently at him.

Keese rolled his eyes and turned. "Ramona, will you please step over here?"

She arrived. Perry stared at her and actually licked his lips. "Got a cuppa coffee for me?" he asked.

"No, I don't have anything for you."

"Sure?"

Ramona asked Keese: "Where'd you find this hillbilly?"

"Honey," said Perry, "you got the mouth of a smart-fart."

Keese leaned close to her and said: "Don't whip him up. He's a kook."

Ramona shrugged and went inside. Perry hacked up a gob of vileness and spat it on the ground.

"Say," he asked Keese, "where'd you find a whore like that out here?"

"Don't talk like that," said Keese. "We're doing you no harm."

Ramona returned. She held the largest butcher knife from the Keese kitchen. "Hey, rube," she said to Perry, "I'm gonna cut you." She seemed in ebullient spirits, grinning and waving her weapon.

Perry lowered his axe. "I didn't mean anything."

"You put the fire out?"

"Yes, ma'am." Perry dropped the axe altogether and removed his helmet, holding it before his belly in both hands.

"Then haul your ass out of here," said Ramona, "and don't come back unless there's another blaze."

"O.K.," said Perry.

"And don't forget," Ramona said. "You know why?"

"No, ma'am."

"Because I got your number," said she. She took Keese's arm and led him inside the kitchen, where she threw the knife clattering into the sink.

Keese said: "You certainly took care of him."

"I despise that type," said she. "No class. Now, where were we?" She scratched her temple. "Eat! We were thinking of how to get to town to get something to eat. Hey, we could hitch a ride with that asshole: he must have transportation."

"Naw," said Keese, "that would make me uncomfortable. Besides, he might even now be planning a savage revenge."

"Not him," said Ramona. "He's done, mark my words. I cooked his goose."

"Is that right?"

"It's the idea, see," she said.

"Oh, yes?"

"That's exactly it." She smiled at him.

"Now I know your secret," said Keese. "So you can't use it on me."

"Oh, you do, do you?" She put her hands on her slender hips and rocked back and forth, producing a Santa Claus laugh: "Hohoho."

He found himself liking her immensely. Now that they were alone, just the two of them at the end of the road, what had previously seemed disagreeable about her, perhaps even warped, now appeared as robust, freewheeling in the good sense, and above all, generous.

"You haven't worn your turban for a while," said he.

"Better with or without?"

"Without, I think, but I like it *with* a lot too."

"Elaine swiped it from me," said Ramona.

"Uh-huh," said Keese. "I'm afraid that's her problem." He lost at least some of his good humor. "It is certainly an obstacle in her path to achievement."

"I think she wanted to impersonate me. That's the real reason I let them take Baby."

"He goes with the turban?"

"Well, it's a style," said Ramona. "You know."

"Sequences are all-important, too," Keese pointed out, "and timing in general."

"I'll tell you this, Earl," Ramona said, "I'm getting hungry as hell."

"Damn right!" Keese cried. "I'm going to call a cab from Allenby to take us to the city! Can you imagine the cost of that? We'll sumptuously wine and dine and stay at the finest hostelry. We'll roam the boulevards with a supercilious smile for all, and glide through smart shops exchanging glib remarks. I'll sport a thin Malacca cane and thrash anyone showing insolence."

"Your concepts seem to date from a bygone era," said Ramona, "but I like them, Earl."

"Well then," he said, "I'd better get into some decent clothes." He felt his unshaven chin.

"On the other hand," said Ramona, "it's certainly comfortable right here. It's not really necessary to go all the way to the city."

"Uh-huh," Keese said. "Are you telling me you'd *rather* stay here? It's just that I thought of you as the city type."

"But to go in on Saturday from the country is not a city thing, if you see what I mean."

Keese leaned against the refrigerator. "Yes," said he, "it's a thing done by people who live in the country. . . . We don't have to go to the city. There's a well-known restaurant outside Allenby."

"Would that be La Nourriture?"

"Yes, it would," said Keese. "You've eaten there?"

"Only a hamburger," said Ramona. "It was O.K."

"The place I meant is luxurious and expensive," said he, somewhat peeved by her obvious confusion of it with a lunch counter. "Their dishes run to turbot and saddle of lamb and asparagus soufflé."

"I just had the hamburger," said Ramona. "It wasn't bad, either."

"I have to get cleaned up and dressed," Keese said. He went upstairs and shaved and showered. He donned a tan suit, a blue shirt, and a blue necktie figured in tan.

He returned to the kitchen. He saw Ramona through the window and went out to join her. The ruins were still smoking, as Perry Greavy had predicted. Keese touched Ramona's shoulder.

"It really is too bad," he said. "You didn't even get a chance to live there one whole day."

"I don't give a damn about that," Ramona said. "I was just thinking about Baby. Maybe I made a mistake. I really miss him."

They returned to the kitchen. Keese seized the phone book and looked in the Ns and could not find La Nourriture, then searched the Ls and found the number.

When the answer came he asked: "Are you still serving lunch?"

"As a policy or with reference to today?" This voice was accented and male.

"A table for two, please, as soon as we can get there."

"No, no, you will not find admittance. It is complete for today."

"It's too late?"

"Go away."

"Now, don't be rude."

"*Launch is gone away,*" cried the voice. "Kiss my phallus."

"How dare you abuse me?" cried Keese.

"This is no malice, I repeat," said the man. "We close. Eat tit! Closed!" Or had he said: "I repeat it"?

Keese gave him the benefit of the doubt. "I'm sorry to have bothered you," he said. "I didn't look at my watch."

"*Merde!*" shouted the voice. "I do not wish to look into your crotch!" The line went abruptly dead.

Keese turned slowly. "They think it's chic to misunderstand. I suppose that seems charming to a vulgar kind of clientele, but I won't put up with it."

"Couldn't make a connection?" Ramona asked indifferently. She had obviously lost all interest in going to lunch.

"I got all cleaned up," Keese said. He had inspected his clothed person in the full-length mirror behind the bathroom door. Oddly enough the scales had told him that after twenty-four hours without food he weighed a pound and a half more than he had a day earlier. Still, he was always slenderized by a suit. "Sure a relief to get those old clothes off," he said, "and shave."

Ramona said impatiently: "I think I'll go out for a walk."

"You don't want me to call the Allenby taxi?"

"If you want to."

Keese sighed and loosened the knot of his tie, though knowing full well that just such a minor adjustment would make a man of his figure look like a tramp. "It's not successful, is it, Ramona?"

"It's probably too early to say."

"I don't think it's working out."

"Well, Earl, all it takes is one person to kill it."

"You're blaming me?" Keese looked at the floor. "You may be right, but let me point out that I wasn't consulted on the arrangement in the first place. When I first heard of it it was already an accomplished fact. You might say I have no great responsibility to make it work."

"I hope you're not insulting me," said Ramona.

"You're doing a good job!" said Keese. "I think you're a fine girl, Ramona. I really like you."

"But I'm not right here?"

"Well," said Keese, "it's—"

"I agree," she said. "I'm wrong here. I don't know why, but I'm wrong."

"I wouldn't use that word," Keese said.

Ramona shrugged. "I'm going for a walk."

"Towards the village?"

"I don't know. Why?"

"I was thinking," said he. "I wouldn't want to load you down, but do you think a roll or two might be possible, and a few slices of liverwurst?"

She shook her head. "I don't want to bother with that, Earl."

"Mixed nuts?" Keese pleaded. "Couple small plastic bags?"

"Naw," said Ramona. "Too much trouble. Sorry." She smiled vaguely and slipped out the back door.

Keese stared dully after her for a while, and then, alone in the house, he knew no restraint. He found a patch of bare kitchen wall, and he threw a tantrum against it, pounding with both fists and stamping on the floor, crying: "No food . . . no sleep . . . no company." But part of this was in irony, for he did not forget at any moment that he had lived half a century: the old carefree rages of childhood were no longer accessible.

When he had had enough of this he thought he would go upstairs and change into the old clothes once more: a suit and tie seemed to mock his current existence.

But before he moved Ramona came in from outdoors.

"Harry's coming back!" she said.

"Alone?"

"I'm sure that Baby is with him."

What an egoist she was! "I wonder about my women," said he.

"How do I know?" said she. "I just see the car coming."

CHAPTER **15/**

WHEN Keese got
outside, the car was turning into his drive. Harry saw him and
sounded the horn. He pulled up around back and leaped out.

The rear doors of Keese's automobile were flung open simultaneously and Enid emerged from the left one; Elaine from the
right, leading the wolfhound.

Harry led Keese around to the trunk. He was dressed in
fresh, perhaps even new clothing, and his face was clean. Even
his black eye seemed to have faded somewhat.

He unlocked and raised the lid of the trunk. "Take a look
at this," said he.

A mélange of fragrances assaulted Keese's nostrils, and he
saw paper bags, cardboard boxes, and containers molded from
shiny substances, even makeshift carriers fashioned from pairs
of paper plates with facing concavities, lids stapled.

"Lend a hand," said Harry, beginning to fill his arms with
burdens.

Keese lost his appetite immediately. Nevertheless he took an
armload of food and carried it indoors. Neither Enid nor Elaine
turned a finger. His daughter, not wearing the turban, but
leading Baby on a long leash that looked thin as a hair, went
to Ramona and kissed her on the mouth. Enid, dressed in a suit

that was the female counterpart of his own, presumably had gone upstairs.

Two trips each were required of Harry and Keese. On their second, the latter said: "You got an awful lot."

Harry plucked up several candy-striped bags. "The way things have gone for us this weekend, we must always shop with a catastrophe in mind."

Keese arranged a series of cardboard boxes along his forearm, which he held close against his chest. They had all the earmarks of Chinese provender. He had already carried in what from the aroma and leaking sauces would seem Mexican, and still left in the trunk were the flat pizza containers, the stapled pie plates holding whatever, the very white boxes imprinted with a baker's name in blue, and the standard brown bags dispensed by supermarkets and delicatessens.

"May I ask a question?" Keese said, looking over the burdens in his arms. "Your intention just now, from start to finish, was only to go for food?"

"What else could it have been?" asked Harry.

"Enid and Elaine went along for the ride?"

"They were in the market for an outing," said Harry. "Say, Allenby is quite the metropolis, isn't it?"

"Then you weren't heading for the horizon, but got cold feet and turned back, and picked up this food merely so you'd have an excuse for the trip?" Harry stared silently at him as they walked towards the house. "Forgive me," Keese said. "I'm thinking out loud and obviously not to the point."

They entered the kitchen. Keese felt a further explanation was necessary. "I didn't mean to cast aspersions," he said. "It's just that someone tried to give me an impression which seems to have been chicane."

"Sounds like Ramona," Harry said, putting his goods on the kitchen counter. "She tends to heighten the moment if she can manage it." He dug into one of the bags and produced what he proceeded to term "a flask of fiery spirits."

"I'll get glasses," Keese said. "What are we drinking?"

"Rum, me hearty!" Harry cried, as if from the thicket of a beard, and he raised one foot and hopped about the kitchen with the implication that he had a peg leg, and he shouted snatches of bogus sea-talk: "Belay that! Avast, ye lubbers!"

Keese returned from the dining-room cabinet with two squat tumblers.

"Reef the t'gallant!" cried Harry. "Lower the tops'l and top the bottoms'l." He poured Keese a generous serving of his amber potion and took an ample measure for himself.

"Ice and mix?" asked Keese.

"Never!" cried Harry. He threw back his head and drained the glass.

Keese prudently sipped at his own: he had nothing in his stomach. Moreover, he had drunk no spirits in ages.

Harry smacked his lips and said: "Now for a gastronomic tour of the world." He began to open bags and boxes. "Cooked," said he, "by the scum of all nations."

Keese toasted him. "For a man who has just lost all his material possessions, your morale is incredible. Have you decided to rebuild with the insurance money?"

"I didn't have any insurance on that house," said Harry.

"No, no," said Keese, "that's impossible. The bank wouldn't give you a mortgage."

"I didn't have a mortgage," Harry said. He unwrapped a Chinese egg roll and inserted one end into his mouth, dropping his hands.

"You paid *cash?*"

Harry bit off the end of the egg roll. The larger piece fell into the cupped hands he brought from nowhere, just in time. He chewed for a moment.

"I didn't own it," he said.

"Rent?"

Harry finally swallowed what he was chewing. "The old lady went to a nursing home when the old man died, right? Then she died, and they didn't have any heirs, so the house went to the state. Well, the red tape will take years to unravel."

Keese drank a hearty share of the rum in his glass, almost all of it, in fact. "Can I be right," he asked, "in my feeling that you and Ramona simply moved in over there without any financial arrangement?"

"All they could have done was throw us out," said Harry. "You don't get the electric chair for trespassing on public property."

"God damn," Keese said in admiration, striking the countertop and reaching for the bottle. "You're all right, Harry." He opened the bag and found half a chicken breast. This was sensible, with rum on an empty stomach. But the chicken was dead cold, with a dull glaze of grease over its insipid breading. Keese got no further than one bite. But he didn't want a case to be made of this: therefore, when Harry was getting something more to eat for himself, Keese slipped the piece of chicken into one of the empty brown bags in which another item of food had been transported.

"How's the Kentucky Fried cluck-cluck?" asked Harry. He had yet to make his next choice. He turned and saw no chicken in Keese's hands. "God, what a trencherman you are!" He seized the bottle and poured more rum for Keese. "Better wash that down."

Keese patted his abdomen. "That'll probably hold me. I could use losing a few grams. Of course, I was never skinny, not even when your age."

"Look in these bakery cartons," Harry said, folding back the cardboard tops. "Lemon meringue pie! Napoleons! Prune danish! . . . Am I tempting you?"

Keese drank some rum. "I'll have something more when I finish my drink. . . . Well, what will you do now, Harry? Look for another house in the same situation?"

"They're not come across that frequently, Earl. I simply have to be alert to whatever opportunity comes my way."

Keese drank some more. "I suppose it keeps you hopping. But it's an interesting way of life. You can't deny that." He chuckled. "What about your furniture?"

"It wasn't museum stuff, Earl." Harry was roaming through the foods. "Can it be . . ." He ripped open the mouth of a bag and plunged his head at it, almost into it. "Yes, it is: *ribs!*" He reached into the interior and brought forth an oblong covered with aluminum foil. He peeled back the foil, and a feeble wisp of steam arose.

Keese accepted the warm rack of barbecued spareribs, which was considerably heavier than it appeared. He found a carving knife and separated a section of three ribs, and then cut those into individuals. They glistened redly, and Harry offered a plastic cup brimful with more sauce. Keese turned this down but found a shaker and salted the meat lavishly.

Harry gulped some rum. "The suspense is killing me," said he.

After Keese found a box of paper napkins in the cupboard he was ready. He took a bite of pork. It was still warm. The meat was abundant, lean, and tasty. The sauce, pungent without excessive acidity.

"These are very nice," he told Harry, waving a rib at him.

"Damn right," Harry said, pushing one end of a taco into his own mouth and spilling a good deal of its contents from the other end—which cleverly he held over an open paper bag that stood on the countertop. After he had chewed awhile he said: "We can have a lot of fun here."

Keese ate more from the rib and took another drink. He had now had just enough of the latter to feel a sense of well-being that seemed natural and not the result of alcohol. This equilibrium was not simple to maintain, especially when in the company of someone with another tolerance.

Harry said: "Do you agree, Earl?"

"With what?"

"That it's nice here."

"Yes," said Keese, "this is really nice, Harry."

"Whereas," said Harry, "if *your* house was burned too, then none of us would have anything."

"I couldn't disagree with that," said Keese.

"You're not going to burn this place down, are you, Earl?"

Keese took a while to digest this remarkable speech. Then he said: "It never occurred to me, Harry."

"I don't know," Harry said, "you were looking mighty wistful."

Keese took the bottle and replenished his glass. "What I actually *was* thinking, a while back, was that you might want to take this house off my hands, but obviously that's not possible now, if you haven't got any insurance money coming."

Harry shook his head. "Besides, where would you go, Earl? Where else would you be likely to feel at home?"

"I was thinking of the city," Keese said, "where the idea of feeling at home has different values from those in the country."

Harry had opened the packages piecemeal and at random, but he now began at the outer edge of the counter and worked back, removing each bag or carton altogether and exposing the food. He did not however ignore Keese.

"You might be bored," he said. "It's all very well to think that the city's where the life is, but that's probably an illusion. And your style, Earl, is pretty out of date so far as the city goes, if you'll forgive my saying so."

"Of course," Keese said, having had a drink, "I go there every day to work, don't I?"

"Do you?" said Harry. "Yet my point still stands, no? It's not working in a place that makes it home, it's living there. For example, I've known city people who commute to the country to work and then return at the time that everyone else is leaving. But what do they know about the country?"

Keese couldn't decide whether to eat a second rib. Actually he did not like barbecued spareribs, nor Chinese food, nor tacos, nor much of anything else that Harry had yet revealed. Therefore what he ate now was a question of what he disliked least. But tastes were tastes, and he didn't blame Harry for the selection.

Nor did he care for rum. Yet he finished what was left in the glass and poured more for himself. Harry had meanwhile freed all the food from its wrappings, and now was arranging the dishes by nationality. The empty cartons and bags had been pushed away as far as they could go, but the counter soon ended at a wall, and the rubbish was elastic: it began to emerge from its compression.

"Let me get this out of your way," said Keese, and he squeezed the lot together and punched it and rolled it, and he went outside to the garbage cans. When he had made his deposit and turned to come back inside, a pickup truck was rolling silently up his driveway. It stopped and old Greavy got out. *Oh-oh*, thought Keese.

But Greavy waved loosely, and when Keese reached him he was grinning amiably.

"Say," he said, leaning towards Keese and speaking in a confidential tone, "I hear you got a whore here."

"No," said Keese, "I haven't."

Greavy frowned. "That's what I heard."

"You heard wrong."

"You ain't got a whore here?"

"No."

"You wouldn't know where I could find one?"

"No, I wouldn't."

Greavy shook his head. "Well, if one shows up, you let me know." He turned, walked back to the pickup truck, got in, and backed down the driveway. He swung around and headed away.

When Keese returned to the kitchen Harry said: "Greavy wasn't looking for me, was he?"

"No."

"I thought for a minute he might think I should pay him for the moving job."

"It probably wasn't a good idea, going into the city," said Keese. "It never did appeal to Enid. She intended to ask you to rent her a room in this house."

"I'll be damned," said Harry. "Is that right? Enid's a prize, Earl. I hope you realize that." He worked free from its bonds of gluey cheese a precut triangle of pizza. "Here." He offered this wilting thing to Keese, who shook his head. "No? Have you eaten anything else today, Earl? You've hardly touched these things."

"They all look delicious, Harry. It's just that I'm off my feed at the moment. It can't hurt me to fast a bit. I've been supposed to lose weight for years. Blood pressure, you know."

Harry looked horrified. He snatched the glass from Keese's hand. "Then you've had enough of this, my friend! We can't afford to lose you now!"

"Harry!" Keese protested. "Give me that glass! Rely on me to take care of myself, please." But Harry put the glass in the small of his back and moved away. "All right, then," Keese said, and seized the bottle itself.

"Oh, come on, Earl, this is no joke."

Keese was touched. "Gosh, you're serious, aren't you? My condition isn't *grave*. I'm sorry to have worried you! I've just got a little high blood pressure, really. Supposed to lose a few pounds and do a bit of exercise to be on the safe side. Of course I haven't done either. You know how that goes."

"Oh, yeah?" Harry asked wryly. "Well, my friend, you're going to fall out three mornings a week from now on for a workout." He approached Keese. "And hand over that bottle."

Keese said: "You really are a friend, aren't you? I never knew anyone else who cared that much about my health." Moved as he was by Harry's concern, he had no choice but to surrender the rum.

"Yessir," said Harry, "we're going to get you in shape, Earl." He put the bottle down and looked at the spread of food. "And what a choice to make! There's no nourishment in this junk. I should have got yoghurt and wheat germ and fresh fruit, and fish."

Ramona entered the kitchen at that point, accompanied by a skulking Baby, whom she took to the door and let out.

"Hey, food," said she, and came to the counter. She smiled sweetly at Keese. "May I feed you something, Earl?"

"No," said Harry, "Earl's in training, Ramona. He's not to get any of this trash nor anything alcoholic."

"Harry's spoiling me," Keese said, his hands rising. "No need for it, but it's flattering."

"Well," Ramona said, "you're precious to us, Earl. Anything happens to you, what would we do?"

Hearing this, Keese became apprehensive for the first time in recent hours. Being their friend was well enough, but why had he suddenly become an object of such value?

"Look," he said, "don't worry about me, either of you. I'm O.K. *You're* the people with difficulties, I'm sorry to say. It's my fault that your car won't work, so why not borrow mine for the rest of the weekend, anyway? Meanwhile you can decide where you're going from this point. For my part, I'll call a garage in Allenby and get them going on your car."

"I doubt they can fix it in what remains of the afternoon, Earl," said Harry. "It's five fifteen. And surely they don't work on Sundays. And you'll need transport to the railroad station on Monday morning . . ."

"Give me a lift to Allenby now," Keese said, "and I'll rent a car."

Ramona was eating a jelly doughnut.

"Needless expense, old pal!" Harry howled. *I'll* be your chauffeur, for free."

"No," said Keese, "there's no need to bother. You'll have plenty of needs of your own. Maybe you'll have found a new home by then."

"Don't worry about that," Ramona said. Her mouth was smeared with crimson jelly. "Your interests come first with us."

"No," Keese said. "I won't hear of it." He marched to the counter where the directory lay, picked it up, and found the car-rental section of the Yellow Pages. He had been prepared to see that Greavy's Garage offered cars for hire locally, and he was not disappointed. He then perused the two listings for Allenby and the adjacent ads for each.

He dialed the first number. "I'd like to rent a car."

"We don't do that any more," said the man. "There simply wasn't enough business."

Keese called the other place. "Sorry," said the woman, "we won't have a free car till a week from next Wednesday. We can't keep up with the business, no matter how many vehicles we put on the road."

Enid and Elaine came into the kitchen as he hung up.

"I just offered Earl my services as chauffeur," Harry said to Enid.

"He's a marvelous driver, Earl," Enid said. She got a plate for herself and some cutlery, and prepared a very tidy arrangement of various Chinese dishes, and when she was done she presented it to Elaine.

Elaine stared at Keese and said, finally: "You're very lucky, Daddy."

"In fact," said Harry, "we might look into the costs of taking you all the way into town by car. I'll wager to say it compares favorably with the price of the train ticket. You could ride in comfort, take coffee in a Thermos . . ."

"And after dropping you off," Elaine said, "Harry could turn right around and come back here. After all, it's the parking that costs the real money." She began gingerly to eat rice, only a few grains at a time.

"I can't ask Harry to take a trip like that," Keese said stubbornly. "He's got plenty on his hands, looking for *a new place to live.*" But he wondered whether he might have put too much offensive emphasis on the phrase, and he smiled sweetly at Harry to take the possible edge off.

"And you can be sure I'll do that, *after* I have delivered you in town," Harry said triumphantly.

Keese regretted his moment of doubt. "Actually, with gas and wear and tear it would still be much more expensive than the train," he said firmly.

"Then he will just take you to the station," Enid said. "So that's settled."

"But—"

Ramona drowned Keese out with a strident: "You've been voted down, Earl! From now on you're going to get the V.I.P. treatment whether you want it or not."

"I think we've got nowhere to go but up," said Elaine, with the disagreeable edge that had become habitual. It seemed an eternity since Keese had thought of her with any approval or pleasure, and yet until the night before he had really given them unconditionally to no one else. He supposed that in one way he was freed of certain bonds.

Enid said: "Earl, why don't you eat something? Everything's O.K., I promise you. You can relax now and enjoy your meal. May I fix your plate?"

"Just take care of yourself," said Keese. "Don't worry about me. I know what I'm doing." He seized the bottle and turned his back on them, not wishing to be observed while he poured.

"But do you?" someone asked, he couldn't say who. It was in a feminine voice, but it could have been Harry speaking in falsetto.

He whirled, splashing himself with rum.

"How disgusting," said Elaine.

And Ramona said: "Looks like you bepissed yourself, Earl."

"I knew someone wouldn't be able to resist making that observation," said Keese. "I'm aware you all think I'm drunk."

Harry shook a chicken leg at him. "Earl, I thought you weren't going to have any more."

Ramona howled: "I haven't had *any!*" She made a dash and grab at Keese's bottle, but he was too quick for her.

"You're all so superior, aren't you?" he asked. "And yet I'm the only one who earns a living." He lifted the bottle and drank from its throat.

Harry made a gesture of pain. "Don't talk like that, Earl. You're the Chief!"

"God almighty," said Ramona, "you're the Big Boss, Earl! Who could forget that for a minute?"

"Damn right I am," said Keese, waving the bottle. "All this is mine, and I'm responsible for it."

"We're not arguing," said Harry.

"But my own family are strangely silent," Keese said. "Do you notice that, Harry?"

"All right," Harry said to the Keese women, approaching the table where they sat, "let's have an expression of loyalty to Earl."

Enid shrugged. "Sure," she said.

Elaine's sullenness was working to a boil, but Harry stuck his finger in her face. "You say something nice to your dad, girlie, or I'll whip your smart little ass."

Keese got so much satisfaction from witnessing this that he feared he might be too far gone, but with an effort he regained his composure and stated hypocritically: "It doesn't really matter."

"Sure it does," said Harry. "A man in your situation doesn't have to take any shit from anybody under his own roof." He banged his fist on the table very near Elaine's plate, the food on which sprang into the air in one mass but came down severally and splattered. "Did you hear what I said, missy?"

"Yessir," said Elaine, showing real fear.

"Say: 'I apologize, Dad, for being so rude. I owe you everything. Without your help, where would I be?' "

Elaine complied in a weak voice. Keese's pleasure was gone now.

"All right," said Harry. "Now say: 'I shall be respectful and obedient in the future, because if I'm not Harry will beat me up.' "

"Just a moment," said Keese. "This is going beyond a joke."

Harry threw his hands into the air and backed away from Elaine. "Just as you say, Earl. You won't have to tell me anything twice, I promise you."

Ramona said submissively: "You won't have to tell *me* more than once!"

Keese threw back his head and took a taste of rum. He swallowed and made a face. "I don't like rum," he said.

"Sorry about that, Earl. I didn't know," said Harry.

Keese pointed the neck of the bottle at Harry, but he meant all of them. "And I don't care for this kind of food. I want a real meal, and served on a china plate, with a full set of silver and a napkin made of cloth. I don't insist on a bread plate, with a butter knife, but it would be nice."

Ramona said: "Enid, show me where that stuff is kept."

"I don't think he means here, Ramona," said Enid. "Besides, we have no food here except this."

"I should think," said Keese, "that after all I'd gone through, you'd have brought home something better than this."

"Ignorance, Earl," said Harry. "We mean well, but we don't know enough. That's why we need your help." He put his hands on his hips and looked at the food on the counter.

"You're right, of course: this is garbage. I'll bring in a can." He started for the door.

"Wait a minute," said Keese. "I didn't say throw it away."

Harry returned. "I don't think we can take most of it back for a refund. Maybe with the pizzas, but certainly not with the tacos."

"Maybe we could give it to some poor family," said Ramona. "Leave it on their porch anonymously, so as not to hurt their pride, so they wouldn't feel beholden."

"You know," said Elaine, "you're really a *kind* person, Ramona."

Keese drank some more rum.

"Earl," said Enid, "I won't dwell on this, but hadn't you better go easy?"

"I need strength," said Keese. "I'm thinking. Harry, am I right in supposing you bought this food with the money I gave you last night?"

"I'm afraid it required a bit more than that," Harry replied.

"Do I owe you something?"

"Forget it, Earl. I want to do my part."

"I thought you had no money?"

"A few bucks maybe."

"He paid by check," said Enid.

"In Allenby?" asked Keese. "Do they know you there?"

"People trust me," Harry said, smiling.

"Well, so do I, in a way," Keese said, and put out his hand. "Let's see it."

"What?"

"That checkbook protruding from the back pocket of those new trousers."

Harry looked for a moment as if he might resist, but apparently he decided otherwise, for he surrendered the checkbook.

Keese opened it. The checks were imprinted with his own name, followed by his address.

"I thought it looked like mine," Keese said, "but don't they all?" Then he said to Harry: "They always ask for identification in Allenby. Let's have yours."

Harry took a billfold from his other back pocket. Keese claimed it as his own. "Unless you have some objection, Harry? It's full of my papers."

"Oh, it's yours all right, Earl, no doubt about it."

"You helped yourself during the brief period you occupied our bedroom, no doubt," said Keese, "and you probably got the checkbook from the desk in the living room."

"Gosh," Harry said, "it'd be hard to say by now. Probably somewhere convenient, that's for sure."

"Yet," said Keese, "you could have run away with them, but you didn't. You stuck around and bought junk food and a modest shirt and pair of pants. You're an unusual fellow, Harry. Every time I see you as a criminal, by another light you look like a kind of benefactor."

"Always trying to be a good neighbor, Earl."

Keese nodded. "I believe you."

"If you'll lend me your checkbook and driver's license again, I'll go out and get you that real meal you want. That is, I'll buy the ingredients and Ramona will cook them. She kids around a lot, but actually she can be very useful."

"There's a whole lot of things I can do," said Ramona. "I just need the opportunity. I can even speak some German."

"I know you can make paper flowers," Elaine said worshipfully. "You told me that."

"I'm sure you're a valuable person to have around," said Keese. "And no doubt it would be only until you both got on your feet again."

Enid said: "Do you mean what you are saying, Earl, or is that the liquor speaking?"

Keese put the bottle on the counter. "Who are you trying to fool?" he asked Enid. "Did you not tell them they could move in here? For all I know, either you or Elaine burned their house down so that they would! I have been aware of your game for ever so long. The only question was what I'd do about it."

"Gee," said Ramona, "I hope you'll be friendly. I get along best with people who are nice."

"We hurl ourselves on your mercy, Earl," said Harry. "We're pathetic creatures."

"Now that," said Keese, "is the ridiculous kind of approach that offends me. You're not helpless at all! You're both young and healthy, and you have a great deal of cunning, whatever additional gifts you may possess, and I'm sure you have many. It's not my business why you want to be parasites but please don't pretend you have no other option."

"We're just a pair of shiftless zanies," said Ramona. "We'd do anything for a chuckle."

"I want you to know that I admire you enormously," said Elaine, with a grim expression.

"The essential thing, Earl," said Enid, "is that you go into this with your eyes wide open. You mustn't think you're the victim of a swindle of any kind."

"Ha!" Keese went to where the food was spread out. The pairs of paper plates, now unstapled, had, it turned out, held a selection of Italian antipasto. He stared at a discolored chunk of tuna fish, poked at an oily green olive. "Bread," he said bitterly. "There's not even a piece of bread amidst all of this! Or a hunk of cheese, a glass of wine. There's nothing basic!"

"But that's what we're saying," Harry cried. "You're the only one with a real foothold on this shifting ground. We need a clue."

"Of course that's flattering to hear," Keese confessed. "But how'd you get along in life till now?"

"Superficially," said Harry.

Keese stared at the bakery goods, shaking his head. "Why did you get all this sweet stuff?"

"I'm childish," Harry said.

Elaine said to her father: "How dare you criticize our friends?"

Harry stepped smartly to the table and slapped her face. "I warned you about your smart mouth!"

Keese cried: "Harry!"

Her face reddening from the blow, Elaine pointed her hand at Keese and shouted: "Don't you dare touch Harry!"

This was enough to stop Keese, but Harry said: "Oh, you want more, do you?" He drew back his large hand.

Keese ordered him away. "Yes, Earl," Harry said, returning to the counter.

"I'll behave, Harry," said Elaine in her obsequious manner.

"Elaine," said Keese, "I'll come right out with it: why are you so defiant with me and a complete sycophant to Harry?"

She grimaced. "Because with him it's a matter of positive principle."

Keese thought with wonderment: *Can Harry be a more virtuous man than I?* He seized the bottle and drank some rum.

Enid said: "Earl, you really ought to give this food a try. It won't be as bad as you think."

"I don't see you eating any."

"I'm not hungry," said Enid. "I ate something when we were down in the village." She rose. "Let me fix you a plate. Just try it, so that you won't ever have reason to reproach yourself."

Keese rolled his eyes. Enid got a plate from the cupboard and began to place food upon it.

"I suppose," he said to Harry, and he included Ramona in these remarks by turning his head towards her at random, "you could hang around here for a while until you got on your feet. You do have some idea of what will be your next port of call?"

"None whatever," said Harry.

"I didn't mean that in a geographical sense, really," Keese said. "What I meant was what you'll do next in life—?"

"Pretty much," said Ramona, "what I've done thus far."

"Ditto," said Harry.

"You certainly aren't encouraging me to allow you to stay," said Keese.

"That would be awfully vulgar, wouldn't it?" Harry asked. "And any lies we told would soon come home to roost."

"In other words, you might never leave once you were ensconced?"

Harry shrugged.

"Earl," Ramona said, "you old Teddy bear you."

Keese asked: "Is it the spare room you've got your eye on?"

"That won't do," Harry said. "I've looked in there, and I don't like it."

Enid came to Keese with the laden plate. "There, doesn't that look good?"

Keese accepted it, along with the fork she brought, and he took a taste of what would seem a chicken enchilada. "This," he said, "is just as bad as I thought." He returned the plate and fork to her. To Harry he said: "Well, it's got a lot of old living-room furniture in it at the moment. It's a nice room."

"Naw," Harry said, "it's not for me."

Keese thought he should be miffed. How could a beggar be so demanding? Nevertheless he said: "Sofa's in good condition. Pulls out at night to a double bed. In the daytime you could have a living room."

"If you're *ordering* me to take it, then I will without question," Harry said. "You know that, Earl. But if I'm being *asked* then: sorry, but no."

Keese tossed his hands in the air. "What am I doing, asking you these things? As if your opinion is important! Why don't you just leave?"

"Earl!" Enid cried. "What manners!"

"Manners by now have no meaning," Keese answered. "We have too long and intimate a history, haven't we, Harry?"

"We're not asking any special consideration," said Harry. "We have to take whatever we can get."

"Speaking for myself," Ramona said, "I feel I'm lucky if I can just get through another day without being shot."

Elaine said adoringly: "I love the way you talk!"

Ramona looked at her and sneered. "You love my possessions, too. That's my ring you're wearing. And where's my scarf?"

Elaine hid one fist in the other hand. "I'm sure you're mistaken," she said.

Keese groaned. "Then what room do you like?"

"The one facing the road," said Harry.

"The master bedroom? Our bedroom?" Keese looked at his own fingernails: they were unusually dirty. "Now you're being silly."

"Well, you asked," said Harry. "I didn't say it to annoy you."

"Looking at it from another perspective," said Keese, "I take it your contribution would be to make yourself useful around here: you are offering your services?"

"Such as they are," said Harry. "I can't do much heavy work: an old rupture."

"Lawn and garden?"

"Not really: allergies restrict my outdoor activities."

"Can use a cleaning woman," Keese said to Ramona.

"God knows I'll give her plenty of work, cleaning up after me," Ramona said. "I'm a real pig."

"But you'd drive me to the station, Harry?"

"I certainly would, Earl, and perhaps you'd return the favor when I wanted to go somewhere?"

"Chauffeur you in my own car? You who were living off me, contributing nothing, eating the food I paid for, and even sleeping in my bedroom?"

"Sure, Earl," Harry said, smiling. "Because we could always be blamed."

"Blamed?"

"For everything," said Harry. "Also, if anyone wanted anything you didn't want to give them, you could always tell them to talk to Harry. Or suppose someone criticized you for doing something. 'Why,' you could say, 'I didn't do that. Harry's the culprit.' "

"What would you do?"

"Isn't that *my* worry?" asked Harry. "What do you care? You simply don't want to be bothered."

Ramona said: "And like if you're asked, 'Who was that lady I saw you with last night?' why, you can say: 'Ramona,' and that's O.K., you see."

"It is?"

"Sure, Earl. You could take me anywhere you wanted to, dressed in any way, and once you got there you could forget all about me, and it would be perfectly O.K. And any time you were in a tight corner anywhere, you could get out by saying, 'I've got to go see Ramona,' and nobody would question your motives."

"Why not?"

"Because they wouldn't, take my word. It's an effective name to mention."

Keese rubbed his chin. "To tell you the truth," he said, "I've never been that crazy about the front room. It's noisy when they come to pick up garbage, or to plow snow in the winter. Also, sometimes people come down here in cars to turn around." He tapped his fingers on the counter. "What do you think, Enid?"

She had returned to sit at the table. "I'm staying there."

Keese moued at Harry. "There you are. I'm sorry."

"But," said Enid, "*you* could go to the back room, if you wanted."

"And Ramona could move in with me!" cried Elaine. "That would be perfect."

"Let's see then," Keese said. "That leaves me alone in what used to be the guest room."

"I could come in to see you whenever you wanted, Earl," Ramona said, "but I always seem to annoy you sooner or later."

At that moment the telephone rang. Keese seized it. The caller was Marge Abernathy. She spoke in a rush.

"Earl, are you and Enid coming to tonight's dinner?" She was heard to gasp for breath. "Please don't abuse me again."

"Marge!" said Keese. "Listen, I'm sorry about last night's remarks. Harry made me say those terrible things. You know Harry: not much can be done about him."

"Dear Earl," said Marge, "say no more!"

"And I'm afraid we can't come tonight. Because of Ramona, I'm afraid."

"Of course," said Marge. "We understand perfectly. You're still our best friends. See you whenever's convenient." She hung up. Keese could scarcely believe it.

"Damned if you weren't right," he said to his former neighbors.

"It never fails," said Ramona. "Ours are good names to bandy about."

"You're so widely known?"

"They're just good names to mention," said Harry. "It gives you an air of authority to mention these names."

"Why not Joe or Bob or Peggy?" Keese asked. "If it's just a name you need."

"They don't strike the right note, I don't know why," said Harry.

"They sound like people who are confused," said Ramona. "That's why."

"I tell you," Keese said, "with all respect: I just have to think it over."

"Fair enough," said Harry, clapping his hands. "That's it, then. Ramona, call Baby and let's hit the road."

"You're actually leaving?" asked Keese. Elaine began to sob, her face in her hands. Enid glided past Keese, and only when she was at the other side of the room did he see she had taken the rum and the glass and was pouring herself a robust drink.

"You'll see, Earl," said Ramona, "you'll miss us. Sometime when you could badly use a lift you'll say: 'Gee, how I wish my pals were still here!' Or you'll have to deal with something unpleasant on the phone, and what will you say?"

"Of course, for that matter I could still mention your names," Keese pointed out. "I could still blame you, couldn't I?"

"It wouldn't work," Harry said, "because it would be a lie. Whereas if we were here, it would be true: we really *would* be to blame."

"What a strange idea to have of oneself," Keese said aloud.

"I'll tell you, Earl," Harry said. "Sometimes it can be as inspiring as any other." He went to the door. "Come on, Ramona."

Keese followed them outside. He said: "Take my car, Harry. Just let me know where you've left it when you're finished." Ramona was calling Baby's name.

"I couldn't do that, Earl," said Harry. "I might just want to keep driving."

"Then let me run you to the bus station in Allenby. Only one train a day operates on weekends, and it would be gone already."

"I don't have the money for a ticket."

Keese looked over at the smoking ruin next door. He saw the wolfhound coursing about there. For some reason this sight made him philosophical. "Look at that," said he. "You wonder whether he knew that was to be his home for the foreseeable future, and if so whether he wonders why it was burned down.

Or if he merely accepts everything as chance?" He glanced at Harry and saw him picking his nose. It was clear that Keese could expect no help in his serious deliberations.

Ramona came along, still shouting for Baby, but the pet paid her no attention.

"He's really a handsome animal," said Keese. "And certainly no trouble around the house, for so large a dog."

"Oh, God," she groaned, "that reminds me: I forgot to clean up his puke in the bedroom. He dug up a mole, I think, and ate it. That always upsets his stomach."

"You and your stupid cur," said Harry.

Ramona shrugged. "Where you keep your wet mop, Earl?"

"Don't worry about it," said Keese. He got out his wallet. "I'm going to give you my registration," he said to Harry. "Wait a minute." He went to his car and found a ball-point pen under the maps in the glove compartment. He put the registration slip on the roof of the car and signed his name. "Now," he said when he rejoined Harry, "here you have a document which makes this automobile your possession. You can enter your own name in the appropriate place, or you can leave it blank until you arrive at your destination, where, to get some ready cash, you can sell the car to someone, putting his name thereupon." He presented the slip to Harry.

Harry looked as if he might burst into tears. "Earl," he said, "I'm really overwhelmed. Nobody's ever been this nice to me in all my life."

"It's only right," said Keese. He felt a kind of humility in the presence of himself.

"Wow," said Ramona, "what a friend you are, Earl!"

"More than a friend," said Harry, clasping Keese's hand. "You've been a real *neighbor.*"

Ramona pressed her body to Keese's and plunged her tongue down his throat, her teeth clashing against his. When she finally pulled away, the three of them walked to the car.

Harry opened the passenger's door and pointed to the glove compartment. "Want to clean that out, Earl? Any valuables? Do you keep your condoms there, or a pistol?"

Keese chuckled. "Whatever you find is yours."

"Good-bye, pal," said Harry. They shook again.

Ramona called Baby, who was still, as it were, grazing. The dog raised his head and peered in their direction.

"I'm sorry it didn't work out for you here," Keese said.

Harry said: "There's always a certain sense of anticipation when you point your nose at the horizon." But Keese detected a weary note in this, and probably a false one as well.

"You never know what's at the end of the rainbow," said Ramona with strained gaiety. "It might be a pot of shit." Her expression changed to impatience, and she shouted: "Baby! Damn you! Come on, you fag! Kiss my ass, Baby."

Harry went around and got in behind the wheel. He started the engine. At this sound the dog came galloping. Ramona opened the rear door on her side. Baby sprang in. He stared smugly at Keese though the closed window.

"So long, Earl," said Ramona. Keese was in some suspense as to whether she would kiss him again, but she did not. She had already gone in spirit: it seemed an anticlimax when she got inside and closed the door.

Keese went around to Harry's side. "Take care of yourself, Harry." They peered at each other and then simultaneously broke into wide grins.

"Some night, eh, Earl?"

"You'd better not drive too long," said Keese. "You didn't have much sleep."

Harry said: "Hey, remember how I took a shot at you? I'm sure glad I missed!"

"Thanks, Harry." Keese could think of a lot more things to say, and Harry seemed to be waiting for some statement on his part, perhaps a summing up, but he had always felt that sentimental departures were in bad taste. He ended up stepping back one pace and saluting Harry with a forefinger to the right eyebrow.

Harry backed to the road, then swung around and headed away. He produced one mournful blast on the horn.

Keese decided he had had enough of watching a vehicle until it reached the vanishing point from his perspective, and he went back inside.

Elaine was eating her Chinese food with gusto. She spoke on a rising note and in a friendly tone. "You really should try this shrimp, Daddy."

"Good heavens," said Keese.

"Mmm, I'm so hungreee," Elaine said through a mouthful of food. "It's probably my relief that those awful people have gone."

Enid had after all drunk little of the remaining rum. She was now rummaging in one of the cupboards. "Ah." She brought out a jar of instant coffee. "I had this hidden. Do you want a cup, Earl?"

Keese said soberly: "The performances given by you both this weekend have been hoaxes, is that still your position?" asked Keese. "Designed to lull Harry and Ramona into a sense of false security?"

"To discourage them," said Enid. "To put them off."

"Uh-huh."

"And it seems we succeeded, at long last." She pointed at the window. "I saw them leave. They stole our car."

"No, they did not," Keese said flatly. "And there's nothing wrong with them. They may not share your tastes, but they are all right."

"You wouldn't say that if you knew Ramona better!" said Elaine. "She'd make your flesh creep."

"I know her very well," said Keese, "and though she's a bit raw sometimes, I see that as an abundance of animal energy.

They're free spirits, Harry and Ramona, and the world would be a worse place without them."

"Well," said Elaine, having cleaned her plate, "that's that. I've got to be going. God, is that the right time!" She pushed her chair back and dashed from the kitchen.

"Will you tell me what that means?" Keese asked Enid.

"She's being picked up at six fifteen," said Enid. "Do you want a cup of coffee, Earl? Might not be a bad idea, after all that rum."

"Picked up?" asked Keese. "By whom?"

"By another student, who's giving her a ride back to school."

"She's returning to college?"

"Of course."

Keese's capacity for emotion was exhausted. "Good," he said, taking the seat that Elaine had just left.

"Yes," Enid said cheerily as she began to bustle about the kitchen, "we're all back on an even keel, with no harm done. We can go ahead now, as always."

As she came by on one of her excursions, Keese handed her Elaine's soiled plate. "Go ahead?" he asked.

"Yes," said Enid, "as soon as I saw *they* were going to leave I called Marge Abernathy and said we'd be there tonight."

"I think you're right," said Keese.

"It's a relief to hear that," said Enid. "Unless you are planning to get into a brawl there."

"I may," said Keese, "and I may not. I respond to the particular situation."

Elaine returned, carrying her overnight case. "Hey, you guys, I wouldn't have missed this for the world," said she. From behind she kissed the top of Keese's head, then exchanged embraces with Enid, who came to her. "Got to run!" She left on a trot towards the front of the house.

"Elaine no longer makes sense to me," said Keese. "That's something that has happened just this weekend."

"It wouldn't be a problem if you thought of her in the same old way," Enid said. "She's the same old Elaine, really."

"All wool and a yard wide, I suppose," said he. She made no response to his irony. He sighed. He suddenly missed Harry & Ramona. He admitted as much to Enid.

"That squalid couple!" she said. "They made a fool of you, Earl."

"No," said Keese, "you're wrong about them, Enid. They were all right. They were good people. They were helpful in this neighborhood. I know I sang a different tune at first, but I was totally misguided. Actually, Harry and Ramona are probably the finest people I've ever met. It just takes a while to perceive their unique quality, but once you do, you're not the same."

"They corrupted your mind," said Enid. She brought him a cup with a measure of powdered coffee already in it. She went to the stove, where the water was steaming in the kettle.

"No," Keese said, "you know nothing about them."

She came with the kettle and made coffee of the powder. "Now, drink up," she said, "and then better get dressed: we're due over there in twenty minutes."

" 'Dressed'?" he asked, incredulously. "I'm wearing my best suit."

"Oh, so you are. I guess I wasn't thinking."

"No," said Keese, "you weren't." He resented receiving direction from such a poor observer. "And I don't want this coffee, for that matter."

"I thought it might give you some energy before having to go out and face people," Enid said.

"Don't try to manipulate me for my own good," he said. "There's nothing wrong with me."

Enid's eyebrows seemed to quiver, unless that was his imagination. She did a strange little thing that may have been affection: passing behind him on her route out of the kitchen, she lingered for an instant to drum her fingertips on his right shoulder.

Keese reached for her hand, probably also in fondness, but already she was gone. He decided after all to drink his coffee. It seemed more of a soporific than a stimulant. If he relaxed his will at all, his head fell forward. This would never do. At last he pushed himself into a standing position.

When he reached the front hallway he could not hear a sound from upstairs. Perhaps he *had* napped for a while in the kitchen and Enid had already left for the Abernathys, a walk of only a few minutes. While he was thinking about this, the door-gong made its sound.

He turned the knob without his habitual apprehension. He could not have cared less who it was—until he saw who. It was Ramona! He seized her and hugged her and lifted her off her feet.

When he put her down she made a fist and fondly punched his arm. "So how are you, Earl?"

"I'm not at my best," said Keese. "I miss you people."

"I guess it's pretty obvious that we return the feeling," she said. "Here we are. We didn't get far."

Keese felt that his eyes were damp. "You're going to stay, of course?"

Tears welled from Ramona's eyes, and this time it was she who hugged him. Looking over her head, he saw Harry beckon.

"We need you, old pal!" Harry shouted. Then Keese saw the dog come into view in the rear window. Baby had probably been sleeping on the rear seat.

"I'll tell you," said Ramona, pushing Keese away so that she could look at him, "it was simultaneous: I stared at Harry and Harry at me. 'What's wrong?' we said. 'It's Earl, that's what! It's not worth doing without him.' "

Keese shook his head. "I've never had friends like you two."

"How often in life do you find somebody who becomes your oldest friend overnight?" said Ramona. "And then you leave him behind?"

Harry shouted merrily: "All aboard! Pottsville, Partridge Hollow, and Peanut Town! Connections to all points of view. All aboard!"

"You mean you want me to come along?" asked Keese.

"Damn right," said Ramona.

"You don't want to stay here? Lots of room!"

"No," Ramona said. "The moment for that has passed. It's essential to keep the initiative. Lose it, and they'll run you ragged. Your sequences will be off."

"Golly," said Keese. "Let me think about that for a minute."

"No, Earl, it's no good if you hesitate. The gears won't mesh, and you can't roll. They'll nail you to the wall."

"C'mon, Earl, while we've got the wind!" Harry shouted from the window of the car. "Open the scuppers and belay the fo'c'sle. Grog for all hands!"

The wolfhound continued to stare inscrutably.

"Where would I ride?" asked Keese. "I don't know if Baby likes me."

"Sure he does!" said Ramona. "He thinks the world of you, Earl. C'mon, I'll prove it to you." She turned and went down the path.

Keese followed her for a step or two, then stopped. "Wait a minute," he called to her. "The lights are on and all that food's spread over the kitchen counter . . ."

"You've got to make a choice, Earl," said Ramona.

Keese looked up at the windows on the second floor. Was Enid there? For that matter, was Elaine still at home? Had her departure been another hoax?

He turned back and said to Ramona: "You're right, of course."

"Hi, fella," said Harry when he reached the car. Harry

leaned across and shook hands. Keese felt something that tickled.

Harry opened his fingers and revealed that on one of them he wore a little round device which faced palmwards.

"My God," said Keese, "can that be a Joy Buzzer? I haven't seen one of those since I was a kid. I didn't know they made them any more."

"Get in, buddy," said Harry.

"I don't know about the dog," said Keese. He looked through the window at the impassive Baby.

"Get in the front."

"No," Keese said, "that would be dodging the issue."

"He's got a point, Harry," Ramona said, and she reached around to the crank of the rear window and wound it down. Baby gingerly put his long white snout on the sill. It occurred to Keese that if he had seen only Baby's eyes he might have thought them those of a human maniac.

"Give him your hand, Earl," said Ramona.

"Would he bite it?"

"That's what we're going to find out."

Keese sighed and extended his hand towards the wolfhound. Baby looked steadily past him. "I suppose he's neutral." He patted the dog's head, which beneath the thin layer of white fur felt hard as marble. Still without looking at Keese, Baby produced a wet red tongue and licked his hand briefly.

"See?" said Ramona. But it was she who climbed into the back with the dog.

"Or do you want to drive, Earl?" Harry asked. "It's still really your car."

"No, no," Keese said, with a fending-off gesture of false horror. "One choice is enough. I wouldn't know which way to head."

Harry started the engine. "The important thing is that we're a team."

Keese said: "I hope it works out as well as being neighbors."

They rolled past the smoking ruin, reached the corner, turned left, and soon were behind the screen of trees that would have concealed the car from Keese had he only been watching from his front lawn. He had his fatal stroke not long afterwards. He was helplessly conscious for a time while it was under way. He was aware that his friends recognized his predicament as genuine and not as some device of guile.

Harry sped up the engine. He said: "I'm certainly not going to think the worst of you, Earl, old pal."

Dying, Keese realized that Ramona had leaned forward to pat his shoulder.

She said: "Earl, it could happen to anybody."